I loved *Angela's Treasures*. I am a voracious reader, usually having three or four books going at one time. This book brought back many thoughts about my parents.

Jill Rossin Amerling
Co-national publicity coordinator
Choose Life License Plates

Marian's background as a journalist carries forward into this novel. There is captivating action and an intriguing plot with a welcome underlying wholesomeness.

Steve Saint, Missionary
Author of *End of the Spear*

Marian Rizzo is a gifted storyteller, whether it be for news reporting or fiction. She has a keen eye and ear for the intricacies of a story, which translates into very powerful narratives. Marian can turn the mundane into the magnificent through the masterful weaving of character, context, and scene-setting.

Susan Smiley-Height
Local news editor, Ocala Star-Banner/ocala.com

Highly recommended. Marian Rizzo gives us a poignant, often heartwarming story of immigrants struggling to overcome the harsh realities of the Great Depression.

David Cook
Historian, Journalist, Author of *The Way It Was*

Angela's Treasures

Angela's Treasures is a work of fiction. All References to persons, places or events are fictitious or used fictitiously.

Cover concept and design by David Warren.

Published by WordCrafts Press
Cody, Wyoming 82414
www.wordcrafts.net

Angela's Treasures

a novel

Marian Rizzo

To my longtime friend and sister in Christ, Cindy, who kept me laughing even when I didn't feel like it.

CHAPTER ONE

ANGELA

SEPTEMBER 2008

It's a sad thing when a major part of your life ends up at the bottom of a trashcan. That's what's happening to me, and I have absolutely no control over the situation.

My daughter Dorothy barged in this morning with an armload of paper towels, a bucket of cleaning supplies, and a box of trash bags. The wheels have begun to turn to move me out of my house. Dorothy's used so much bleach, the place smells like a swimming pool

Cupboard doors stand wide open. The shelves are nearly bare. I'm glued to this kitchen chair, unable to stop the flow, yet I grasp for a yesterday that's disappearing before my eyes.

A lump settles in my throat. I try to rinse it down with a sip of the tea Dorothy made for me. The warm liquid fails to ease the ache in my heart.

My daughter has turned my kitchen into a jobsite. Three large packing boxes are lined up along the wall. They're marked with the words, *Family*, *Yard Sale*, and *Charity*. Another carton—a smaller one—stands alone in the corner. It's labeled *Mother*. So far, nothing's gone into *that* one. The other three are filling up fast.

Dorothy glides past me with an armload of my stuff. She doesn't pause to ask my opinion, just tosses my personal things into whatever box fits her whim. Or she feeds my precious items to the trashcan. Then she moves on as if I'm not even here.

As each item leaves my daughter's hand, I travel back to another time and place. There's the torn flyer from the 1939 World's Fair. Faded movie ticket stubs for *Gone with the Wind* and *The Wizard of Oz*. A bill of lading with my husband's signature scrawled at the bottom. A bent spoon from the soup kitchen where I volunteered to feed the homeless. A bullet casing from the assembly line where I worked during the war. And a strip of black-and-white photos of Fredo and me making funny faces inside a booth at Coney Island. A painful tear comes to my eye. I blink hard and it spills onto my cheek.

The other day, Dorothy and I had the fourth of what I refer to as our moving-out discussions. My Plus-size daughter loomed in front of me and crossed her arms.

"Daddy's been gone for five years," she said, a no-nonsense tone in her voice. "We need to sell this old house and get you into assisted living. Or, you can move in with Barry and me."

I let out a grunt. Some choice. Assisted living sounds like one foot in the grave. And why would I want to live with that insufferable son-in-law of mine? He smokes like a chimney. He grumbles constantly about his failing real estate business. And I suspect he's got his eye on my Social Security checks.

I glared back at my daughter. "I want to stay in my own home. I've done okay since your Daddy died."

But Dorothy shook her head. "You can't take care of yourself anymore, Mother. That stroke left you paralyzed on one side. You can't walk without assistance. You can't cook for yourself. You barely can comb your own hair."

I drew myself up as straight as an old lady can. I was facing a tough adversary, but I wasn't about to back down. Not when the rest of my life was at stake.

"My therapist said I should be able to ditch that contraption soon." I nodded in the direction of my walker. "And, if I keep fiddling with that little red ball he gave me, my hand will get back to normal, too. I just need a little more time."

"Sorry, Mother. You're gonna move, and I'm *not* going to discuss this again."

But we did discuss it. Over and over. Each time, I spoke my mind. And each time, I lost. Okay, I'm not the vital, capable young woman I used to be. That person is gone, and in her place is a white-haired, shriveled up bag of bones who's debating with a 66-year-old fuddy-duddy.

A few tears make their way to my eyes and settle there, flooding my vision. Dorothy lets out a tired sigh. "Mother, you're going to have to trust me." She leans close and brushes a stray curl from my forehead. The lines on her face soften. "Tell you what... I'll save some of your precious things. We'll just have to find a place for them when you move—"

"I don't *want* to move."

She straightens. "Well, you can't stay here, and I can't keep running back and forth from my house to yours." She sweeps her hand toward the row of boxes. "This job is going to take several days, if not weeks. Do you know what you've become, Mother? You're a hoarder."

Insulted, I lurch backward against the chair. "A hoarder? How can you say that? I'm not like those people who pile trash all over their house and live with rats and bugs." I raise my chin. "I keep a neat home."

"That's not what I mean. Yes, on the surface your home is

neat and clean. But you've packed your cupboards with things most people would throw away." She's raises her voice now. "Your pantry is full of outdated food. Torn packages have spilled rice and beans and pasta all over the shelves. Most of your canned goods are way past the expiration dates. Some of them are so swollen they're about to burst. Don't you know you can get botulism and die?"

"It never hurt us in the past," I say with confidence, then I quickly chew my bottom lip. There was that time Fredo ended up in the hospital with intestinal cramps. They had to pump his stomach.

Dorothy places her hands on her hips and scowls at me the way parents do when they're about to reprimand a small child. I cringe and brace for the attack.

"It's not only your kitchen," she says. "The whole house needs a good cleanout. I think you've kept every piece of clothing you ever bought. Your dresses have gone out of style. Your closet shelves are packed with purses you never use. You own a ton of shoes you never took out of their boxes. And your dresser drawer is full of nylons you haven't worn in years." With each mention, Dorothy's voice rose another decibel.

My daughter's mouth continues to move, but I've tuned her out. I turn my eyes away from her flapping lips and take another sip of tea. The lump in my throat doesn't budge.

With a huff, she spins away, stomps off to the pantry, and sticks her head in. I glare at her backside. I'd like to give it a good, swift kick.

Seconds later, Dorothy emerges with a familiar cup in her hand. *World's Best Dad* is scrawled on the outside in bright red paint. She's moving past me to the trashcan just beyond where I'm sitting.

I make a grab for the cup. "That was your father's favorite."

She jerks her hand back. "Daddy's not here anymore."

"*I* can drink out of it."

"No, you can't. Look. There's a crack down the side. It'll leak."

She gives me a smug look, then she heads for the trashcan and releases the cup. It strikes the inside of the metal container ... and shatters. My heart breaks along with it.

I stare at Dorothy in disbelief. What has become of the curly-haired child who climbed on her daddy's knee on Father's Day sixty years ago and proudly handed him that hand-painted cup? More tears rush to my eyes. I blink them away along with the image of that little girl.

The grownup Dorothy remains, and she's bent on trashing everything that matters to me. And, even things that don't matter. Like my jar of rubber bands, my empty margarine containers, the pile of grocery bags, and the plastic forks I washed after every picnic. I kept telling her we might need those things someday, but she gave a disgusted shake of her head and dumped them.

I suppose I should appreciate my daughter. Since my release from the hospital six months ago, she's brought meals to me every day. She plunks them on the table, spends a couple of minutes in idle conversation, then rushes out to do whatever an unemployed office worker does.

Over the last few days, she's been whirling through my house like a white tornado. Soon this place will look as empty and uninhabitable as if a real storm had torn through here. And, just like those people in Kansas who rise from the debris and pick up the broken pieces of their lives, I'd like to put my own life back together.

Dorothy is marching toward the trashcan again. In her hand is a beat-up, old cigar box. I smile at the scratched-up image of a white owl on the lid.

"There's no reason to throw that away." I put out my hand, but she scoots around my outstretched fingers.

"It's empty, Mother. See?" She shakes the box and the lid flies open.

"I can put rubber bands in it. Or postage stamps." I give her a hopeful smile.

She drops the cigar box in the trash, and, without another word, she turns her back on me and disappears inside the pantry again. I reach for my walker. If I can get to the trashcan, I can retrieve that old box and slip it under the table. I stretch my arm to its full length but my walker is too far away. With a resigned sigh, I settle back in my chair, my eyes on the trashcan, my heart aching for the cigar box at the bottom.

Now, my husband never smoked cigars. He preferred a pipe and a scented tobacco that made our apartment smell like cherries. His friend Giorgio gave us that box after he smoked all the cigars in it. During the first few years of our marriage it held our extra cash. When the banks failed, people stuffed their hard-earned cash under a mattress, or they buried it under a rock in the garden, or they wrapped it in newspapers and hid it inside their refrigerator—if they were lucky enough to have one. Fredo and I used the cigar box.

Every Friday, after paying our bills, my husband put what was left in that box and slid it underneath our sofa-bed. We dropped our loose change in a Mason jar on the shelf above our stove, and we made a rule not to touch the cigar box money until we used up what was in the Mason jar. That cigar box served us well until the day we couldn't shut the lid anymore. That's when we switched to shoeboxes.

Our shoebox fund kept us going through the Great Depression, through World War II, through the birth of three children, and all the way into our retirement years. We never used a bank. Never needed to.

I press my lips together and stifle a chuckle. My eyes wander down the hall to the first door on the right. I can hardly wait until Dorothy starts poking around in that spare bedroom. Chances are she'll come across those old shoeboxes. I'd love to be standing there when she pulls off the lids.

CHAPTER TWO

THE BRONX, NEW YORK

1929-1933

I was fifteen years old when the stock market crashed. That same week, seven hundred banks closed. My parents hurried to their bank only to find the doors locked. They lost their life savings that day.

From the moment he stepped off the boat at Ellis Island, my father worked as a handyman for people who, like himself, spoke only Italian. But, his American dream died when the economy crashed.

"I no should leave Italia," he'd said more often than I needed to hear it.

I'd gotten half-way through high school when my father hurt his back and had to quit working.

"I want to drop out of school and get a job," I told my parents one afternoon.

Papa lowered his newspaper and Mama stopped stirring the potato soup. They both stared at me but said nothing.

"I've finished two years of high school," I persisted. "I've learned enough office skills to get a decent job. Let me help out."

Papa grunted and went back to his newspaper. Mama went back to stirring the soup. The next day, I quit school and applied for a job typing invoices at a meat refrigeration plant. The owner said he'd try me out for a while at $5 a week. I leaped at the opportunity. The extra income would keep our pantry stocked with beans and potatoes and rice.

I fell into a routine. Out the door of our apartment at the ungodly hour of six-thirty in the morning. Grabbed a cross-town bus. Got to my desk by eight o'clock. At five p.m. I headed for home. Such was my boring life. After supper, I curled up on my bed and stirred my imagination with library books written by F. Scott Fitzgerald and Ernest Hemingway. The next day, I repeated the whole scenario.

My older brother, Tomas, landed a job two years before I did. He worked in construction making $45 a month. Every morning before sunrise, a construction crew honked outside our apartment building. Tommy dragged himself out of bed and grabbed a piece of toast on his way out the door.

"I don't like getting up so early," he griped. "It's not human. What do those bosses think I am ... a rooster?" Then, he stumbled down the stairs and climbed onto the bed of the truck with the other guys, and off they went.

"I don't feel sorry for you, Tommy," I told him more than once. "At least you have a ride. I have to walk five city blocks and catch a bus."

I felt like the postman, trudging through the streets, no matter what the weather—rain or shine, sleet or snow. The buses weren't heated in those days. I would tuck my bare legs under my coat and pray for more riders to come aboard and warm up the bus.

The view from the window showed me a world that was a step down from my own. I gazed with pity at the beggars on street corners, the winos asleep in doorways, entire families rising from rusted out cars where they must have spent the night. If nothing else, it made me appreciate the little bit my family had.

Tomas had witnessed the harsh reality too. He came home every evening with stories about people struggling to survive in the back alleys where he worked.

"Can you believe it?" he said at dinner one night. "People are rigging wires to their electric meters to stop the wheels from spinning." He chuckled and leaned toward Papa. "Maybe we should try that too."

Papa glared at my brother. The old man didn't have to say a word. We may not have had much, but Papa always insisted we come by it honestly. Tomas slumped back in his chair. "Just kidding, Pop," he said, his voice weak. "I would never do anything like that."

Our younger brother, Benito, cocked his head, his eyes on Tomas, a smirk on his lips. "Tell us, Tommy. What else do you see in the back alleys? You know ... when you're supposed to be working?"

Tomas straightened. "You wouldn't joke if you seen what I saw," he said. "Little kids come out on the street and scrounge for pieces of wood or lumps of coal, whatever they can find." He shrugged. "Some of us guys toss 'em a few coins. Who knows what they do with the money? Or if they get to keep it."

He took a bite of potato and got a far-off look in his eyes. "When we get married, Donatella and I are gonna have a big family. I'll make sure I have a steady job with good pay. I don't want *my* kids to have to beg like that."

Mama gave Tommy one of her crooked smiles and ladled another helping of soup in his bowl. "*Mangia, mangia*. Eat. You talk-a too much."

Most of our suppers went the same way, with Tommy sharing stories from the streets of New York, and the rest of us swallowing whatever he said along with the potatoes or the rice or whatever else we were eating that night. Except for our evening radio programs, Tommy's stories were about the most entertainment we had back then.

The five of us had crammed together in a small apartment in the Bronx. Ten concrete steps led from the sidewalk to a glass-fronted entry. Another set of steps—wooden ones—rose from a musty foyer to our place on the second floor. A solitary light bulb hung on a chain from the ceiling. Whenever the front door opened, the bulb swayed and cast eerie shadows on the wall. Anyone could have been hiding there. At the end of a workday, as the sun was setting beyond the buildings, I scrambled up the steps, trembling, until I unlocked the door and walked into our brightly lit apartment.

I'd find Mama by the stove, her cheeks flushed from the steam rising out of a pot of something, and Papa, as always, in his easy chair, his face partially hidden behind his *l'Unita* newspaper, his unlit pipe clenched between his teeth.

Our apartment originally came with two bedrooms. Papa walled off the dining room to create a third bedroom for my brothers, which meant the five of us—and any invited guests—had to crowd around the kitchen table for meals. I didn't mind. I sat comfortably wedged between my two brothers. Our conversations always became animated to the point of pushing and poking. And laughing.

Of the three of us, Benny got the best grades and dreamed of going to college. He surprised us during supper one night when he said he wanted to quit school and get a job like Tomas and I had done.

Mama let out a wail and pulled a handkerchief from her apron pocket. "*O, Dio mio. O, Dio mio.* No break-a my heart."

Papa banged his fist on the table and made all the forks jump. Benny never asked again. It was a good thing, too, because a few years later, he graduated with honors and received a college scholarship. Mama raved about her son, the scholar, to anyone who would listen.

It didn't bother me that I never graduated from high school. In those days, a diploma was a useless piece of paper for a girl. Like most women born into ethnic families, I was expected to marry well or spend the rest of my life taking care of my parents.

Anyway, I had gotten enough schooling to satisfy my boss at the refrigeration plant. Back then, we didn't have all the modern-day FAX machines and computers to confuse the heck out of us. I used a filing cabinet, a phone, and a pad and pen. I wrote out bills of lading, which I passed to the men in the warehouse.

At the end of each week, I slipped a few coins in a sock at the back of my lingerie drawer, and I handed Mama the bulk of my pay envelope. She dropped the bills in what my brothers laughingly dubbed the "Cookie Jar Bank & Trust Company." After giving Mama a big chunk of his pay, Tomas spent what was left on Donatella.

Back then, I didn't hang out with my friends at shopping malls. We didn't have any malls to hang out in. We made our own clothes or wore hand-me-downs. We walked everywhere or took the bus. Mama stretched a single chicken into four meals. Papa cut my brothers' hair with a pair of hand clippers. Mama trimmed mine with kitchen shears. I assumed everybody did that.

That is, until I went to work for Sam at the meat refrigeration plant.

My boss drove a big car. We didn't even have a little one. Sam wore expensive store-bought suits, and he chain-smoked cigars like he owned Cuba. Despite his wealth he didn't act like a big shot. Though he lived in a huge house on the north shore of Long Island, he never behaved like he thought he was better than anyone else. He gave his employees bonuses on special holidays, and he talked to me as if I were his next door neighbor, not a nobody he'd hired off the street.

"Angela," he said, one morning, his voice sounding like he'd swallowed gravel. "You only have to watch the signs to know what's going on with the stock market. When the numbers began to fluctuate this past summer, I started selling off my stock." He strutted back-and-forth in front of my desk and puffed cigar smoke into the air. I coughed, but he didn't seem to notice.

"The same thing happened after World War I," he rambled on. "We had a few prosperous years, then the economy started to go downhill. When I saw the numbers starting to change, I figured it was time to get out."

Unlike Sam, a lot of investors didn't foresee the crash. When Black Thursday hit, they leaped out of buildings or shot themselves. Over what? Money? If they'd been like my family, poor to begin with, they wouldn't have ended their lives when they lost everything.

Sam had an opinion about that too. "It's the 1920s all over again," he growled. "People partied. They gambled. They bought things on time, and they signed away their lives to purchase houses they couldn't afford." He shook his head and spewed cigar ashes on my desk. "I'm tellin' ya, Angela, if not for

Hoover, we wouldn't have a prayer. He's gonna fix everything."

I thought about our President's campaign promise—"a car in every garage and a chicken in every pot." Like most low-income families, we didn't own a car. We didn't even have a garage to put one in. And chicken? If we were lucky, we'd get one a week.

"Hoover's a good man," Sam said. He peered at me through a gray cloud. "Did you know when Hoover got elected he refused to take a salary? Why, he could have had seventy-five grand a year. Just you wait, Angela. Hoover's got a plan that will fix the economy and put people back to work."

I wanted to believe such a promise, but, to be honest, I was growing a little tired of potato soup. Occasionally, Sam tossed me a package of ground beef or sausage links that were about to go bad. Mama simply trimmed off the green part and tossed the rest in the pot with the potatoes.

One evening, she opened the door of her pantry and scratched her head. "We have potatoes and beans. That's all. If Tomas bring home a bag of flour, we add a little water, a little salt, an' what-a you know? We have *pasta fajioli* for supper." She turned to look at me. "Watch an' learn, Angela. We no starve yet."

While the rest of us pooled our money to fill Mama's pantry, Papa became a visitor in his own home. With no drugs to relieve the pain in his back, he sat in his chair all day or took short walks around the block. Mama didn't allow smoking inside our little apartment, so Papa either perched on the front stoop and puffed away, or he took his pipe to the corner store and sat in a smoky circle with his Italian friends. One evening, I caught sight of him there on my way home from work, and my heart ached for him. His mop of hair was turning gray faster than it should have. And his shoulders had started to hunch over, either from age, or discouragement, or both.

The DiPolo boys next door had lost their own father to a heart attack. Poor Mrs. DiPolo didn't have much income except for a couple of cleaning jobs. One morning, her sons left home and hopped a train in search of work out west. One of them was only twelve years old. My brother Benito stared out the front window and watched them go.

"Don't even think about leaving, Benny," I warned him. "If those boys don't find work, they're gonna end up on the side of the road begging. Do you want that to happen to you?

"Shut up, Sis. I'll do what I want."

Mama shot Benny one of her eagle-eyed stares. As soon as he turned his back, the hardness left her eyes and they filled with tears.

Shortly after her sons took off, Mrs. DiPolo moved into one of those shacks the President set up on the outskirts of the city. "Hoovervilles," people called them. But when they needed a place to live, they stopped mocking and scrambled to get their families settled there.

Despite the swell of poverty, the Empire State Building opened on May 31, 1931. Sam strutted into the warehouse with a "Play Safe With Hoover" button pinned to his jacket.

"The President is going to dedicate the building from his office in Washington." My boss puffed out his chest. "I intend to be there when the lights go on." He paused by my desk. "You know, Angela, lots of folks are calling that amazing structure a worthless waste of money. But, I disagree. The tallest building in the world is going to set us miles above every other country."

Then, he grabbed a handful of cigars from his desk drawer, strode out of the building, and headed for town.

As some people had predicted, most of the offices remained empty for a long time. The project was beginning to look like a failure. But whenever I went into town, the spire at the top had me looking up, and, for the moment, it looked like Hoover might rescue us, after all.

Nevertheless, when Franklin D. Roosevelt ran against the incumbent, I followed the crowd. I didn't tell my boss I voted for the opposition. He wouldn't have fired me, but I wanted to keep peace in my workplace. After the votes were counted, Sam stomped around the building with a frown on his face. He dropped cigar ashes everywhere and shouted obscenities at the help.

After Roosevelt's inauguration, the newspapers were filled with negative articles about our new President. He was shot at, ridiculed, and accused of being a dictator. All the while he kept saying, "The only thing we have to fear is fear itself."

"That man lies," Sam huffed one day. "He promised us 'no new taxes,' but he signed that blasted 'soak the rich' tax. Why, if I bring in more than $100,000 a year, I'll have to pay a big chunk in taxes. I might as well shut everything down."

I shuddered at the thought. If Sam closed the warehouse, I'd be out of a job. Who would hire me when nearly thirteen million Americans were out of work? Every morning, I scanned the headlines and tried to anticipate my boss' mood before he walked in my office. Trouble in the stock market? He stomped in, growling and gnawing at the end of his cigar. A boost in the economy? He literally danced through the door, smiling and humming a tune.

As for me, I settled for the simple life. Away from the office,

I could forget about politics. I went to the movies with my best friend, Katie O'Malley. I read library books. I helped Mama with the cleaning and the cooking. I didn't expect my life would get any more exciting than that, until the day a humble Italian immigrant walked into my office, winked a sky blue eye at me, and changed my life forever.

CHAPTER THREE

THE BRONX, NEW YORK

1933-1935

His name was Alfredo Busconi, but I got to know him by the nickname the warehouse crew had given him—Fredo.

He wore the same type of clothes every day—plaid flannel shirts, pants that barely skimmed his ankles, white socks, and beat-up loafers. In the winter, he donned a Navy pea-coat with the collar turned up against the cold. Dark brown curls poked out from under a knitted cap, and his shocking blue eyes had me questioning his Italian heritage.

He wasn't what you might call handsome—not like Errol Flynn or Clark Gable—but he had a sweet meekness that set him apart from those plastic faces on the movie screen.

Every Tuesday and Thursday, like clockwork, Fredo backed up his truck to the dock. When he finished loading, he came into my office and went over every detail of the bill. At first, I thought he wanted to make sure he hadn't been cheated. But I discovered the opposite, one morning, when he dropped the bill on my desk and shook his head. "This say I get twenty chickens. I no get twenty, I get twenty-five. I no wanna cheat my friend Sam."

I left him standing there with his woolen cap bunched up in his hands. I stuck my head out the door and called out the discrepancy to the loading manager. He shouted the number. "Twenty-five." I went back to my desk and corrected the paperwork. With Fredo leaning over my shoulder, I was embarrassed to find I couldn't breathe. Heat rushed to my face. Trembling, I handed him the revised slip, then dared to look into his face. The sparkle in his eyes sent ripples down my spine.

He glanced at the bill, nodded, and left the building. I sat for a long time after, just staring at the door, until Sam walked in and snapped his fingers in front of my face.

Many nights I had prayed for a good, honest man to come into my life. My prince didn't have to be handsome and rich ... although handsome and rich would have been okay, too. What I wanted—*needed*—was a man I could look up to, a man of integrity, like my Papa.

On the days when Fredo came to the warehouse, I showed up for work early and spent several minutes in front of the bathroom mirror trying to get the tangles out of my hair. I cursed the day I was born with that mop of thick curls. What I wouldn't have given for Donatella's ebony blanket that hung almost to her waist.

With a resigned smirk, I returned to my desk and tried to busy myself with filing. All the while, I kept an eye on the plate glass between my office and the loading dock. I thought up all sorts of things I might say to Fredo. But when he walked through the door, the words lodged in my throat and all I could do was choke out a pathetic, "Good morning."

He responded with a nod and a soft, *"Buon giorno,"* and, after paying his bill, a simple, *"Ciao,"* as he left my office.

This went on for several weeks. Then one day, Fredo dawdled beside my desk. He shifted from one foot to the other, his cap crumpled up in his hands. He made a comment about the weather, then he smiled and raised his eyebrows, as if a thought had struck him.

"Angela, you wanna go *Italiano restaurante* where I deliver meat? Good food. Good music. We go—*come si dice,* how do you say—Saturday night? No?"

I blinked back my surprise. "S-Saturday night? Y-yes, sounds wonderful."

"We go." He nodded. "I pick-a you up. Sette?"

"Yes, seven o'clock is fine."

I wrote out my address and handed the slip of paper to him. With another nod, he put on his cap, then he backed out the door, still smiling and nodding.

My heart was pounding. I typed the next invoice three times before I got it right.

Saturday night, Fredo showed up promptly at seven o'clock with a broad grin and a bouquet of cut flowers. After enduring a grilling by my Papa—in Italian—my quivering suitor ushered me outside into the coolness of dusk. We each took a long breath of fresh air, then Fredo grabbed my hand and helped me into the passenger seat of his truck. I expected to be overwhelmed by the residue of bloody meat products he'd delivered over the past week. Instead, I inhaled the lemony aroma of Murphy's Oil Soap, familiar to me because it was the only product Mama trusted to clean her kitchen floor.

During dinner, I got to know this fascinating immigrant who had stepped off the boat at Ellis Island two years before. In broken English, Fredo told me he'd left Italy with a pocketful of lire he'd earned while working in the grape arbors in Tuscany. Shortly after his feet touched American soil he got a driver's license and bought a used pickup truck. He installed insulated bins in the bed, loaded them with ice, and for seventeen cents a gallon for gas, he began to deliver meat to restaurants and markets all over New York City. He lived alone in a rented room, but he dreamed of one day having a house and a family of his own.

I hung on every word. No other guy—not the boys I had known in school, not the workmen in the refrigeration plant, not any of my brothers' friends—were able to hold my attention the way Fredo did. He never failed to compliment my clothes, and he gave me a pet name—*Angelina*—which stayed with me for the rest of my life.

Our first dinner date turned into more evenings out, more dinners, and occasional trips to the local movie house. Mama complained that I never stayed home. To appease her, Fredo started spending evenings in our apartment. We sat on the living room sofa with a respectable distance between us, while Mama and Papa eyeballed us from the kitchen. I feared they might scare him off. Then, one day, at my Papa's prodding, my brother, Tomas, asked Fredo what his intentions were. I shrank back in embarrassment.

Fredo stood to his feet and faced my brother. "I proper," he said. "I hope for me nice-a future with Angelina." Then he turned toward Papa and said the same thing in Italian.

My folks smiled and nodded their approval. I waved my brother away, grabbed my boyfriend's arm, and led him to the landing. Scowling, I shut the door against the smiling faces inside the apartment. I gazed into Fredo's silvery blue eyes and hoped he couldn't hear the pounding of my heart. He put his hand on my waist and pulled me toward him. Every part of me went limp. His face came close to mine. A wave of heat rushed to my cheeks.

"*Domani,*" he whispered.

He brushed his lips against my cheek, missing my mouth entirely. Then, he danced down the stairs and out the door, leaving me wishing I had turned my face a fraction of an inch and gotten a real kiss.

After that, Fredo and I went everywhere together. More kisses came—real ones, but always in secret. I didn't care. Everyone could see we were falling in love.

Even the guys at work noticed our blossoming romance. They taunted Fredo when he came in for a load of meat. They winked at me when he left my office. I ignored them and tried to concentrate on my work. But when Fredo's truck pulled away I craned my neck and peered out the window. The guys burst out laughing. I glared at them, and they went back inside the warehouse shaking their heads and cooing to each other.

Though Fredo and I tried to find time alone, my parents insisted we spend weekday evenings in their apartment. Most of the time, we sat in the living room with Mama and Papa and my brother Benito. Some nights, the five of us gathered around our kitchen table and listened to *Jack Benny* or *Will Rogers* on the radio. Benito laughed out loud over their silly skits. I was distracted by more important things, like the way Fredo nudged my knee under the table, or the unspoken messages that traveled between our eyes.

Occasionally, Papa would tune in one of Roosevelt's *Fireside chats.* In a calming voice, the President began his message with, "My friends," and ended with a recording of the "Star-Spangled Banner." Fredo sprang to his feet and placed his right hand over his heart. The rest of us just sat there, astounded that this immigrant had a greater attachment to his new country than we did.

I think my life might have gone on that way forever, if not for the night Fredo took my father aside. I watched them from a chair in the living room. They talked for several minutes, shook hands, and hugged each other. With a huge grin on his face, Fredo came over to me, and, right in front of my folks, he got down on one knee and asked me to marry him. My heart racing, I mumbled a tearful acceptance.

The next morning, I hurried across town to show Katie my engagement ring. I didn't care if the diamond was the size of an apple seed. I held out my left hand with pride. On our tenth wedding anniversary, Fredo replaced my first diamond with a larger stone, and I put my little ring in my jewelry box for safe keeping. Every now and then, over the years, I would take it out, slip it on my finger, and remember the night my Fredo proposed. Now I hope and pray my daughter won't think my ring is a piece of junk and throw it away.

The day Sam spotted that engagement ring on my finger, he gave me a $2-a-week raise. I filled my socks with the extra cash and began to plan my wedding. Fredo and I continued to work during the day, and in the evenings we either went out to a restaurant or a movie, or he came to the apartment and we sat around like two concrete statues, afraid to touch each other with my folks watching.

Tomas beat us to the altar after he found out Donatella was four months pregnant. He moved in with her folks, but he kept giving Mama a few dollars every week.

Fredo's business took him to shops owned by other immigrants, people who spoke his language, and some who came from other countries—Poland mostly, and Ireland. Despite the language barriers, they got along fine and even held international block parties on Saturday nights. We attended for the street dancing and the ethnic foods, but also for the chance to get out from under my parents' scrutiny.

Then, one Saturday night, Fredo took my hand and led me to the center of the street. A small combo was playing "I Only Have Eyes for You." He twirled me a couple of times, then he dipped me backward until my curls brushed against the pavement. With both of his hands on my waist, he raised me up, and pulled me toward him.

"No more wait," he murmured, his lips close to my ear. "We call-a the church."

I didn't need any convincing. Four weeks later, on March 30, 1935, I put on Mama's faded wedding dress, and I walked down the aisle to become Mrs. Alfredo Busconi. Happy tears streamed down my face. For the moment, anyway, I had no idea of the tragedies that awaited us.

CHAPTER FOUR

THE BRONX

1935-1936

Although my parents invited us to live with them, like most newlyweds, Fredo and I wanted a place of our own. The thought of bringing my husband into my bedroom with a paper-thin wall separating us from my parents' sleeping quarters revolted me. When I moved out, Benito took my place, and Papa turned my younger brother's bedroom back into a dining room.

We settled in a small flat over Giuseppe's Italian Market, paid $20 a month rent, plus a dollar for electricity and fifty cents for gas to light our stove. A friend of my mother's gave us some used furniture—a sofa-bed, a kitchen table, and two chairs that didn't match. For baths, we kept a large pan in the corner of the kitchen and filled it with water we heated on the stove. I used the same tub and a washboard to do our laundry, which I hung to dry on a line in our bathroom.

Giuseppe installed a two-burner gas stove and a small "ice-a-box," as he and Fredo called it. As wedding gifts, we received several practical items—a toaster, a coffeepot, a few pieces of cookware, and a partial set of bargain basement dishes. We managed quite well without any of the conveniences I have today. It's true what they say, "What you don't know won't hurt you."

Between the two of us, we managed to pay our bills, and we put a little aside for a rainy day. When money was tight, we looked for the best deals at the market. Mama had taught me how to stretch a single chicken into a whole week of dinners by adding rice or pasta. I also made my mother's potato soup recipe, usually with a few whole potatoes, but sometimes with peelings I salvaged from Giuseppe's bins. We had salt but no milk, bread but no butter, beans but no onions. And we survived.

"Look," Fredo said one evening after dragging himself home from work. "Mario give me nice hunk o'beef. It tough like my boots, but maybe okay if you pound good."

He pealed open the brown paper and revealed a pathetic looking slab of meat. I gave him a big hug, lay the beef on the table and got the hammer out of our catch-all drawer.

Fredo crossed his arms and stepped away from the table. "No break-a my hammer," he said, laughing.

I glanced at him out of the corner of my eye and gave him a sly grin. "Don't worry, Fredo. You'll still have your hammer when I'm done." Then I raised the tool above my head, and snarled like I was about to kill an animal, and the two of us broke into hysterics.

Mama once told me laughter can help a marriage survive anything. If not for Fredo's sense of humor, I might have sunk into despair many times. Even when we were down to our last dime, he'd find ways to cheer me up. A few times, he suggested we take a walk to the corner store and spend a couple of nickels on two bottles of Coke. All the way over and all the way back, he told funny stories about things that had happened at work that day. He had me laughing so hard I couldn't take a drink without spilling some.

Like Charles Dickens wrote in one of his books, "It was the best of times. It was the worst of times." In spite of all our struggles, the Great Depression set the stage for a sixty-eight year marriage that produced three children, four grandchildren, and a whole lot of happy memories.

When other men's businesses failed, Fredo picked up more clients. Every Friday, he'd come home with a pocketful of money. He'd give me enough for household expenses, and he'd put the rest in the cigar box under our sofa-bed. That little box held up for a long time, but eventually we needed something bigger, so we switched to shoeboxes.

"Let's hang onto our cigar box anyway," I said. "For old times' sake."

After all, that little box had held more than money. In a symbolic way, it held our dreams. Who in the world would trash something like that?

Though we had to tighten our belts, we counted ourselves among the more fortunate. Ten million people were out of work, but we both had jobs. Together, we brought home about $1,700 a year. We began to save anything that still had life in it. I grabbed a mess of tangled rubber bands my boss was getting ready to throw out. I tucked them in our kitchen catch-all drawer along with a broken stapler and some torn envelopes. Fredo came home from work with a handful of rusty nails he'd found on the ground along his route. He plunged them in a sink full of soapy water, scrubbed them clean, and then he took my meat-tenderizing hammer and pounded the bent ones straight.

I made a deal with Giuseppe to clean his shelves and the stairwell in return for leftover vegetables. More often than not, we ate beans instead of chicken, potatoes instead of beef, and rice mixed with anything we could find in our pantry.

"We joost-a fine," Fredo said one Friday night when I had curled up beside him on our sofa-bed. "I poot five dollar in shoebox today. You take tomorrow. Buy flour and tomatoes. Make-a spaghetti."

I snuggled up to him, not caring about flour and tomatoes at the moment. I tucked my forehead against his neck. I didn't mind the perspiration that clung to his chest after a hard day on the road, or the residue of grease on his hands from working on his truck. No amount of soap or deodorant could erase the vestige of the man I had fallen in love with. My Fredo hadn't walked off the cover of a magazine. Nor did he smell of men's cologne and cigar wrappings, like my boss Sam did. With my Italian lover's arms wrapped around me, I felt safe and content, and that was all that mattered.

But one summer night, when the steamy streets began to cool and a mist hung in the air, my sense of security plummeted. We had left our kitchen window open to allow in a breath of evening air. The sheer curtain gave a lazy flutter, then hung lifeless. With strains of "Blue Moon" playing on our radio, Fredo and I drifted off to sleep in each other's arms.

At midnight we awoke to static on the radio and the sound of breaking glass downstairs.

Fredo slipped out of bed and shuffled to the window. He raised his hand and cautioned me to stay back. I tiptoed to the radio and turned off the noise.

Fredo backed into the room. "Three men outside Giuseppe's store," he whispered.

There was a scuffling of footsteps below. Bins overturned with a crash, followed by the plunking of produce dropping to the floor. Then came the ka-ching of Giuseppe's cash register, the rustle of bags, and, finally, the scraping of shoes on the sidewalk out front.

Fredo ventured another peek out the window. "They look up." He jerked his head back, and I caught my breath. He turned toward me and raised a finger to his lips.

I edged closer to my husband. We had no weapons. No gun. No club. Only a couple of dull kitchen knives. I considered my iron skillet. My wooden rolling pin. I sized up my wiry, little husband. He'd be no match against three desperate hoodlums.

Fredo pulled back the curtain and risked another look out the side of the window. "They run away," he said, relief in his voice.

I drew close to his side and caught a glimpse of the robbers stumbling across the street, their arms weighted down with paper sacks. Fredo wrapped an arm around me. I couldn't stop trembling. I gazed into my husband's face and was surprised to find calmness there. My Fredo may not have looked like Errol Flynn or Clark Gable, but at that moment he was my hero.

Gently, he released his hold on me. "I go downstairs to phone. Call Giuseppe." Placing his hands on my arms, he settled me on the sofa-bed. "You stay. No worry."

He left the apartment for only a few minutes. I sat on our sofa-bed and held my breath until Fredo returned. When he walked in, I started shaking. I burst into sobs. He stared at me, his brow wrinkled with compassion. He settled beside me and caught me up in his arms.

"No, no, *mio amore*. This happen in Italy all-a time. People no have food. They beg. They steal. But we safe. Giuseppe no in store. Nobody harm."

I shook my head. He couldn't possibly understand the reason for my tears.

"Those men—" I mumbled. "Maybe they have wives—and children. Maybe they wouldn't have had to resort to stealing if they had a job." I searched his face for answers. "Don't you see, Fredo? If things don't get any better, we might find ourselves in the same situation as those men. How bad will things get before *we* have to steal to survive?"

My husband's cool, blue eyes didn't flicker. He stroked my hair and smiled. "We fine, Angelina. No worry."

"You know the economic situation is going to get worse before it gets better, don't you?" I didn't try to keep the tension out of my voice. I wanted Fredo to understand—as I did—this was only the beginning.

I didn't sleep that night. Fredo snored away as though nothing had happened.

The next morning, we talked over breakfast while we waited for Giuseppe to show up at the store.

"They've started rationing milk and butter," I told Fredo. He shrugged and took a bite of his toast. "And coffee," I continued. "It's only a matter of time before the refrigeration plant closes and I lose my job. Your delivery business could fail too, and—"

He shook his head and smiled sweetly. "No worry, *mio amore*. This better than old country. Over there, I work long hours. Not much pay. Here—in America—I have truck. I have my own business. We fine."

"But, what if—"

Fredo leaned across the table and pressed his index finger against my lips. He gave me a firm stare. "Be calm, Angelina. I take care you."

From downstairs came the stomping of footsteps, the slam of a door, and a loud shriek. Giuseppe had walked in on the mess. Fredo gulped down the last of his breakfast and went downstairs to help our poor grocer-friend clean up his store. I opened the kitchen window and listened to the cacophony of renovations—the scratching of brooms, the stirring of shards of glass, the banging of hammers patching wood over the broken window, and the clunking of tables and shelves being righted. Now and then, Giuseppe wailed out a curse in Italian. Fredo's voice followed with soft words of comfort.

I busied myself pressing the wrinkles out of my husband's shirts. While my iron drew heat from the stove, I filled an empty soda bottle with water and sprinkled the collar of his dress shirt. I lifted the fabric to my chin and sniffed Fredo's masculine scent. It was the next best thing to touching his skin.

After I hung the last of my husband's shirts in our little closet, I put together a simple stew with a potato, a couple of wilted carrots, an onion, and a can of beef broth. If I'd had a stone I could have made a pot of soup like the one in the storybook I would one day read to my children. Though the concoction on my stove didn't amount to much, it sent a hearty aroma out the window to the two men working downstairs.

"Smells good," Fredo called from the street.

I leaned over the window ledge. "It's not ready. Give me a few more minutes."

I sliced mold off a piece of cheese and set the good part on the table with a loaf of stale brown bread that would soften up once they dipped it in the broth. I put a set of mismatched bowls and three spoons on the table, and then I laid out some blue napkins I had made from an old tablecloth. I set the pot of soup in the center, along with a vase of red artificial flowers. Then I stepped back and surveyed my setting, thinking it every bit as nice as a restaurant might offer.

Satisfied, I stuck my head out the window. "Fredo! Lunch."

Seconds later, there was a thumping on the stairs and the two men burst into the apartment. They brushed the dust off their clothes and washed their hands in our little cubicle of a bathroom. I chuckled at the sight of two grown men—one a scrawny little Italian, the other a robust gorilla—huddled together over our tiny washbasin.

Giuseppe emerged first. Before me stood a stocky man with a grizzled chin and red-rimmed eyes. With the ties of his white apron crisscrossed in front of him, he looked every bit the owner of a grocery store. Giuseppe's smock was as much a part of him as his bulbous pink nose and his bushy eyebrows.

Fredo and Giuseppe took our only two chairs at the table. My husband bowed his head and blessed the food. Then the two of them dug in like two hungry bears.

Giuseppe tore off a chunk of the bread, immersed it in the soup, and shoved the dripping morsel in his mouth. Gravy ran onto his beard. His eyes smiled. He made a circle with his thumb and forefinger and gave them a loud kiss. "*Deliziosa!*"

Fredo beamed. "My wife—she queen of the kitchen."

I stifled an embarrassed smile, shook my head, and fixed myself a bowl of soup. While the two men fell into their native tongue, I settled on our sofa-bed and ate in silence. Though my parents had come from Sicily, I rarely spoke their language. I grew up in America. I had an American education. I hung out with American friends. In fact, my best friend,

Katie O'Malley, was Irish. But, I knew enough Italian to understand Giuseppe when he said the robbery had caused him to consider closing his store and selling the building. I set down my spoon and stared at him. Where else could we pay $20 a month for such accommodations? I shifted my gaze to Fredo. He slurped up his soup as though he hadn't heard a word Giuseppe had said. Once again, I started to worry about the future.

Three weeks later, things did get worse. My husband came home from work early, his face drawn, his shoulders hunched, his eyes moist. "I joost-a hear—my friend, Georgio, he go back to Italy. Deported."

I tossed aside the dish towel I was holding and rushed over to him. "No. Not Georgio. But why? What did he do?"

"He no do nothing. Men complain where he work, say jobs belong-a to Americans. They strike—march outside. Same thing happen all over. So, government no renew visas, shut down immigration, send Georgio and others back to old country."

My heart sank. "Wh-what about you, Fredo? Your competitors—they could force you out of business. Will the government send *you* back to Italy, too?"

"No, *mio amore*. I married," he said with a wink. "But I make-a sure." He tapped his forehead with his index finger. "I know what I do. I stand before judge. I say—*come si dice?*—I say *Pledge*. Then judge say, 'Alfredo Busconi citizen. No deport.'"

I stared in amazement at my courageous, young husband. Despite his limited command of the English language, I had no doubt he'd be able to recite the oath. For immigrants like Fredo, American citizenship opened a door to jobs without opposition. It gave them the right to vote, the right to hold local office, and, of course, the right to pay taxes. But, in the late 1930s, another door was about to open. Soon, the government would create the draft. American males between the ages of 18 and 25—including naturalized citizens—would be required to sign up. A few years later, the United States would enter World War II, and my beloved Fredo would be among the first to go.

CHAPTER FIVE

SEPTEMBER 2008

I wipe away a tear and shift my attention to the park across the street. The stillness of morning erupts with life as three small children rush toward the jungle gym. Their shrill laughter penetrates my window. They tumble down the slide and swing from the monkey bars. Their mother is sitting nearby on a park bench. Her head's buried in a book, but she knows where her children are and what they're doing. I know this because it's exactly what I used to do when my kids were young and we went to a neighborhood park. No matter what I was doing, I had one eye on my kids.

When we first moved here, the property across the street was nothing but three acres of scrub grass with a murky pond in the middle. Our town leaders cleaned up the pond, then they planted a few seedlings that eventually grew into mature oaks. I loved watching the scene change and grow. In more recent years, the city added white flowering shrubbery, a picnic pavilion, several benches, and the playground. Then, of course, the park filled up with people too.

We found this house in a real estate ad that listed it as a "historic home overflowing with small-town charm." And so, thirty-six years ago, after Fredo retired, we moved to this rural Florida town, population 4,304.

"Angelina," Fredo said, a big grin on his face. "Now, there be four-thousand, three hundred, and *six.*"

At the time, our son Jack was in his final year at the University of Florida and was working on his PhD in family counseling. He lived in a dorm in Gainesville. Patricia had divorced her husband and though she came down and stayed with us for a while, she missed the New York society set, and she soon left us. Dorothy and her husband, Barry, followed us down here and bought their own place. A former car salesman, Barry got into real estate, and our eldest daughter found a secretarial job in an Orlando law office.

From the beginning, Barry—the big real estate expert—told Fredo we'd bought the wrong house. He got right in my husband's face and raised his voice the way some people do when they're talking to senior citizens.

"This house is over a hundred years old," Barry shouted. "It has too many things wrong with it. I'm afraid you bought yourself a money pit, Pop."

Fredo backed away and shot me one of his annoyed glances. He ignored Barry's advice and went ahead with the deal. In fact, most of the time, both of us ignored our son-in-law. For one thing, he wasn't Italian. Plus, he'd been a lousy car salesman, so we didn't expect him to do much better in real estate.

Okay, maybe Barry had a point. We *had* purchased an older house, and our place *did* have some flaws we discovered after we moved in. For instance, the fireplace had a clogged flue. A little over $2,000 took care of that. Barry said we didn't need a fireplace in Florida, but we disagreed. Our New York house had one and we liked it. So, on chilly evenings, my husband got a blaze going during those couple of weeks they call winter down here. Then, we cozied up together on the sofa with cups of hot chocolate and a bowl of popcorn, and we watched the flames flicker and dance.

Since Fredo passed away, I haven't lit another fire. I had no idea how much work it took for my husband to haul in those logs. Nor did I relish the chore of cleaning up the ashes. So, when the weather gets cold and damp, I simply turn up the thermostat.

The outside of this place also had some weak spots the newspaper ad never mentioned. Fredo had to reinforce the balcony outside our bedroom so we could sit up there during Founder's Day celebrations. From up there we enjoyed the scene but avoided the sweaty crowd and the children scampering around with balloons and cotton candy in their sticky hands. We passed our one set of binoculars back and forth between the two of us and got a birds-eye view of the demonstrators showing off their skills in the park.

Pretty soon, Founder's Day will roll around again on the third weekend in October. A parade will circle the block and pass right in front of my house. Storytellers will come to the park and talk about the Seminole Indians who once camped around the pond. And, the air will carry the aromas of barbecued wild boar, fresh-baked bread, and apple cider.

I take a deep breath and sip my tea. The golden liquid has cooled, but it still tastes of orange spice, one of my favorite brews.

A flash of heat lightening streaks across the sky beyond the pond. It's followed by a low rumble. I can't help but compare it to the storm that's building inside my heart, a faint stirring for now, but chances are it too could build into a violent storm, if I let it.

I turn my attention to the fountain in the center of the pond and a sense of calm stills the tempest inside me. Many an evening, Fredo and I sat on our front porch and watched that fountain spew crystals in the air while colored lights cast a rainbow across the mist. At least once a week, Fredo would stop rocking and he'd shoot me a sideways glance. "How much you think it costs to keep that thing runnin'?" he'd say.

I'd simply smile. "It doesn't matter. I like it."

He'd nod and say he liked it too. Then he'd set his rocker going again with a steady creak-creak-creak. How I miss that sound.

We must have repeated the same dialogue a hundred times during the last two years of Fredo's life. I never corrected him, no matter how many times he said it. That's love, isn't it, to let the other person say whatever they want and not correct them?

We didn't only talk about the fountain. We also discussed how our bushes needed trimming, how our house could use a fresh coat of paint, and how our front porch swing needed oiling. Those things never got done. We merely sat there and talked about them.

As the evening wore on, neighbors walked by. Sometimes we gave them a wave, sometimes we stepped off the porch and joined them for a stroll around the pond. When we returned home, Fredo paused and saluted the American flag he'd hung from a bracket out there. I'm ashamed to say I didn't raise my hand to my heart. I just stood there and waited for Fredo to get through his patriotic ritual.

I never felt the kind of loyalty Fredo had developed. Our government had demanded so much from my husband I grew to resent the symbol of our country. To me, the flag stood for struggles beyond anything I could have dreamed would happen to us. It stood for an economy that had gotten so bad I lost my job. It stood for young men going off to war, some of them never coming home again. Most of all, it stood for losing my husband to a war I didn't support.

Twice Fredo was taken away from me—once when he joined the forest service to help stop the flooding along the Ohio River, and again when he ran off to fight in a war that left him crippled both physically and emotionally. That's what I remembered when I looked at the flag.

After my husband died, I stashed his flag in a corner of his tool shed and bolted the door. Salute the flag? He should have been glad I didn't burn it.

I take a deep breath and soak up the scene across the street. This may be my last chance to enjoy it. If Dorothy has her way, I'll be out of here by tomorrow.

The storm is starting to move off. I'd love to get out on the porch and feel the static in the air, but I don't have the strength to move without my walker, and I'm not about to ask Dorothy to help me.

During Fredo's last year, we rarely left our front porch. The last time we were out there together, he turned to me and said, "Let's go down to the park."

I took his arm and guided him down the steps. He felt like one of those rag dolls, almost weightless and without any muscle tone. I no sooner got him settled on a bench by the pond than he fell into a coughing spell. I held my breath and kept my eyes on him until he was able to settle down. Afterward, he slipped his arm around me and we snuggled so close our shadow looked like our shirts were sewn together.

When the last orange streaks settled across the pond, we

shuffled back home. Fredo paused on the front lawn and raised his arm in a weak salute. Then he gripped the railing and struggled up the porch steps, halting now and then to catch his breath. I braced his elbow until he reached the top. Gasping, he sank into his rocker, and I ran inside to get his medicine.

At night, I made Fredo use the oxygen tank his doctor had prescribed.

"I no like," he said. "Too hot. Too much noise."

I feared he might not live through the night without the breathing apparatus.

"I'll lie here beside you," I said. "We'll both put up with the heat and the noise."

I settled close to my husband on his hospital bed and we listened to the pulsing of the machine. After Fredo fell asleep, I slipped into my own bed on the other side of the room. From there, I could pray, and weep, and toss and turn without disturbing him.

As time passed, Fredo's condition worsened, though he never complained. Once, I came into the living room and found him coughing into a wad of tissues. He caught me standing there, crumpled up the hanky and tossed it in the fireplace. He didn't move fast enough to hide the splotch of red. I pretended I didn't see it.

Right up to the end, Fredo downplayed his sickness. He'd shoot me one of those ear-to-ear smiles of his, the kind that sent a web of lines trailing from the corners of his eyes to his hairline.

"Maybe we go for ice-a cream?" he said one night after supper.

"I have some in the freezer, dear. Let's take a couple of bowls out to the porch."

It didn't take much coaxing to get Fredo outside with a bowl of rum raisin. If he struggled with the spoon, I helped him bring it to his mouth. He simply smiled and smacked his lips.

Five years have passed since Fredo lay, pain-free, in a casket. Clad in his pale blue suit and dress shirt, he resembled the man who stood waiting for me at the altar many years before. That's the image I hold onto. It's how I want to remember my husband. But sometimes, I have trouble picturing his features. They've faded to a blur, and I'm afraid I might forget his face altogether. That's when I pull out our old photo albums. They help me remember him the way he used to be. Healthy, active, his sky blue eyes dancing with delight over the silliest little incident. I get my Fredo back again, if only for a few minutes.

CHAPTER SIX

ANGELA

SEPTEMBER 2008

Soon I'll have nothing left. Nothing but the clothes on my back and whatever little trinkets Dorothy decides I can keep. It's like reliving the Great Depression all over again. I have this nagging sense of urgency, a lingering fear that something will go wrong and I'll be completely destitute.

In a matter of hours, I'll reach the point of no return. My three children will force me to decide where I'm going to live. I can't imagine spending the rest of my life with any of them. Nor do I want to go into a nursing home. There's nothing but a bunch of old people there. What am I gonna do? Play cards? Bingo? Sit in a wheelchair and watch TV until the drool runs down my chin?

It's not like my kids are fighting over who gets me. They're all busy with their own lives. I think Dorothy has resigned herself to the fact that she'll have to take me in. It's not what she really wants. It's not what I want either.

Nor could I live with Patricia. After her divorce from Ed Carpenter, my youngest daughter came to stay with us for a short time. It didn't last. She missed her fast-paced life up north. Her modeling days over, she ended up in Burlington, New Jersey, where she took a job as a buyer of women's apparel in Riche's Department Store. Today she earns a six-figure salary and lives in a condominium in a high-rise building. She hardly knows I'm alive. Anyway, I wouldn't be able to take that ice cold climate again.

One summer, I went up north to visit her. Patricia rushed in and out of her condo and left me to fend for myself.

"There's yogurt and some other stuff in the fridge," she said as she went out the door. "Root around and help yourself, Mother. See ya later."

In the evening, she barged in with a bunch of her rowdy friends, whipped up some snacks and partied till two in the morning. I retreated to the spare bedroom, but I couldn't sleep for all the noise. The next day I went home.

I could almost tolerate living with Patricia if not for Billy Beckman. His pretty-boy face was plastered all over the covers of decades-old magazines strewn across their coffee table. Billy's twenty years younger than my daughter, but, at forty-three, he's pretty much over the hill in the world of photographic modeling. With him hanging around there, the place would seem way to crowded to suit me.

If I wanted to live with any of our kids, I'd choose Jack, my youngest. We bonded from the day he was born. Even as a toddler, he rarely left my side. I had to watch my step while I was cooking, he'd be under foot every time I turned around. I was extra careful not to spill hot water on him or drop a knife or a fork when he was beside me.

While growing up, Jack talked to me about everything—his school work, his ballgames, his dream to become a doctor one day. He even wanted my opinion about the girls he dated, and he never left the house without first asking if I needed anything.

So, why hasn't Jack come to my rescue? He should have

taken charge of this moving-out drama. If only he didn't live so far away.

After Jack got married, his wife dragged him across the country to California so she could be close to her parents. They have a big, beautiful home with enough room for me, but a few weeks ago they took in their son, Freddie, and his family. The poor boy was laid off from his job at the newspaper. His house went into foreclosure, and neither he nor Marcie have found another job. So, they went home to Papa, dragging along their three children and cramming their belongings in the shed behind Jack's house.

Now I'm facing a major decision. Assisted living or Dorothy's place. I'm guessing the final choice won't rest with me anyway.

When I move, I'll leave behind a big part of my life with Fredo. I stare at the empty chair on the other side of the table. I sniff the air expecting to get one more whiff of my husband's pipe tobacco. Instead I breathe in the harsh sting of disinfectant.

Dorothy has come up beside me and she's wiping her hands on a towel. She strokes my back. I'm surprised by the comfort in her touch.

"You don't have to worry about anything, Mother." Her tone has softened and catches me off-guard. "I'm going to take care of you," she says, her voice sweet. "You'll see. Once you get settled, you'll have no more worries, no more housework, no more—"

"Independence?" I raise my eyebrows at her.

"Come on, Mother. All I'm saying is, you'll be able to relax and enjoy life."

I look into her eyes. They shine with genuine compassion. Maybe Dorothy *did* get some of Fredo's genes, after all.

I'm about to beg for more time when Dorothy's cell phone sounds off. She pulls the noisy thing out of her pocket and stares at the screen.

"Hi, Hon. Yeah, we'll be home in twenty minutes."

She shuts off the phone and turns to me. "Lunchtime."

Ten minutes later, we're cruising down my tree-lined street toward Dorothy's house about three miles away. I shudder. In another day or two, lunchtime is going to last longer than an hour. It's going turn into an overnight stay. Then, my overnight stay will turn into the rest of my life.

I stare out my window at the manicured lawns and the brick-and-mortar homes scrolling past my window. Occasionally, there's a break in the string of inhabited dwellings and we pass an unkempt yard, an empty shell of a house, and a "foreclosure" sign out front. Those lifeless houses send a wave of sadness through me. They remind me of another period in American history, one that I wouldn't want to live through again. Not without Fredo.

I glance at my daughter. She isn't the only person who has the power of eviction. From the looks of things, the banks and mortgage companies have it too. Nor am I the only person who's being uprooted. The same thing happened to the people who once owned those empty houses.

We turn the corner and pass through an iron gate into the community where Dorothy and Barry live. The houses are bigger here, the yards smaller. The uniform dwellings have conformed to the rules of the homeowner's association. No trash cans by the curb, no fences, no free-roaming pets, no sheds, no boats, no trailers, no parking on the street. No life. No freedom. No individual creativity of any kind.

I purse my lips in disgust. Giuseppe had one rule. "You need anything? Joost-a let me know. Anything at all. If I can do, I make it happen." How I miss him.

We turn the corner and there's Barry, pacing the sidewalk, cigarette smoke trailing upward past his squinty eyes. I grumble under my breath. We pull into the drive and he tosses the butt on the sidewalk. He doesn't bother to stomp it out. He approaches my side of the car and opens the door, and I'm hit with a wave of tobacco residue.

"Hi, Mom," he shouts in my face. "Let me help you out."

He bends close to me and I'm repelled by the stale cigarette odor on his breath. I'd like to get out of the car under my own power, but before I can grip the door frame, Barry tucks his hands under my armpits and lifts me like I'm a three-year-old. I get my footing, and Dorothy comes around with my walker.

"I'm okay," I insist. "I can make it inside."

Pushing my walker, I limp to the side entry where Barry has installed a ramp to the kitchen door. I suppose I should appreciate my son-in-law. After all, he didn't *have* to build a ramp for me.

Once inside, I'm struck by the aroma of marinated beef sizzling under the broiler. If nothing else, Barry's turned out to be a pretty fair cook. If his real estate business fails, maybe he can get a job in a restaurant.

Dorothy gets me seated at the kitchen table. She heads for the refrigerator and pulls out a salad. Barry slips his hands inside two oven mitts and takes a broiler pan from the oven. My mouth waters at the sight of the charred roast with its juices dripping through the grate to the bottom of the pan. Like the TV chefs recommend, Barry sets the meat aside and lets it rest while he scoops potatoes into a bowl and tops them with a glob of butter and a sprinkle of fresh parsley.

Dorothy pours me a glass of lemonade. The ice cubes tinkle against the sides, and momentarily take me back to my front porch swing and summer nights with Fredo. Like a knife going into my heart, the elusive memory leaves behind a lingering ache.

Dorothy heaps potatoes on my plate and Barry adds a slice of roast beef. They reach across the table, passing the bread, butter, salt, pepper, ketchup—never uttering a word.

Dorothy's cutting up my steak. Barry's already eaten halfway through his own generous portion. There was no blessing of the food. No polite waiting for the rest of us to start eating. I raised Dorothy better than that. My Fredo never let our kids lift a fork until we thanked the Lord. And, no one took a bite until I did. Where I come from, it's called etiquette.

I whisper my own words of gratitude and start eating.

Dorothy takes a sip of lemonade and turns toward me, her eyebrows raised, like she has something important to say.

"We've renovated our dining room into a bedroom for you, Mother, on the main floor, so you won't have to climb any stairs. It's right off the kitchen, and you'll have the downstairs bath all to yourself."

I'm about to dig into my salad. I hesitate and glance at her. What am I supposed to say? Thank you? Thanks for moving me out of a three-bedroom house and into a box?

"Let's have you try living here for a while, Mother. If it doesn't work out, you can go into assisted living. There's a nice facility about two miles away. I visited the place a couple of months ago. The rooms are spacious, and they serve meals in a dining room that looks like a fancy restaurant. The residents get together and watch TV. They play cards and bingo, and they celebrate each other's birthdays."

She let out the whole spiel without taking a breath. I couldn't interrupt her if I wanted to. I let out a sigh and focus on the pile of potatoes on my plate. There was a day when all we had in the pantry were potatoes. I fried them, baked them, and boiled them. And, of course, I made my mother's potato soup. Simply add a few pieces of onion, a stalk of celery, and a little milk. Of course, mine never turned out like hers.

"My last contract fell through." Barry's talking with his mouth full. "I haven't had a sale in six months," he whines. "The real estate market has declined steadily for the last three or four years. By the end of this year, a million people will have lost their homes to foreclosure. Everybody's hurting, Dottie. Builders. Insurance agents. Those of us who stuck it out in real estate got hit the worst. If we can't get a foothold soon, we're gonna have to dip into my IRA."

He glances up at me and keeps eating.

I slip a piece of steak in my mouth and grind it between my back teeth. I don't feel sorry for my son-in-law. He should have been around in the 1930s when people got sucked into loans they couldn't afford and fell for promises that were never fulfilled. Instead of making their lives better, people lost everything. Now, here we are, more than seventy years later, and the whole scene is repeating itself. What was it someone said about making the same mistakes over and over and expecting different results?

Dorothy pats her husband's wrist. "Be patient, Barry. It's bound to get better."

In my opinion, she pampers him too much. The piece of

meat in my mouth goes down hard. I drink a little lemonade to soothe the ache in my throat.

"You'll see, dear," Dorothy croons. "Once we get Mother settled, I'll put a few job applications in town."

"Right." Barry's smirking now. "You just turned sixty-six. Who's gonna hire you? Maybe it's time you started collecting your Social Security."

Dorothy sets down her fork and glares at Barry. "You don't understand. I like the idea of getting back into the workforce. I used to work in an office. It'll all come back to me."

Barry snickers. "Keep dreaming, Dottie. With your limited office training, what are ya' gonna do? Times have changed, my dear. Everything's done on computers now."

"I'm not stupid, Barry. Whatever I don't know I can learn. The local college offers classes. Or, I can ask our grandchildren to teach me. Maybe it'll get them to visit us more often. Picture it. We'll sit in front of a computer, and they'll show their grandma how to do spread sheets and documents."

"And online games," Barry adds with a chuckle.

They laugh and the tension eases a little. Barry smiles at her. Dorothy raises her eyebrows and smiles back at him. He winks and takes another mouthful. Between bites, I look back and forth at the two of them. Their facial expressions say a lot more than their spoken words do.

I can relate. Fredo and I could communicate without saying a single word. I guess when couples stay together for that many years, they really do become one.

Barry chomps on another slice of meat. "So, how's the packing going?"

"I'm making progress, but Mother has way too much stuff."

"Can I help?"

"Maybe. I'll have a couple of trash bags ready for you to take to the dump tomorrow."

I stop eating for a second and catch my breath. I hadn't pictured my things going into one of those dumpsters. This is really happening.

"I'll come by in the afternoon," Barry says. "Anything else?"

"No, dear. I can take care of the small items by myself. In a couple of days you can help with the bigger jobs—the furniture and cleaning out Dad's shed."

"Right. I'll get a U-Haul and—" Barry's eyes flash. "Say, what do you have planned for Mom's furniture?"

"I'm not sure." Dorothy suspends her fork in mid-air. "*We* certainly don't need it." She takes a bite of salad. "I don't know. It's still in good shape. Maybe we can take it to the women's shelter."

"W-wait up. I have an idea." Barry leans back and cocks his head. "Do you think I might use some of Mom's furniture to stage one of my empty houses?"

"Like a showroom?"

"Yeah, when it's done right, the houses sell faster."

Dorothy shrugs. "Take it all if you think it will help."

I'm sitting here like a dead person watching other people decide what they'll do with the remains. They talk right past me. I'm about ready to speak up when Barry pushes away from the table, lets out a belch, and takes his plate to the sink. He pulls a pack of cigarettes from his shirt pocket and heads out the side door.

Dorothy cleans the table and tackles the dishes. There was a time when I would have gotten up and helped. But now, I sit and watch the stack of dirty plates disappear into the dishwasher. That's my life. I'm nothing but a used-up dirty dish. My belongings are like the scraps of food being scraped into the garbage disposal, and I'm heading for the wash cycle. Just clean her up and put her back on the shelf.

CHAPTER SEVEN

THE BRONX

1937

It was May 6, 1937. Tragedy struck when an airship crashed in Lakehurst, New Jersey, less than eighty miles from our apartment. Giuseppe hollered up the stairwell for Fredo to turn on our radio. We huddled together in front of the speaker as a reporter choked out a detailed account of the fiery accident. I wept over the graphic descriptions of people leaping to safety while others were trapped by the flames.

I learned later that thirty-six people had died and many others had suffered terrible injuries. I imagined the horror. The unexpected drop to earth. The burst of flames. The screaming nightmare.

A newspaper article said the Hindenburg's passengers had paid $450 apiece for the trans-Atlantic crossing. I absorbed the information with a touch of bitterness.

"Can you imagine spending that much money on one ride?" I griped to my husband. "If we had $450 we'd buy food. Or clothes. Or we'd help somebody else. Anything but splurge it on a joy ride."

Fredo tilted his head and smiled at me. "Angelina, open your heart. Those poor people no see the part of life we have. Only know what they have. Not their fault if they blind to the poor."

I hated to admit my own shortcomings, but my dear Fredo had a much more tolerant attitude than I had. Fredo and I bought only what we needed and tried to ignore the frills. For entertainment, we went to the movies or took walks around town. Some nights Fredo moved the furniture to one side of our living room, and we'd turn up the radio and foxtrot to some of our favorite songs, like "A Fine Romance" and "Cheek to Cheek." That's how he held me, with his cheek pressed against mine and our arms and legs so intertwined we must have looked like a pretzel.

When we got tired of dancing, we cuddled on the sofa and tuned our radio to one of the nighttime serials that held our attention from one episode to the next. Except for the dollar a month we paid for electricity, it was free entertainment.

Fredo and I were in our second year of marriage when the government started handing out food, clothing, and blankets to the poor. We took a couple of quilts to Mama's house and stayed for a dinner of rice and beans. Benito joined us, and, as I expected, the conversation turned to the economy.

"Well, things are looking up," my college student brother said. He raised his chin and grinned like he was about to spill a ton of secrets on the rest of us imbeciles. "My professor went over the numbers in class yesterday." He ignored the smirk on my lips and went on. "If Roosevelt's Second New Deal can get support from the conservatives, it'll mean more benefits for the poor."

"Like us?" I said with an air of sarcasm.

Benito bobbed his head. "Yeah. Like us and a whole lot of other folks who are far worse off than we are."

I decided to challenge him with a little knowledge of my own. "My boss told me the President has ordered farmers to plow their fields under and to let the fruit rot on their trees. And dairy farmers are dumping their extra milk along the side of the road." I shook my head in disgust. "People are starving and they're wasting food. Kids can't even get a glass of milk and they're dumping it. Where are the benefits in all that?"

My smarty-pants brother jumped right in. "You don't understand, Sis. They're trying to force the prices up in order to fix the economy." He stared at me wide-eyed, like I didn't have a brain in my head. "You'll see. In a few years, everything will stabilize and it'll all make sense to people like you."

I scooped a spoonful of beans in my mouth and glared at my brother. I was no match for him.

"Wasn't your boss a Hoover fan?" he said with a sneer.

I shrugged and kept eating.

"Trust me," he went on, an arrogant tone in his voice. "Roosevelt is surrounded by advisors who know a lot more than any of us do." At least he had included himself in the word *us*. "He's got college professors guiding his decisions. They've studied the successes and mistakes of past administrations. I'm telling you, things are going to improve. You're just gonna have to wait and see."

I rued the day my younger brother started college. Overnight he turned into an expert on nearly every subject. Benny raised his eyebrows, and his lips curled up at the corners.

A flash of heat rose to my cheeks. "Stop laughing at me."

"I'm not." He lost his smile. He picked up his empty soup bowl and rose from the table. As he passed my chair, he patted me on the head. I gritted my teeth. I used to baby-sit that kid.

I have to admit, Benito's prediction wasn't too far off. The day came when things *did* appear to be getting better. The news reports said FDR's jobs program had put more than eight million people back to work building bridges and highways and campgrounds. As I rode the bus to and from work, changes started to take place right before my eyes. Artists painted murals on the walls of buildings and had them looking clean and fresh again. Workers in coveralls swept debris from the streets. "Help Wanted" signs went up in store windows.

But the uplift was temporary. A few months later, mom-and-pop stores closed, foreclosure signs appeared on shops and on houses, and beggars started showing up on street corners again. People started calling the drop "Roosevelt's Recession."

Thankfully, Giuseppe's market survived, but he had to raise our rent to $25 a month. The poor man shed tears when he gave us the news.

A couple of times, we hopped in Fredo's truck and took a drive to another part of town, a million worlds away from our home in the Bronx. We witnessed a fantasy land where a privileged few attended ballgames, horse races, concerts, and the theater. We drove past women swathed in diamonds and minks, and men wearing tuxedoes and top hats. They stepped out of limousines and fancy cars. Neon lights flashed up and down the street. Music blared from nightclubs. Department store windows displayed the latest fashions. Dollar signs were everywhere.

I looked at Fredo and shook my head. "They don't even notice the rest of us," I said. "They could drive those limousines right past a food line and they'd never see the folks in tattered clothes or the little kids with their hands out. They're blind to our part of the world."

Like always, my husband had a different perspective. "You

blind too, *mio amore.*" His words bore a hole in my heart. "You say we poor, but we have more than my family in the old country. Here, we have nice apartment. Food. Clothes. In Italy, I leave behind six brothers an' three sisters. We share clothes, maybe one or two shirts, then pass down to the next one. We have four beds, pack with straw. Our house look like a box. No windows. One door, always open. Pigs and chickens run all over, outside house, inside house, wherever they wanna go." Then he chuckled. "Someday, they be dinner."

I couldn't help but laugh at the image. But, my husband's smile faded and a sadness filled his eyes. "I eight years old when I go to work. My brothers and me, we pitch in. Still, my family no have much. Not like here, in America. Look around you, Angelina." He waved his hand. "No look at what those other people have. Look at what *we* have. Next to my family, we *rich*."

Ashamed of myself, I chewed my bottom lip. Fredo wrapped an arm around me. "We rich, *mio amore,*" he said, his voice soft. Then he stared off in the distance, like he was remembering another time. A tear squiggled down his face.

My throat tightened. "I'm sorry, Fredo. You must miss your family."

"Si." He brushed the moisture from his cheek.

"I guess I forgot you had a life before you came here. Please, forgive me."

He let out a sigh. "We have a good life. No?"

Fredo had gotten me to see that, despite our circumstances, there was always someone worse off. Not just in Italy, but right there in New York.

I began to notice them as I rode the bus to work. Derelicts

slept in doorways of abandoned shops. Children rifled through garbage cans. Once, when my bus slowed to make a turn, a small boy peered back at me from the curb, his dark, sunken eyes piercing mine.

That night, I lay awake in bed with that little boy's image hovering over me. I gritted my teeth and wept. My husband had done what no one else had been able to do to that point. He'd helped me to see my own depravity of heart.

One cold December morning, Fredo decided we both needed a lift. He grabbed our woolen coats and swept me out the door of our apartment. "Come on, *mio amore,* we go for—*come si dice*—an adventure."

Without another word, he helped me climb into his drafty old truck and we drove into the heart of the city. Patches of snow and ice littered the streets. Fredo's truck bounced over the lumps and bumps. He laughed aloud.

I grabbed the dash and tried to hang on. "Where are we going, Fredo?"

He laughed again and kept driving. Moments later, we merged with a slow-moving line of cars at the entrance of the Lincoln Tunnel. My dear husband paid the fifty-cent toll and we sat there shivering for almost an hour just so we could say we were among the first to drive underneath the Hudson River.

Fredo wrapped one arm around me and started singing, "I've Got My Love to Keep Me Warm." His boisterous, off-key rendition soon got me smiling and singing too. Then, we turned around, paid another toll, and drove back through to the other side. To most people, such a flight of fancy might seem as frivolous as buying a seat on the Hindenburg. But it was the highlight of the year for me, and, in a way, it helped me understand why someone would throw away money on something so trivial.

Three days later, we spent Christmas at my parents' apartment. I put together a pot of steamed vegetables. Somehow, my brother Tomas was able to get a ham. He came to dinner with his pregnant wife and their two-year-old twin girls.

Benny stood in three separate ration lines and came home with two loaves of pumpernickel, a small block of butter, and a bag of nuts. Mama made her famous almond cookies, and Papa went to the corner store and picked up a cheap bottle of wine.

We exchanged home-made presents, sang Christmas carols, and toasted with the first glass of wine we'd had in months. Some people don't know this, but we Italians rarely have a holiday dinner without a bottle of *vino* on the table. So, a glass of the purple grape on Christmas helped us feel normal again, at least for one day.

When the holiday festivities ended, reality set in. The new year brought another economic shift downward. I heard on the radio that thirteen million people were out of work.

That spring, Tomas' wife gave birth to their third child, a boy. My older brother could hardly contain himself. He finally had a son. I took his call on Giuseppe's phone. Tommy laughed and cried so hard, he could barely get out the news.

Of course, he could no longer help Mama with money, so Benito cut a few of his college classes and put in more hours at his job prepping vegetables in a restaurant. I visited my folks whenever I could, brought them leftovers and cans of soup whenever I could find a good deal on them.

Once a month, Fredo pulled the shoeboxes out from under our sofa-bed and counted every dollar. Then he emptied our jar of coins on the kitchen table and made individual stacks of quarters, dimes, nickels, and pennies. Yes, pennies. In those days, you could buy a loaf of bread with ten of them or a block of cheese with twenty.

While Fredo and I were counting pennies, Congress was approving billions of dollars for the President's projects, many of which affected individual businesses. The minimum wage went from 25 cents an hour to 30 cents, then 40. Sam complied with the law and raised my wages to $16 a week. He came into my office one morning, shaking his head. He was so upset, he didn't even light the cigar in his mouth.

"Lots of businesses are cutting back." Sam began his usual pacing, the unlit cigar shifting from one side of his mouth to the other. "My best friend let some of his employees go and has started hiring only part-time help. Another buddy of mine stopped hiring altogether. I'll tell ya', Angela, it's a tough world, and with Roosevelt at the helm it's gonna get tougher."

Somehow, Sam managed to maintain a full crew, with me in the office and six workmen handling the warehouse. He did the same at his other three plants across town.

"I don't have the heart to let anybody go," he said. "I'll simply have to drum up more business."

So, for the time being, I still had a job. As long as Fredo and I could keep going as we had been, maybe we could survive until things improved.

But I soon learned that tragedy can strike in a multitude of ways. The reality came one afternoon when Giuseppe hollered up the stairwell with urgency in his voice. I raced down the stairs ahead of Fredo and grabbed the phone out of Giuseppe's hand. Mama's voice came over, loud, but not clear. She screamed something in Italian. I couldn't make out what she was saying, so I passed the phone to Fredo, so he could translate.

He listened, then looked at me, his eyes wide. "You Mama say you brother—Tomas—he have accident at work. Steel beam poke his face."

I grabbed my husband's arm. "Oh my Lord, is he okay? Where is he?"

He spoke to Mama and then to me. "Fordham Hospital. We need to go."

Fredo couldn't get anything else out of my mother's frantic rambling. He held the phone away from his ear. Her cries echoed in the stairwell. "Tomas! Tomas, *O Dio mio*. Tomas."

I ran upstairs and grabbed my purse. Fredo and I jumped in his truck. He pressed the pedal to the floor. We skidded around corners, bounced over ruts in the road, and we made the half-hour drive to the hospital in less than twenty minutes, in heavy traffic.

We found my brother lying in bed with the right half of his face wrapped in bandages. His wife and kids flooded into the room and swarmed around his bedside. Donatella shrieked something in Italian. The twins drowned her out with ear-piercing wails. A nurse rushed in. Her whispered "Shush" went unheeded.

I tried to round up the twins, but they scooted out of my grasp. Fredo stepped up, wrapped a gentle arm around Donatella's shoulder, and led her to a chair in the corner. "Come. Sit." His voice died amidst the shrieks and cries from Tommy's children.

Donatella cuddled her baby boy close to her breast. She was sobbing uncontrollably. Fredo grabbed a box of tissues off the bedside table and placed it on her lap. Then he tucked one of the twins under each of his arms and took them down the hall to a waiting area where there'd be plenty of books and building blocks to keep them busy. Their cries diminished and Tommy's hospital room fell into an anxious silence.

Donatella settled down and was weeping softly. I laid my hand on top of Tommy's. My brother turned his head toward me and acknowledged my touch with a wink of his good eye.

"Where's Mama?" I asked him.

"Don't know, Angel," he said, using his pet name for me. "They probably had to grab a cab."

"What happened, Tommy?"

"Oh, I got stupid, that's all. I thought I could handle the girder by myself. The blasted thing went out of control and rammed into my face." He reached up and touched the bandage. "I must look a sight."

"Well ... " I didn't have the nerve to tell him about the bruises on his chin or the cut on his forehead.

He surprised me by letting out a chuckle.

I leaned close and planted a kiss on his brow. "You big dope, you should be more careful."

"I'll be okay." Tommy shrugged and kept smiling. "Soon as I get out-a this joint, I'll go back to work."

I raised my eyebrows but said nothing.

Fredo returned from the hall. Then Mama and Papa surged in and the chaos started all over again. Mama blubbered something unintelligible close to my brother, and Papa sent up an anguished plea in Italian. Benito stumbled in behind them and pelted Tommy with questions about the accident. The nurse returned and told us to quiet down or we'd have to leave.

As it turned out, Tommy lost the sight in his right eye. He could have been fired from his construction job, but his boss kept him on and made him foreman. Tommy called it a "blessing in disguise." When he went back to work the following week, he had a raise in pay and he didn't have to do hard labor anymore.

We were just getting back to normal when two more of Fredo's clients closed their doors. I still had my job, but for how long I didn't know. As long as I had a few dollars in my pocket, I could still shop for food.

Once a week, I went to the butcher shop and picked out a freshly killed chicken from a whole row of them hanging by their feet from a rafter. Shopping for food wasn't like what we do today. We can go to a supermarket and buy a cleaned and dressed bird bound up in plastic wrap. Back then, we went home with a whole chicken, feathers and all. At least I didn't have to kill the bird like Fredo used to do back in Italy.

Like my Mama taught me, I soaked the thing in hot water, plucked out the feathers, and singed the stubborn pins over a flame on our gas stove. Those burnt little buggers left a terrible stench in our apartment. Even with the window open, the odor didn't clear for a couple of days.

Occasionally, on a Saturday morning, Fredo's friends, Pietro and John, took him out on a row boat. They'd come home with a mess of pathetic-looking fish, cleaned and ready for the stove. We fried part of our catch for supper and cured the rest for future meals. After a while I preferred the crisp and salty flavor of the cured fish. A couple of slices could turn a pile of rice or potatoes into a tasty dinner.

Somehow, we had something to eat every day. One of Fredo's clients occasionally tossed him a slab of tripe. I cooked it the way he liked it, simmered in tomatoes and garlic. Whenever we ran out of food, I'd go downstairs and grab Giuseppe's leftover vegetables before they went into the garbage heap. I could steam them, roast them, or toss them in a pan of beans. "Beggars can't be choosey," Mama always said, and now I was saying it too.

CHAPTER EIGHT

ANGELA

SEPTEMBER 2008

I read in the paper this morning that nearly thirteen million people are out of work. Interesting, since only ten million were jobless in 1938, when we were in the midst of the Great Depression.

Okay, so the population has grown and today's so-called experts talk about percentages instead of actual numbers. They're calling what we're experiencing a recession, but to thirteen million people, plus those of us who are old enough to remember—it's another depression.

But, who am I? Just one more senior citizen who lived through it, a woman who couldn't even argue economics with her younger brother. So I file away the latest news, and I focus my attention on the changes going on inside my home.

Sadly, I hardly recognize my own house anymore. Most of my treasures have disappeared, leaving me with an even more pronounced emptiness in my heart. I grab my walker and travel at a snail's pace to my bedroom. Groaning, I settle on my bed. Dorothy has piled my clothes on my dresser, my chair, and the chest by the window. I lie very still and wait for her to emerge from the closet. Now she's holding up a hanger with a familiar, pink plastic bag.

I raise my head. "Your father bought me that mink stole for our twenty-fifth wedding anniversary."

Dorothy stares at me, wide-eyed. "I thought you were asleep."

"Not while you're nosing around in my closet."

She frowns at me. "Sorry, Mother," Her tone sounds nothing like an apology. She raises the bag and exposes my mink. "Are you telling me you want to keep this thing?"

"Sure."

"In Florida?"

"Yes, in Florida."

"It's too hot down here for a mink stole."

"Not in the restaurants," I tell her. "They have air conditioning. And the winter nights get pretty cool, sometimes close to freezing."

"Be sensible, Mother. You know you don't go out much anymore, especially not at night." She looks at the stole, then back at me. "I can't recall the last time you wore this stole." She turns the hanger one way and then the other. "It looks to be in good condition." Her eyes dart back in my direction. "Maybe Patricia will want it."

"Patricia?" I scrunch up my forehead. Why would Dorothy want to give *anything* to Patricia? She hates her younger sister.

She shrugs. "New Jersey has very cold winters."

Skeptical, I study her face but say nothing.

"A gift like this might break down the wall between us, Mother. Don't you think we've been at each other's throats far too long?"

I clam up and eye my daughter with curiosity. She must have an ulterior motive.

She pulls the plastic wrap back over the stole. "Maybe it'll get her to come down and help me out here."

I nod my head. *So that's it.*

"Patricia doesn't need my stole. She has a closet full."

"Yes, but she might appreciate something Daddy bought for you."

My mind races. "What if I want to be buried in it?"

Dorothy lets out a chuckle. "Really, Mother. You're kidding, aren't you?"

"No, I'm not kidding. People get buried in all sorts of things, these days. Remember Gladys Shwartz? She wore a black negligee. And Max Wilson? He was all decked out in his fishing outfit, complete with rubber hip boots, and his rod and reel."

Dorothy giggles. "Oh, Mother. That's too funny."

I lower my head to the pillow with a sigh. "Just do what you want with it."

"Okay, tell you what. I'll put your fur aside until you figure out what you want me to do with it. Anyway, what was I thinking? Give it to Patricia? Like it's gonna get her rushing down here? She hasn't been to Florida since Daddy's funeral."

"I hope she doesn't wait until *my* funeral to come down. I'd like to see her while I'm still kickin'."

Dorothy's cell phone rings. She pulls it from her pocket and gawks at the screen. "Speak of the devil," she says.

She leaves the room for a few minutes. Her voice carries in from the hall, but I can't make out a word she's saying.

Minutes later, she returns to my bedroom with the phone pressed to her ear. "Um-hmm ... really? I can't change your mind? Well, okay. Whatever ..."

She puts the phone away and heads toward my closet. She doesn't say a word about the phone call.

I raise my head off the pillow. "What did Patricia say?"

Dorothy smirks and gives me one of her, *If you must know*, looks.

"Not much. She's *not* coming down here if *that's* what you're wondering. She's in her own little world up there. She said she's got a life that doesn't fit in with ours."

"Didn't she ask to talk to me?"

"Not this time."

I turn my face away. Tears trickle down the side of my cheek and strike the pillow.

Dorothy comes close and sits on the side of the bed. She strokes my hair. I relish her gentle touch, a rare experience anymore.

"Don't fret over Patricia, Mother. You've put up with her behavior long enough. You must know she's not going to change." She pulls a couple of tissues from the box on my nightstand. "Here. Let it out. You've got a lot going on right now."

For the moment, Dorothy's let out the tender side of herself, the side she keeps hidden most of the time. She's a confusing mix of softness and grit. I just wish she'd release the softness more often. Maybe we'd get along better.

I had three children and they were all different from each other. I don't always understand them, but each one holds a precious place in my heart.

I choke out a sob. "I miss Patricia."

Dorothy pats my shoulder. "Of course you do. The separation must hurt a great deal."

"Don't you miss her, too?" I look her in the eye. "She's your sister. You shared a bedroom for years. You played together when you were kids."

"Yeah, and we had a lot of sibling rivalry, too."

“Isn’t that part of growing up? Siblings fight. And they make up. But they never stop loving each other.”

“Right, thank God I grew up, even though *she* didn’t. I don’t know, maybe I’ve developed a thick skin over the years. It’s hard to forget the damage and go back to what we were.”

I blot the tears from my cheeks. My family broke apart years ago, and I couldn’t stop it. My dear husband died knowing his two little girls didn’t get along with each other.

Dorothy rises from my bed and goes back to my closet. Our moment of intimacy gone, I roll onto my side and shut my eyes.

I don’t know when I drifted off, but I awaken to the last rays of a setting sun peeking through the edge of my curtain. I search the dimness for signs of life. Dorothy has left my room. The closet is empty. My dresser drawers lay open. Piles of clothes are stacked everywhere.

The rattle of my good dishes drifts from the dining room. Great. Dorothy’s gotten into my china cabinet.

With a grunt, I push myself to a sitting position and search for my walker. It’s within reach at the side of my bed. I manage to stand and make my way to the bathroom, take care of business, then move with baby steps down the hall to the dining room.

Dorothy must have turned on every light I own. I blink my eyes against the brightness. A surgeon could do an operation in here. My daughter’s placed my fine china on the dining room table. Plates, cups, saucers, platters, and bowls are piled like leaning towers ready to topple.

I settle in an empty chair. Dorothy’s pulling my soup tureen from the hutch. It’s trimmed in gold and has a hand-painted flower design around the outside.

"Your father paid a lot of money for that," I tell her. "In fact, all of these dishes came from Italy."

She turns as if she's hasn't noticed me till now. With a sigh, she lowers my soup tureen to the table. "You haven't used this stuff in years, Mother."

"It's for holidays and special occasions."

The side of her mouth lifts, like she's getting ready to say something sarcastic. Instead, she shakes her head. "I'll box it all up and put it in my attic. Maybe we can use these dishes for Thanksgiving dinner, that is, if anyone comes down here to eat with us. And who knows? One of your great-grandchildren might want it someday."

I scowl at her. "*Great*-grandchildren? What about my grandchildren?"

Dorothy pauses and puts her hands on her hips. "Mother, you're talking about Generation X. They're a whole different breed of animal. They prefer to eat off of paper plates. They like picnics. Not Thanksgiving dinner."

"What makes you think my great-grandchildren will be any different?"

She raises one shoulder. "I don't know. There may be a collector in the family."

I picture my treasures hidden away in Dorothy's dusty old attic, and I want to scream. My tureen will be forgotten by generations to come, like a relic in a time capsule, pulled out decades later, so our descendents can joke about how primitive we were. My favorite dishes might even go into a museum someday.

Dorothy frowns and walks to the serving table at the far end of the room. She hits the power button on my TV set. It's one more dinosaur I own. It has a twelve-inch screen and no remote control. Fredo set it on that table twenty years ago, and it still works fine. Every evening, he and I watched the six o'clock news while we ate supper. Then we went out to the front porch and sipped lemonade or hot cocoa, depending on what season it was.

The TV emits a string of static and a flash of light, and a news anchor appears in mid-sentence. He's talking about a local charity and the need for stuffed animals for the children's ward at the hospital. Then, his smile fades.

"More banks have gone under," he says with a grimace. "Congress is discussing another hike in taxes. The unemployment numbers have risen across the nation—double digits in some states, with the highest figures in Michigan and Florida."

"Florida?" I blurt out. "Sound's pretty bad." I turn to my daughter. "Don't you think that's pretty bad, Dorothy? What are you and Barry going to do?"

Dorothy changes the channel to a soap opera. "It's bad all over, Mother."

"Then I guess I should give up on Patricia or Jack ever coming home again."

"They wouldn't find a decent job," she says. "Not here anyway." She starts wrapping my good china in newspapers. I cringe at the thought of ink stains on those fragile plates. I could say something, but she won't listen, not to me.

I'm simply an actor in a stage play. Someone else has written my dialogue, and another faceless person is directing. All I have to do is follow the cues and recite my lines. No ad libs. Not in this place.

I gaze out the window at the darkening sky and quietly seek help from the Creator of the universe. Years ago, my best friend, Katie, tried to tell me about a God who cares. Now, here I am, silently pleading for him to rescue me.

CHAPTER NINE

PATRICIA

NEW JERSEY, 2008

If there's one thing Patricia Carpenter enjoys after a long day at work it's to stand on the balcony of her high-rise condominium with a glass of wine in one hand and a cigarette in the other. From the tenth-floor balcony she scans her empire—the shopping district of Burlington, New Jersey. Her eyes sweep over the lighted storefronts, beads of traffic on the streets below, and shoppers rushing along the sidewalks. Most of them are spilling out of Riche's Department Store, their arms laden with items Patricia personally stocked on the shelves.

She sips a little Merlot and breathes in the chilly September air. Her cell phone buzzes in her slacks pocket. She releases a sigh. *It's gotta be Dorothy again.*

She flicks the cigarette butt over the railing and pulls the phone from her pocket, ignores Dorothy's text, and punches the *return call* button. She presses the phone to her ear and frowns at the sound of her sister's harsh, "Well, finally. What's the matter, Patti? Didn't you get any of my messages?"

"Messages?"

"Don't play dumb with me. I've been calling you all day."

"I've been working." She swallows another sip of wine. "What do you want, Dorothy?"

There's a heavy sigh, then silence.

"Well?" Patricia's about to hang up.

"I need your help. Mother has way too much stuff. I can't finish the job by myself."

"So?"

"So, say you'll come down."

"Sorry, Dottie, I told you yesterday, I can't leave right now, not with the winter holidays right around the corner. I have to take inventory. I need to bring in the winter stock. I can't depend on those idiots who work under me. Too many things can go wrong."

"If we work together it'll take us less than a week. Maybe only a weekend."

Another moment of silence passes. Patricia tries in vain to think up a more convincing argument.

"Come on," Dorothy persists. "You can't imagine what I'm going through down here. Mother has saved more junk than you and I ever thought possible. We could open a gift shop with all the knick knacks she's held onto. And clothes? I'm having a hard time deciding what to keep and what to take to a thrift store. Mother isn't making it easy. She wants to keep everything. I need help, but neither you nor Jack have raised a finger to help me."

"What about Bernie? Can't he help you?"

Dorothy's huff comes over loud and clear. "Barry. My husband's name is Barry."

"Sorry."

"I told Barry he could help with the furniture. Other than that, he'd only get in the way. A man wouldn't have a clue what to do with the things Mother's collected. Some of them may be antiques, which I know nothing about, but you do. I need you to decide what to keep and what to toss out. You might even want some of this stuff."

"Just dump it. Dump it all. *I* don't have any use for Mother's things."

"I can't throw it *all* out. What if she has something valuable in here? You have a much better eye for such things."

Patricia lowers her eyelids to half-mast. She can see right through Dorothy's lame attempt at flattery.

"If you think something might have value, take it to an antique dealer. Or a pawn shop."

"Really? You're kidding, aren't you?"

"No. They'll tell you what it's worth."

"That's not good enough. Come on, Patricia. I'm asking for only a couple of days."

There's a brief pause when neither one of them says a word. Patricia gazes at the traffic below. Strings of lights wind through the city streets. Like a diamond necklace it trails across intersections, loops, and then moves in another direction.

"Mother wants to see you again." The last time Dorothy used her begging voice, she needed twelve-hundred dollars to catch up on a late mortgage payment. This time is no different. Her request is more about *her* than about Mother.

Patricia finishes off the wine. "I phoned her two weeks ago. She sounded fine."

"A phone call doesn't take the place of being here in person."

"I told you, I'm busy. I have a job."

"You can't take a few days off?"

"It's impossible right now. I have to move the fall line out and get the winter displays ready. You must know we try to stay several weeks ahead of the seasons."

"You mean months, don't you?"

"Whatever..." Patricia lets the slight pass.

"I'm head buyer of women's clothing. It's our busiest time of the year."

"And I don't have a life?"

"Not like mine. You haven't held a decent job since you got pregnant with Carrie."

More dead air. She can picture Dorothy grinding her teeth.

"Come on, Sis." Dorothy's tone now borders on frustration. "We haven't gotten together in ages. We can chat while we're working, catch up on what's happening in each other's life. After we finish, you can fly home, and I can start hunting for a job."

Patricia stares at the *end call* button and raises her finger over the key. She shuts her eyes. The two of them haven't sat down for a friendly chat in years. She be surprised if they could actually pull off such a feat.

"I don't know ..."

"Think it over, Patti. You know I wouldn't bother you if I didn't need your help."

Patricia lets out a long, labored sigh. "I'm done. I have to go."

"Wait—"

"Good bye, Dorothy." The call ends the way all the others did, with icicles dripping from both sides of the line.

Patricia hangs up without asking to talk to her mother. Why should she? The old girl will plead with her to come down. It's one thing to say no to Dorothy and quite another to say it to Mother. She doesn't need a guilt trip right now, not with all the responsibilities on her shoulders.

The problem isn't so much with Dorothy as the simple fact that she can't go back again. If she were to step inside that house, she might become that miserable little girl again. She'd grown up with a father who worked as a common laborer and could barely speak English. Her mother insisted on making her clothes, and she had an older sister who bossed her around, or tried to, and a younger brother who played jokes on her. If she went back, she'd be stepping into the mundane existence she'd escaped from decades ago.

Did other middle children get shuffled around and neglected the way she had been? Somehow, she'd developed a thick skin. She became competitive, won academic awards, performed in dance recitals, kept plunging ahead until she was able to leave home for a career in modeling and later took a six-figure job in one of the most elaborate department stores in New Jersey. The small-town girl had turned into a big-city career woman. Going home—even for one day—could drag her right back down again.

"Who was *that*?" Billy Beckman has come up behind her.

She turns. Her boyfriend has a bottle of wine in his hand. She lifts her glass and he fills it.

"I returned Dorothy's call."

"I thought you were never gonna speak to her again. What's she want now?"

She shrugs. "Same thing. She begged me to come to Florida to help her with Mother's stuff."

Patricia faces the railing, places her elbows on the top, and coddles the wine glass in her palms. Daggers of sunlight pierce the overcast sky and paint burnished streaks on the office windows across the street. A cloud drifts overhead and the scene fades within its shadow.

"Why don't you put on one of your new dresses and we'll go out dancing?"

She turns to face him. "I'm not in the mood, Billy."

"Why? Your sister got you miffed?"

"No, I'm tired, that's all."

She moves past him through the sliding glass door and enters the living room. She sets the glass of wine on the coffee table, reaches for a pack of cigarettes, and shakes one out. Billy's right behind her. She can smell his cologne. It's that new one she bought him last week.

"My dear sister wants me to help move my mother out of her house," Patricia says." I told her I need to get ready for our winter rush. Of course, I can't expect my out-of-work sister and her lazy, good-for-nothing husband to understand my responsibilities."

Billy stands the bottle next to Patricia's glass, grabs the lighter off the table and touches a flame to her cigarette. Then he strikes a pose, a leftover habit from his modeling days. He tucks his thumbs in the belt loops of his blue jeans, the way some teenage boys do. But on a forty-three-year-old man, the stance looks laughable.

"So, Dorothy's tearing up your mother's house?" He wrinkles his brow, the way he did for that Budweiser commercial fifteen years ago. She shakes off the image and focuses on the way he looks now—balding, sagging, and with a paunch the size of a bowling ball. She takes a long drag on her cigarette and exhales a stream of smoke in his direction.

"Aside from grabbing up a few pieces of Mother's jewelry and maybe her mink stole, I see no reason to go down there." A surge of guilt rises. She dismisses it. "Actually, I don't care *what* happens to her stuff. Most of it's as old as Methuselah anyway."

Billy creeps up close to her and slips his hands around her

waist. "There's always UPS or FedEx. Maybe Dorothy can ship some of your mom's things to you. Then you won't have to go anywhere near the place." He leans back and narrows his eyes. "You aren't thinking about going down there, are you?"

"Don't worry, Billy. Dorothy can plead with me until her tonsils dry up. I'm staying right here."

His boyish smile disarms her. Their relationship began almost twenty years ago with a casual flirtation. Patricia tried to tell herself it was just an ego trip. Now she believes she's in love with the guy, despite their twenty-year age difference. When she doesn't have a mirror in front of her to remind her how old she is, she can imagine herself anyway she wants—youthful, glamorous, desirable—twenty years younger, if she so desires.

She stares at Billy's face. He's still handsome, though he's no longer model material. He mentioned plastic surgery several times in the last two months, but Patricia squashed the idea.

"If I'm going to look older, so are you," she told him. "And there's no way I'm going under the knife. Not for you or anybody else."

She takes a long drag on her cigarette, then squashes the remaining stub in an ashtray.

"So, you think I should have my sister send me some of Mother's things?"

He raises his eyebrows and nods.

"I don't know, Billy. It means Dorothy and Barry will decide what I get. Most likely, it'll be something I neither want or need."

Billy's thick brows come together like two sides of a triangle. "You know what I think?" he says. "I think you have that look again—like you had when your dad died and you ran down to Florida."

"Look, I'm not going anywhere." She backs away from him. "Do you know what'll happen if I go down there? Like when we were kids, Dorothy will give the orders and I'll have to jump. No thanks. I escaped that life decades ago."

Her mother's face comes before her. She wonders what that poor woman might be going through, alone with Dorothy, without Daddy or Jack there to defend her.

"I imagine she's bossing Mother around right now," she says, her tone softening.

"You're gonna let this whole thing guilt you into going down there, aren't you?"

She picks up her wine glass and sips the purple liquid. "I don't know."

"What about the party?"

"What about it?"

"Well, for one thing, it's *your* party. And it's next Saturday."

"I could postpone it. I'd only have to make a few calls."

"Why so much concern about your mother all of a sudden?"

"She's helpless since she had that stroke. I can picture Dorothy pushing her around—"

"Pushing?"

"Not physically. With her mouth. She'll make my mother sit and watch while she goes through all her stuff. Mother saved a ton of things. They meant something to her—and to Daddy. But my sister says it's all trash."

"So? What can *you* do about it? You said Dorothy's pushy. What makes you think *you* can control her? And what if she brings up all the dirt about your divorce again?"

"She won't."

"You never told her Ed beat you, did you? Or that he had a string of girlfriends?"

"Why should I? She'd say I provoked him. Plus, she hated me for not wanting to have children. What? A woman who doesn't want kids? How terrible. Believe me, Billy, Dorothy loves to come out looking like the woman of the year, and it's always at my expense."

Patricia blinks against a rise of tears and turns toward her wall of windows. Darkness has fallen on her domain. In the distance a silhouette of skyscrapers spans the horizon in a multilayered shadow, like a child's set of Legos after night has fallen on the tiny bedroom. It's a picture of the life she carved out for herself, long ago. The buildings are well-constructed, evenly spaced, and reaching for the sky. It would be just like Dorothy to come in and knock them all down.

She releases a labored breath and faces Billy. "I have a strong feeling Mother's in trouble."

His brow wrinkles. "Be careful, Patricia."

She bites her lip, her mind shifting between going and staying.

"So, what are you gonna do?"

His face is overwhelmingly close. He's pressing for an answer.

She toys with the gold bracelet on her wrist. "Do you know what this little trinket cost me? Twelve-hundred dollars, the same amount Dorothy pays on her monthly mortgage. In my safe is a whole pile of these bracelets. And necklaces. And rings. I have a great job, a closet full of expensive clothes, and—" She smiles at Billy. "A hot boyfriend. No wonder my sister resents me."

"Then, that settles it. You're not going anywhere."

CHAPTER TEN

THE BRONX
1938

"You won't believe it," Sam said to me one morning. "My wife made the mistake of handing a sandwich to a guy who begged at our back door. Next thing, a big, white *X* was chalked on the side of our house. It took me an hour to wash the thing off." He lit up a cigar and shook his head. "It's happening all over town. If I didn't erase that mess, every bum within ten miles would have been pounding on our back door. I told Anna not to give out any more sandwiches. It's better if we just donate a few bucks to a soup kitchen or the Salvation Army."

I had an idea what Sam was talking about. In my neighborhood people were tipping over garbage cans to scrounge for food. Vagrants snatched purses from women on the street. Some of the stores near our apartment were broken into. Police car sirens whined day and night.

It looked to me like the middle class didn't exist anymore. People fit into one of two categories. They were either very rich or very poor. Fredo and I weren't completely destitute, but living that close to poverty had me fearing about tomorrow. That's when I started stashing away paper sacks, plastic containers, hairpins, rubber bands, and balls of string. Now, Dorothy's throwing them all out. If only I could make her understand those items have long-term value. A person only has to do without them once to know.

One cold February morning, Giuseppe hollered up the stairs that a market across town was selling eggs for twenty cents a dozen. *Eggs!* The thought of frying eggs for breakfast had me scrambling to get out of our toasty apartment and onto the icy streets of New York. I put on a heavy wool sweater, topped it with my winter coat, and wrapped a bright red scarf around my neck. I grabbed a cross-town bus and scurried over slick sidewalks to the shop Giuseppe had mentioned. The place was packed with customers. I squirmed through the mob, plunked two dimes on the counter, and left with a dozen eggs in a paper sack.

All the way back to the bus stop, I cradled those precious eggs in my arms. I was several yards away when I saw my bus was coming. I picked up my step. I didn't want to wait an hour for the next one. I had almost reached the bus stop when my foot hit a sheet of ice and slid out from under me. I flew through the air.

The eggs! I raised the paper sack over my head, lunged forward, and hit the pavement with a crash. The breath went out of me. I gasped for air.

Nearby, a woman screamed, "Look out! The bus ... " My head and shoulders hung across the curb. I turned my head. A big white-and-blue monster was rumbling towards me. Still gripping the bag of eggs, I squeezed my eyes shut and waited for the blow. There was a screech of brakes. I opened my eyes and found the bus had come to a stop mere inches from my head.

People circled around me. Hands reached down and helped me to my feet.

"Be careful of the eggs," I blurted out. "Please, don't break the eggs."

A man brushed the snow off my coat. He stared at me, his eyes wide. "How can you be worried about eggs when you almost lost your head?"

I was shaking so hard I couldn't answer him. Through a flow of tears I surveyed the damages. Blood oozed out the tears in my stockings. My arms ached. So did my back.

Cautiously, I opened the paper sack and peered inside. Not a single egg had broken. I smiled. Taking a deep breath, I boarded the bus. A young man offered me his seat. Others cast sympathetic eyes on me. I didn't care. I'd suffered no broken bones, and—thankfully—no broken eggs.

Later, when I described the episode to Fredo, he turned red with anger. "For eggs?" You risk-a you life for eggs? *Mio amore*, are you crazy?"

"I'm all right, dear. Just think about the wonderful dinner we're going to have tonight."

Twenty minutes later, the two of us were dancing around the kitchen, humming a tune along with a song on the radio. Fredo lit a fire under the burner and I reached for the iron skillet. For supper we ate brown bread topped with honey along with a pile of the most delicious scrambled eggs I'd ever had.

Highs turned to lows. The shift from good to bad came unexpectedly. In the summer of 1938, my greatest fear became a reality when Sam announced he was closing his plants beginning with the warehouse where I worked. He started by laying off a few of the men, but held onto a skeleton crew, which consisted of three men, and me. I gazed with sadness through my office window as the others filed out, their heads down, a final pay envelope in their hands. Three weeks later, I got a hug from Sam and a small severance pay.

"I'll call you if things pick up again," he said, unable to look me in the eye.

We parted amicably. I would miss Sam, his opinionated outbursts, his political sermons, even the stench of his cigars. He treated me like his equal, right up to the day he closed his doors.

For a while, I escaped inside the books I borrowed from the library. The writings of F. Scott Fitzgerald and Charles Dickens entertained me in the evenings. During the day, I walked the streets in search of another job. I stood in line at every storefront and office building with a "Help Wanted" sign in the window. The signs came down as fast as they went up.

Banks started calling in loans. Fortunately for Fredo and me, we had never borrowed a dime. My husband paid cash for his truck with the money he brought from Italy. We hadn't purchased a home or anything else on time. And, we still paid $25 a month to Giuseppe.

I never expected I would one day stand in a bread line, but after I lost my job I swallowed my pride, and there I stood early one Monday morning, wedged between two bums, the one in front reeking of body odor and the one behind me breathing alcohol down my neck. I was surprised to find that most of the people in line were a lot like me, regular folks—women with small children, old people leaning on canes, and teenagers helping their families. To save my parents the long wait in line, I usually asked for an extra loaf of bread or another wedge of cheese. Sometimes I got them, more often I received an apologetic head-shake.

I looked forward to those days when I could go to my

parents' apartment with a sack of provisions under my arm. Each time the stairwell smelled dingier than before, the paint on the walls had peeled a little more, and the shadows seemed more pronounced. Always, the door opened to the aroma of soup on the stove. My mother would rush over and engulf me in her arms. Papa would remain in his easy chair, his Italian newspaper spread open on his lap. Though he stared back at me, it took several seconds for his eyelids to flicker in recognition of his only daughter.

Without fail, Mama invited me to stay for lunch. At the kitchen table I bowed my head and waited while she recited a memorized prayer from her former church-going days. Then I mumbled, "Amen," though I didn't feel the least bit thankful for those puny little scraps.

We were down to one income, Fredo's. A couple of months later, we were hit with another blow. Sam made a contract with the government to provide food at various worksites. Fredo had lost his supplier. Days passed. Then weeks. He couldn't hook up with another meat supply house in all of New York.

He and his buddies, Pietro and John, temporarily found work in Queens helping to clear the landfill in preparation for the World's Fair that was coming to New York the following year. Fredo came home tired and dirty every night, but we were glad for the short-lived income. Meanwhile, his truck sat idle on the street in front of our apartment.

Then, one afternoon, he walked in and told me he had sold his truck. "I have new plan," he announced, his eyes lighting up like he'd struck gold. "I take job with—how do you say?—National Forest Service. Pietro and John and me—we leave in three days for New York camp."

"Three days?" Weeping, I fell into my husband's arms. "Why didn't you discuss this with me? I'm not sure I—"

"It's a job, *mio amore*. A chance to make some real money. I go for short time—two, maybe three months. Then, I come home, buy another truck, we start fresh."

I wasn't ready for us to be separated. We'd been married for only three years.

"Can I go with you? I'm a strong woman. I can work beside you."

Fredo chuckled and gave me a squeeze. "No, no. This man's work. Hard labor. We live in tents—like soldiers. We dig ditches, plant trees, build dams. No place for women. You stay. Take care you Mama."

My heart racing, I begged him not to go. "We're doing okay, Fredo. We still have one shoebox full of cash. Maybe you can find another job here in New York. Something different from what you were doing before."

He took my face in both of his hands. His callused fingers stroked the sides of my cheeks and caught the flow of my tears. His hopeful blue eyes hid what was really going on inside him. I knew my husband. Deep down, a defeated man was struggling for one more chance to succeed. I knew better than to try and stop him.

More tears came and I fell into uncontrollable sobbing. For the next hour, my dear husband tried to soothe me, but to no avail. Once, for a few minutes, he shed some tears along with me. Then he straightened his back and gave me one of his inflexible stares.

"I no wanna go," he admitted. "I no see any other way. This our chance, *mio amore.* Our chance to keep going."

Two or three months, he'd said. He'd already signed up

with his two buddies, Pietro Lambetti and John Gillis. Though I hated to see my husband leave, I couldn't come up with another answer to our problem. The pay was $50 a month, more money than we'd seen in the last two months.

"I keep a few dollar an' I send the rest home," he promised. "You stay here. Pay Giuseppe what we owe. Buy what you need. Put a little in shoebox. And no worry about me. I be with my two friends. We watch out for each other."

Three days later, Fredo got out of bed before the first rays of sunlight spilled across our window sill. He tossed the last of his underwear in his bag. Pietro and John stood on the street below. They whistled and called his name.

Fredo leaned out the window and gave them a wave.

"C'mon," Pietro shouted. "We gotta catch the bus."

Fredo turned away from them and stepped toward me. He wrapped his arms around me and pressed his chin against my forehead. "Let them wait," he said. He held me for a long time. I clung to him. Then, he kissed me and gazed into my eyes. "I come back. I no lie to you. I come back."

As he turned away, I thought I saw tears in his eyes. He grabbed his suitcase and, without another look back, he stumbled down the stairs and out onto the street.

I leaned out the kitchen window. The three of them strode away, their feet tripping along the pavement, their arms swinging their bags as if they were weightless. I shook my head in disgust. They were three kids heading off to camp.

I took a last, lingering look at Fredo's wiry frame until he disappeared around the corner. Still, I couldn't pull my eyes away from the empty street. A part of me hoped he might change his mind and come back into view. Another part—the more rational side of me—knew he wouldn't. Once my husband committed to something, he didn't quit until he was done.

With Fredo away, the life was sucked out of our apartment. Instead of songs belted out in Italian, a heavy silence hung over our living room. There were no more visits with Giuseppe, no more dancing in the living room, no more shared meals, shared kisses, or shared dreams. No more snuggling at night.

For days, I sat staring at the empty chair across the table from me. I didn't feel like cooking for one person, so sometimes I simply cut up a potato, sprinkle a little salt on it, and ate it raw. Or I'd open a can of Campbell's soup, the latest thing at 25 cents for four cans.

After a week of pining and fasting, I emerged from my shell. It had been a while since I'd gotten together with Katie. After I started dating Fredo, I rarely saw her. We talked on the phone maybe once or twice a month. Now that my husband was away, I sure could use a friend.

I went downstairs to Giuseppe's pay phone and dialed the number of her mother's sewing shop.

Katie answered on the second ring. The lilt in her voice warmed my heart. I hadn't realized how much I missed hearing her voice.

"I need to see you, Katie. Are you free?"

"My mum has a pile of work. I'm not sure she can spare me today."

"I only need a few minutes. Please ..."

"You sound very down. Hold on—" She left the phone for a brief conversation with her mother. Then she was back.

"Come on over. I'll try to get away for a bit. My mum's giving me ten minutes."

Colleen O'Malley had been a widow for twenty years and had raised Katie off the money she made in her little sewing shop. They lived in the back of the shop in one bedroom with a small bath and a makeshift kitchen. I ate many a fine meal back there, the three of us crammed together around a little round table, and Colleen bustling back and forth between their two-burner stove and a tiny ice box.

" 'Tis plenty big enough for the two of us," Colleen told me the first time I visited.

It didn't matter how small their place was. I found comfort inside those four walls. Colleen's kitchen smelled of Irish stew, fresh-baked brown bread, and apple butter. More than that, a visit to the tiny hovel also brought warm hugs, a listening ear, and heartfelt words of advice. Where else would I want to go when I was down and out?

I hopped a bus for Brooklyn and entered the shop to the tinkle of a bell over the door. Colleen greeted me in her usual lilting brogue. "It's grand to see ya', dearie. Come in. Come in."

Katie gave the final fold to a man's dress shirt and set it aside. She looked at my face and her smile faded. No surprise. I would have sworn Katie and I could read each other's minds. Plus, I wasn't one to hide my feelings. Not from her.

She came around the side of the folding table and hurried toward me. "What's the matter, Angela? You look absolutely devastated."

I blinked back a tear and glanced at her mother.

Colleen leaned into her sewing machine, fed a piece of fabric under the needle, and pressed the lever with her knee. The whir of the machine drowned out my weak, "I need to talk."

Katie turned toward her mother. "Do you mind if I take a walk with Angela?" she shouted over the buzz of the machine.

The wheel stopped spinning and a sudden silence fell on the little shop. Colleen glanced at the pile of clothes on the folding table, then turned her eyes on the two of us. A flicker of understanding crossed her face.

"You said I could have ten minutes," Katie reminded her mother. "I promise, I won't stop working until I finish today's load."

Colleen approved with a nod and turned the wheel of her machine. The whirring resumed. Katie grabbed my arm and led me out the door. With the tiny bell announcing our departure, we hit the sidewalk and I stepped into blessed silence.

Katie leaned close. "You sounded miserable on the phone. And, I have to say, you look even worse than I expected." She pointed to the corner bus stop. "C'mon. We can sit on a bench while we talk. But remember, I have only ten minutes."

A wave of guilt washed over me. How could I be so selfish? Katie had troubles of her own. Her father had died when she was thirteen. Her mother couldn't run the shop alone. My friend quit school two years before I did. Growing up, she had little time for fun, and, in recent years, no time for dates either. Without complaint, she plunged into her duties—sewing, ironing, folding other people's clothes. Sometimes, she brought me something she made—a frilly blouse, an embroidered handkerchief, a scarf she knitted from leftover yarn. And, she always made time for me, if only for a ten-minute talk.

We sat on the bench and watched the passing traffic. Then I took a breath and faced my friend. The afternoon sun cast a circle of gold around her strawberry colored hair. I nearly gasped. For a moment, she looked like an angel. She was a tiny thing—five-foot, two, was a little roly-poly and she bubbled with energy. At five-four, I was a couple of inches shorter than my husband, and I was thin as a rail. I looked into her green eyes and marveled at our differences. In contrast, everything about me was dark—my hair, my eyes—yet we'd formed a bond stronger than sisters.

"Well?" she said, arching her eyebrows. "Are you going to tell me what's wrong, or do I have to dig it out of you?"

"Fredo's gone," I blurted and broke into sobs.

"What? Oh Angela." She placed a hand on my arm. "Fredo? Gone? Why? I thought you two were doing fine."

I shook my head and pulled a handkerchief from my purse. The crumpled linen was the one Katie had embroidered for me, with butterflies and rose buds in the corner. I blotted my tears, then chuckled. She'd thought Fredo and I had separated.

"No Katie," I protested between sobs and giggles. "He hasn't left me. Not the way you're thinking. He and his buddies went to work for the National Forest Service."

Katie nodded. "I see." She stared at me, her brow wrinkled in bewilderment.

"He'll be gone for at least two months."

"Angela, how is that a bad thing? Didn't you tell me he lost his business?"

"Yes, I did tell you that."

"So, he signed up with the forest service. What's the problem?"

"He never discussed it with me. Those three blockheads talked among themselves and made up their own minds."

Katie stared back at me, amusement in her eyes, her lips pinched together, as though she were trying not to laugh.

"Who knows what kind of dangers they'll face?" I'd raised my voice, hoping to get her to understand. "They'll be living in tents. No matter what the weather. There may be wild animals out there." My tone turned sour. "They acted like they were going on a big adventure."

Katie stroked my arm. "Oh, Angela, you're too emotional over this. Believe me, they're not on an adventure. Those men will do hard labor from dawn till dusk. Wild animals? I doubt it. The worst problems they'll face might be a little poison ivy and aching muscles. You need to quit worrying. Fredo's a big boy. He can take care of himself."

She chuckled and leaned toward me. "I'm more worried about you than about him. It's important that you stay healthy, both physically and emotionally. That way, when he comes home, he'll find the same sweet woman waiting for him that he left behind."

I stared at the pink and green scrollwork on my handkerchief. "It must have been Pietro's idea," I snarled. "Fredo wouldn't have thought up something that stupid. And John? He comes from a wealthy family. He doesn't need the money. He goes along with whatever Pietro wants to do." My throat tightened and my voice came out like a squeak. "Katie, I could scream. Those big oafs took my Fredo away from me. They're single. They have no responsibilities. But do you think they cared that Fredo has a wife, that maybe I needed him at home?"

I hated sounding like a whiny, spoiled woman, but I couldn't help it. My emotions had boiled to the surface. I'd held them in for days, but the instant I sat on the bench beside my friend, something happened to me, and I unleashed my grief. And what did Katie do? She smiled sweetly and wrapped an arm around my shoulder.

"I can't begin to understand how you feel," Katie said, her voice softening. "I don't have a husband. I don't even have a boyfriend. But, I've seen you and Fredo together. I'm sure you must feel like a part of yourself has left."

I nodded and blubbered into the handkerchief. Katie pulled away, her emerald eyes gazing into mine. "How long will he be gone?"

I shrugged. "He said a few months, but I'm guessing it'll be closer to a year."

Katie shook her head and looked down at her shoes. "It's a pity." She sounded like her mother. With her head cocked to one side and her brow furrowed, she looked like a young version of Colleen. "Where will he go?" she said, raising her head.

"He said a work camp in the upper part of the state. I'm hoping it'll be close enough for him to come home for a weekend now and then."

Katie raised her eyebrows. "Don't count on it, Angela. I've heard about those camps. They're deep inside the forest. He won't be able to just pick up and leave whenever he wants to. Most likely, they'll work seven days a week, without a break."

"I'm worried, Katie. Fredo isn't a rugged guy, not like the other two. Think about it. What has he done since he came to this country? He tossed packages of meat in the back of his truck. He drove all over New York. From the time he stepped off the boat, he's had a roof over his head. Now he'll live in a tent and eat beans out of a can."

Katie giggled. "I doubt it'll be that bad. Some of those places have cabins. And, I'm sure they'll get government rations." Katie's face brightened. "You know, Fredo might learn a whole new trade. Maybe he'll be able to come home and find another job."

"Maybe." I blinked hard and tried to imagine what kind of work my husband might do. "Back in Italy, he didn't do anything except pick grapes," I told her. "But, maybe you're right. Fredo is resourceful. If he doesn't go back into the meat delivery business, he'll find a different job. Maybe something better."

Katie looked at her watch. "I'm sorry, Angela. I have to go. A local mission gave my mum a box of clothes to be patched and washed and ready to hand out to the poor."

I nodded my understanding. "She won't get paid for that job, will she?"

"Not in money. But God blesses."

We stood up and started back to the shop. Katie grabbed my hand. "Be strong, Angela. And, don't forget, Fredo's going to feel like he did something worthwhile. For the country, and for the two of you. Having this job, even temporarily, will restore his sense of pride. You want that for him, don't you?"

"I guess so, but it's hard living without him. The walls in my apartment have started to echo. I don't have a job. What am I supposed to do while he's gone?"

Katie stopped walking and blocked my path. "Listen. I have an idea, but I'll need to check it out first."

"What—"

She raised her hand. "I need to talk to someone before I tell you."

I looked her in the eye. She shook her head and set her crimson curls bouncing.

"Don't ask, Angela. Just go home. All I can tell you is, I think I might know how you can fill your lonely hours and keep from fretting about Fredo. You'll stay busy and you'll be doing some good."

I started to ask, but she held up her hand. "I'll tell you in a couple of days."

CHAPTER ELEVEN

ANGELA

SEPTEMBER 2008

Dorothy's been tearing into my china hutch for the last two days with little regard for the fragile items stored there. I lift one of the cups off the table and examine it. Not a chip or a crack.

"I took extra good care of this set," I tell my daughter. "Take a look at them, Dorothy. They're trimmed in 24-carat gold."

Dorothy tugs a stray curl behind her ear and blends it in with the mix of grays and browns. She stares with obvious disinterest at the array of cups and saucers on the table.

"So?" she says, finally.

I stare at the expensive serving platter in her hand. "You might want to handle my things with a little more care."

She frowns at the oversized plate. "This?"

"Yes. These are not bargain basement dishes. I used this set for special occasions—holidays, birthdays, family gatherings."

"She shakes her head. "You know I've never been much of a collector. One dish looks the same as any other."

"Let me show you something. Hold one saucer up to the light."

She doesn't move.

"Go ahead, Dorothy, hold a saucer up to the light."

With an impatient smirk on her lips, she sets down the serving platter and lifts a saucer above her head.

"Okay," I tell her. "If you can see your hand through it, that means it's valuable."

Her eyebrows go up.

"Now look at the bottom. Check out what's engraved there."

"Hmmm. *Made in Italy.*"

"Right. Those are precious dishes. If you can't underst—"

"Okay, Mother. But who might want this set? I know *I* don't." She pauses, then her eyes flash with an idea. "Patricia gives fancy dinner parties. Maybe you should give them to her."

I huff. "Patricia already has two sets of fine china."

Dorothy's staring at me, a shadow of impatience enveloping her face. "I'm doing the best I can, Mother. I know you don't like to see all of your things end up in a box, but we have to do this. Wherever you go—whether it's assisted living or my house—you'll have a small bedroom and a private bath, nothing more. You'll have no hutch. No cupboards. No closets to store things in."

Dorothy glances around the room. I follow her uneasy gaze to the glass-fronted cabinet and my collection of ceramic birds, then to my wall of Christmas plates, and finally to the row of *Precious Moments* figurines on the sidebar.

"You know?" she says, turning toward me. "You could open your own curios shop." She scratches her head. "Maybe I can list everything on eBay. Some of your so-called treasures might attract a few collectors."

I fold my hands and press my lips together. I don't want my things to go to strangers. Names and faces pass before me.

"Okay, Dorothy. I want my good china to go to Jack and Amy. At least they'll take care of it."

"I can't believe you. Do you honestly expect me to send this fragile set all the way to California?"

"It got here from Italy."

"It's more expensive to ship things these days. I'd have to insure the whole batch. Why, Jack could go out and buy a full set of china for less money."

I view the spread on my table. Dorothy's still complaining about the workload. Her griping fades beneath the last Thanksgiving holiday I hosted in this dining room about seven or eight years ago. My husband stood at the head of the table, raised a glass of wine, and made a toast. All my kids had gathered here with their spouses and their children. Flickering candles lit up their smiling faces. The dining room hummed with conversation. Thankfully, Dorothy and Patricia sat at opposite ends of the table. There was no fighting that day. Holiday music played, and the aromas of cinnamon, brown sugar, apples, and pine needles filled the air.

I surface from the memory to the loud clatter of forks and spoons. Dorothy's sorting through my silverware drawer.

"A little polish should brighten these up," she says. "Somebody's going to inherit a nice set of flatware."

Inherit? Dorothy's never used that word before, at least not around me. It goes along with dying, doesn't it?

"Let Jack have them too."

"Jack again? Does everything have to go to Jack and Amy?"

"Well, *you* don't want any of it."

"You're right. I don't. But I'm not going to ship it to California."

"Do you think he might come home? He can take everything back with him."

"I don't know, Mother. He's got enough problems with his son moving in with them. What a nightmare."

"I just thought—"

"Stop thinking." Dorothy chews her lip and looks at her watch. "Why don't you sit in the living room for a while?"

Without giving me a chance to refuse, she scoots my walker in front of me, shoves her hand under my arm, and lifts me to my feet. We make our way—step by labored step—into the living room. I settle into my Victorian chair with the high back and the velvet cushion. I reach for the remote control and start flipping through channels until I find a cooking show.

I find myself following my daughter's orders, like I don't have a will of my own. I'm like a robot that's been programmed to respond to her commands. And I don't know how to get my old self back, the feisty, strong-willed me who made it through the Great Depression without Dorothy's help.

My daughter pauses next to the end table, opens a drawer, and pulls out one of those little red balls the therapist left for me.

"Here," she says. "You need to strengthen your fingers."

She presses it in my left palm. I feel like a kid with a glob of Play-Doh.

Dorothy heads back to the dining room. I stare after her and squeeze that little red ball almost to death. Then I turn my attention to the TV. A chef is trussing a chicken. The image starts to blur. I try to recall the argument Dorothy and I were having only moments ago, but it slips my mind.

I don't know how long I slept. A different cooking show is on. Another chef is putting together a fancy salad.

Dorothy's shouting something from the spare bedroom.

She's obviously finished with my dishes and has started on another project.

She pokes her head out the door. "Where are your suitcases, Mother? Still under the bed in here?"

I perk up. "Yes, they should be there."

I can't help but smile. If nothing else, her next discovery will bring a little fun into my life.

"I can use your luggage to pack some of your precious dishes. I'll wrap them in towels to protect them. We'll decide what to do with them later, okay?"

I chuckle.

"Did you say something, Mother?" Dorothy's voice sounds muffled. She must be searching under the bed. The image brings another giggle to my throat.

"Okay, I found the suitcases," Dorothy calls out.

There's the snapping of latches followed by a moment of silence. I hold my breath and angle my ear toward the hall.

"Wh-what in the world?" Silence again. Then, "Mother, what is this?"

I'm snickering out loud now. Dorothy emerges from the spare room and I stifle my smile. She's cradling a shoebox in her arm. The lid is off and a bunch of Andrew Jacksons are peering over the top.

"Where did you get all this money?"

"Your father and I stole it."

"What? You *stole* it?"

"Yep. Your daddy and I robbed banks back in the 1930s. Like Bonnie and Clyde. He went in with a gun, and I drove the getaway car."

Dorothy tilts her head to one side. "Come on, Mother. Give me a straight answer."

I grin back at her. "Oh, honey, relax. When lots of people were losing their savings, your dad and I designed our own banking system. We started with the cigar box you threw away. When we couldn't stuff any more cash in it, we used shoeboxes. It's how we survived the Great Depression."

"Do you know how much money you have in here?"

"Nope. Your father did all the counting." I lose my smile. "Listen, Dorothy. In those days, having a shoebox full of cash turned out to be a lifesaver. We never used a bank. Never had to. Never trusted them."

"Mother." Dorothy's shaking her head. "I counted five shoeboxes in there. And they're all full of cash. At some point, you should have put your money in a bank. Don't you know, people's savings accounts have been insured for decades? These days, bank accounts are secure. Plus you can earn interest."

I cross my arms in front of me. "I don't know what all the fuss is about. Your father and I did whatever we could to stay alive. The money you're so upset about? If we'd put our hard-earned cash in a bank, we would have lost it all, like my parents did. Then, where would we be today? We wouldn't have this nice house. And you kids wouldn't have had all the fine things we handed you while you were growing up."

"But saving money in shoeboxes? It's ridiculous."

She turns away in a huff and heads back to the spare bedroom.

I wish Katie were here. My best friend was more like family to me than my own daughter is. Katie may not always have known what I was going through, but she stuck by me. She gave me comfort. And hope. Like the day at the bus stop when I told her how lost I was without Fredo. He was off somewhere at a forest camp with his two buddies and I was alone with nothing to do. Katie tried to console me. Then she said she had a plan.

I had to wait for her to check something out. What, I didn't know, but a spark of expectancy had ignited inside me.

Two days later, Giuseppe hollered up the stairwell and said I had a phone call. I flew down the steps and grabbed the phone out of his hand. It was Katie.

CHAPTER TWELVE

THE BRONX

1938

"Can you come for lunch today?" The lilt in Katie's voice got my heart racing. "I'm ready to tell you my idea. Believe me, Angie, it'll change your life."

"Change my life? How?"

"You'll see," was all she'd say.

Fortunately, I didn't have to wait long for the cross-town bus. When I arrived at Colleen's sewing shop, Katie led me into the back room.

"We'll talk over lunch," she said, a glint in her eye.

There was no sense trying to pull the information out of her. Katie would talk when she was good and ready. I took a seat at their little table with barely enough room for the three of us. But the tiny cove offered an intimacy people don't usually enjoy in a huge dining room where poor acoustics blend your conversations with everybody else's.

Colleen stood at the stove, her cheeks crimson as she ladled stew out of a cast iron pot onto three metal plates. She glanced at me, smiled like she had a secret, and set a plate on the table before me. A whiff of lamb gravy rose from the thick stew. I ran my tongue over my lips.

Katie placed a plate of brown bread on the table and took a seat beside me. We waited for her mother to get settled, then they both reached for my hands. Colleen's blessing of the food sounded like music. I always looked forward to her prayers. They were different every time, not like those memorized ditties I grew up with. This time, she also mentioned the surprise Katie had for me and asked God to bless it too.

The three of us dug into her lamb stew. The gravy soaked potatoes and tidbits of meat warmed my insides. Summer had ended and a chill hung in the air. I ate with relish, but didn't take my eyes off of Katie. All the while, Colleen chattered away about her latest customer, a wealthy woman who'd promised to bring more clients to the little shop. Katie made me wait until she'd scraped the last morsel out of her plate.

"Okay," she said, at last. "I have some good news for you, Angie."

I let out a relieved sigh. "You said it would change my life. What could possibly do that?"

She drank a little water. "First answer a question."

I tilted my head and eyed her with suspicion.

"Tell my mum how your life has been since Fredo left for the forest camp."

I looked at Colleen. Her eyes crinkled at the corners.

"Well," I said. "For one thing, my apartment walls are closing in on me. I've cleaned everything I own until the place squeaks. I've read every book on my shelf three times. And, I've searched endlessly for a job, with no luck. I miss my husband so much I'm about to fall down and die of loneliness. How's that for a thorough description of loneliness?" I sat back in my chair.

Katie broke down in hysterics. Colleen had a sparkle in her eyes.

"Stop being so melodramatic," Katie said, still laughing. "You don't need to have the most immaculate apartment in the Bronx. And, except for something to do, you don't really need a job. Fredo's promised to send money home, right?"

I nodded, but I kept my mouth shut and waited for her big surprise.

Katie lifted her chin, a sly smile on her lips. "You need a project, Angie. Something to get your mind off of your own troubles by helping others instead."

I perked up.

Katie grabbed my hand. "Angela," she said. "There's a ministry not far from here, in fact, it's just around the corner. I had to check with the people who run it. It turns out, they can use an extra hand."

I tilted my head and listened with interest. "Go on."

"It's a soup kitchen. They serve meals to the less fortunate—the homeless, sure, but also people who've simply had a run of bad luck."

Confused, I glanced back and forth between Katie and her mom. They were both smiling now.

"Tell me more."

Colleen leaned toward me. "The first thing you need to realize, my dear girl, is that lots of people are worse off than you." Her smile faded, but there was a friendly twinkle in her eye. "The soup kitchen is operated by the Bartons, a wonderful couple, and their son. Lots of needy folks—men, women, and even children—line up at their door every day."

"Children?" I was shocked.

"Sure, and what a pathetic bunch they are," Colleen said. "They receive a hot meal, but they come away with a lot more. Mae Barton also dishes out plenty of encouraging words.

'Tis amazing how a little kindness can give a person hope for tomorrow."

Katie nodded. "Sometimes, the line stretches around the corner and runs right past our shop. It's heartbreaking, Angie."

"And you think I can help? But how? I don't have much money."

"You'll help by *serving* the food and by helping to clean up after everyone leaves," Colleen said. "And, you can show compassion to the souls who come there. The Bartons—Andrew and Mae—said they're eager to have you join them."

While Katie and her mother cleared the table, I let their idea sink in. The two of them fell silent. The only sounds in the room were the rattle of dishes and silverware, the splash of water in the sink, and the squeaky opening and closing of cupboard doors.

When they finished, Colleen paused by my chair and placed a hand on my shoulder. "It sounds like a grand idea, dearie. There's no need to rush into anything, but you should think it over."

She went back to the shop and left Katie and me to discuss my options. I could step out in faith and help someone else, or I could retreat to my little apartment and wallow in self-pity. At least, that's how my best friend put it.

"So, the line of people runs right past your shop?" I tried to imagine the faceless men and women, and the little children, waiting on the sidewalk for what might be their only meal of the day. I had witnessed similar scenes during my bus rides through the city. The children hit me the hardest. But the images lasted for only a moment. When I walked into my lonely apartment, I retreated into my own self-centered misery. Katie was right. She had offered me the opportunity to escape from a situation that only promised to drag me down.

"I'll do it," I said.

Katie's grin lit up her whole face. She leaned over and wrapped her arms around me. "Come back tomorrow morning around nine and we'll go to the soup kitchen before the line starts to form. Oh, one more thing—" She backed away. "They can't pay you. The position is strictly voluntary."

"Of course. I don't want to be paid. I want to help—anyway I can."

I left Colleen's shop with a spring in my step. For the last twenty minutes, I hadn't thought about my lonely life, not even once. I hadn't mentioned Fredo, hadn't wrung my hands. In fact, I was actually smiling.

The next morning, I returned to Colleen's shop at nine o'clock, as planned. Katie led me around the corner to a shabby storefront. Propped in the window was a makeshift sign with the words, *God's Kitchen,* printed on it. A line of people had already started to form. I tried not to stare at the hungry faces.

We went inside and I was immediately struck by the aroma of tomatoes and garlic wafting from the kitchen. A robust woman in her mid-forties rushed toward us. She had a matronly appearance. Plump breasts, thick arms, almost no waist to speak of, and she was wearing a flowered housedress under a chef's apron, with the ties stretched to their limit around her middle. Her gray-streaked hair was bound in a messy bun in back. A few stray hairs clung to her sweaty cheeks. Around her neck hung a gold cross on a chain.

Katie introduced us, giving my full name, Angela Busconi.

"Ah, a nice *Italiano* girl," Mae's cheerful tone reminded me of Colleen. And, like Katie's mother, Mae displayed the same sweet, welcoming smile.

"Maybe you can cook for us one of these days," she said, her eyes twinkling. "I think our guests would love a bowl of authentic spaghetti."

She shook my hand, then turned toward the kitchen. "Andrew!" she sang out. "She's here."

A short, thin, balding man emerged from the kitchen. I stifled a laugh. They could have been Jack Sprat and his wife. The little man drew up beside Mae and wrapped his arm half-way around her middle.

Andrew's eyes darted toward the ceiling. "Thank you, God, for sending us this much needed help." Then, he turned smiling eyes on me. "And, thank you, miss, for making time to help us."

"Believe me, it's my pleasure. I needed something worthwhile to do, something to keep my mind off my husband. He's away—"

"We know," Andrew broke in. "Katie told us. Hopefully, you'll find peace through our ministry. Believe me, we intend to keep you very busy. You won't have time to fret over your husband."

Katie took that moment to head for the door. "I have to get back to my mother's shop, so I'll leave you to get better acquainted. Call me," she hollered back as she slipped out the exit, leaving me alone with perfect strangers.

I froze, not knowing what I should do or say next. As though sensing my discomfort, Mae spread her arms and engulfed me. I snuggled into the folds of her body until she let me go. Then, Andrew stepped up and pumped my hand.

"We've been praying for a helper," Andrew said. "Until now, we've only had my son, Ronnie, and a sweet Jewish girl, Ariella Steinberg. She brings produce from her father's farm, and she stays and helps serve our guests."

"Guests?"

Andrew nodded. "Yes, guests. We think the word sounds more dignified than calling them homeless or needy. We want them to feel human, despite their situations. Much of the time, whatever has befallen them has not been their fault."

He raised his eyebrows. "So, Angela. Are you in?"

I managed a bashful smile. "Yes." I shrugged. "I'm not sure how much I can do. But if you'll show me ..."

Andrew gestured toward the kitchen. "Ronnie and I do most of the cooking. Mae sets up the serving table. You can help her with that. And, you'll serve the food. You'll catch on quickly enough. After everyone has eaten, I hope you'll stay and help us clean up—you know, sweep the floor, wipe down the tables. So many come to our door, these days, we often have to serve them in shifts. So, of course, we'll have a ton of dishes for you to wash between servings."

"One other thing," Mae interjected. "If time allows, you're welcome to sit and talk to the people. Let them tell you their stories. Sometimes, if it's needed, we share a verse or two from God's word."

God's word? I'd never read the Bible, much less quoted from it. Truth be told, I didn't even own one.

Mae stared at me as though she could read my mind. "It's a part of our ministry," she said. "We listen to their problems. You can't imagine the hard times some of these people have had. So, if we're at a loss for words, we simply look in the Bible for an answer."

I lowered my eyes. My voice came out almost a whisper. "I've never talked about spiritual things to other people. To me, it's a private thing, something I do in church or in the quiet of my bedroom." I couldn't believe I was actually sharing my insecurity with these strangers.

I raised my head and looked from one to the other, certain I must have turned seven shades of red. Neither one of them had an inkling of condemnation in their eyes. I gave a weak shrug.

Mae grabbed my hand in both of hers. My fingers literally disappeared inside her grasp.

"My dear, you don't have to do anything that makes you uncomfortable. In time, you will relax about such things. Right, Andrew?" She cast a hopeful eye at her husband.

"Right," he said, grinning. "You won't be able to help yourself. Mae's spirit tends to rub off on anyone she meets."

At that moment, the front door swung open and a lanky teenage boy entered. His mop of blond hair captured the sunlight streaming through the open doorway behind him. He quickly shut the door and blocked out the buzz of voices outside.

"This is my boy," Andrew said, puffing up his chest. He beckoned the young man closer. "Ronnie, come and meet our new helper." Then, he leaned toward me and lowered his voice. "My son has one more year of high school, and who knows what he'll do after that? Mae and I have a dream for him to go to college, but, it has to be his decision."

"I heard that, Father." Ronnie shuffled up to us.

"Meet Angela," Andrew said.

Ronnie nodded but didn't offer his hand. He flushed a deep pink and bowed his head. I found his shyness refreshing. He was so unlike the boisterous ruffians who hung out in my neighborhood.

Mae rested her hand on Ronnie's shoulder. "My son wants to be an architect."

He lifted his head and straightened his shoulders. "If I keep my grades up, my teacher said I might earn a scholarship. It's probably the only way I'll get into college."

"It sounds like a good plan," I said.

He grinned. "It is, as long as my mother keeps out of it." He shot a sideways glance at Mae.

"To be honest, I was hoping he'd go into the ministry," Mae confessed. Then she ruffled his mop of hair. "Don't worry, Ronnie. I know when to back off." She shrugged. "Anyway, it wouldn't hurt to have an architect in the family. They make a pretty good living."

The front door opened again and a young woman entered. Her bronze skin, pitch black hair, and exotic dark eyes nearly took my breath away. She was absolutely gorgeous. I guessed her age at around nineteen or twenty. She carried a large basket loaded with vegetables.

Andrew nudged his son's arm. "Help Ariella."

The boy rushed toward the girl and swept the basket out of her hands. The back of his neck turned bright red. He turned away from her. The pathetic gleam in his eyes took me back to the day a young Italian immigrant came into my office. Fredo had the same look as he stood there with his hat in his hands, turning it in circles. I could relate to the joyous heartache of young love, even when it's not returned. I felt a stab of compassion for the boy.

Mae peered into the basket and lifted a handful of carrots. "Ariella, these are gorgeous."

Ariella moved closer. Mae introduced us, then wrapped her arm around the girl's shoulder.

"Ariella's family fled Germany a few years ago," she told me. "They sold everything they owned, hid the money in the linings of their coats, and escaped into England. They left behind a thriving bicycle business and several relatives they may never see again. After reaching New York, they bought a small farm in the country." She gave Ariella a squeeze. "Now, they grow vegetables, and they have a few chickens and a cow. They've been very generous toward our soup kitchen."

Andrew waved a hand at his son. "Come on, Ronnie. The soup's a little weak. We need to add Ariella's vegetables. Better start chopping." He flashed a grateful eye on Ariella. "Thank your parents for us."

"I will," she said. Her throaty voice didn't match her soft femininity. I took an immediate interest in Ariella. At such a young age she already had a history that spoke of loss and a struggle for existence. I couldn't imagine having to leave everything behind, particularly people you loved, to start over in a strange land. But isn't that what my Fredo had done?

While the two guys headed for the kitchen with the basket of vegetables, Mae showed me around the place. She explained that the kitchen once served a large restaurant. The proprietor had left behind a four-burner gas stove, a huge Formica prepping table, a full-size refrigerator, and a double sink for cleanup.

I shook my head in awe. "This is terrific. It looks like a restaurant kitchen."

"That's the idea," Andrew called over his shoulder. "We want our guests to feel as though they've gone out to a fine restaurant for dinner."

With a chuckle, Mae ushered me out into the dining area. Two huge tables stood off to one side near the kitchen. "We serve from here," she said. "And our guests sit there." She gestured toward seven long tables in parallel rows across the room. Wood slatted folding chairs ran along both sides of each table.

"What Andrew said is not far from the truth," Mae said. "A restaurant used to operate out of this building. It wasn't fine dining, not with these tables. It was more of a cafeteria. When the economy dropped, the business failed. The owner took an interest in our ministry. He donated the furniture and all the kitchen equipment."

"Where is he now?"

"Far as I know, he and his family went to live with relatives in Canada." Mae breathed a sigh and smoothed a wrinkle from her apron. "Time to get started," she announced.

A grunt drew my attention to the far side of the room. An elderly man, dressed all in black, sat at the head of the last table. He was reading a book.

I caught Mae's eye. "Who's he?"

"That's old Jake—my father. He likes to come in and visit with the people. I guess you might call him our social chairman."

The old man looked up from his book and squinted his eyes at me. I offered a smile. He merely grunted again and went back to his book.

From the kitchen came the rattle of pans, the chopping of a knife on a cutting board, and the running of water.

"Well, we need to get a move on," Mae said. "We keep a tight schedule. A lot of hungry people are standing outside. Come with me."

She went to a cupboard, pulled out a couple of white linens, and carried them to the two serving tables. I helped her spread the cloths. Ariella followed behind us and placed a basket of artificial flowers in the center of each table.

The girl's dark eyes sparkled. She glided into the kitchen and returned pushing a rolling cart laden with bowls and spoons along with an odd mix of cups and glasses. I joined her at one of the serving tables and helped her arrange everything in rows. Then, she scooted the cart back to the kitchen.

I eyed the display of dishes, then looked at my soft, pink hands. I'd been designated dish washer. I hated to imagine what my skin would look like at the end of the day.

Mae went to the kitchen and returned with Ariella's basket, now filled with sliced bread. Ariella took a position behind the beverage table and started pouring water into the cups and glasses. The aroma of vegetable soup gripped my stomach. I'd only had an apple for breakfast that morning.

"Soup's ready," Andrew called from the kitchen. He and Ronnie came out carrying two steaming kettles. I joined Mae behind the serving table. She grabbed a soup ladle and directed me behind the basket of bread. Ronnie went to open the door.

"You have a well-organized operation here," I said to Mae. "I only hope I can help without getting in the way."

She smiled at me. "You've already fit in, dear. You'll see. As the day goes by, I'll have plenty for you to do."

As the first of our "guests" walked through the door, old Jake looked up from his book and followed them with his eyes. They came straight to the serving tables, collected their bowls of soup and cups of water and started toward the seating area. Like the master of the house, Jake nodded, set aside his book, and beckoned them to his table with a wave of his hand. While they ate, he carried on multiple conversations at once, like a wealthy host who had invited his friends to a lavish dinner party.

A lump came to my throat. The people didn't seem at all like what I expected. Sure, a few derelicts approached my table. It was easy to spot them. Unshaven. Wearing torn and stained clothing. Their breath reeked of cheap alcohol, and they were hunched over, like they were ashamed of the choices they'd made or simply couldn't hold up under their burden anymore.

But most of the people in line could have been my neighbors or my own relatives. Men and women in decent clothes, their hair combed, their hands clean. Families with small children in tow. Teenagers who punched each other's arm, told jokes, laughed, and came back for seconds. If I didn't know better, I would have thought I was in a cafeteria, and these people were on a lunch break from work or from school.

Mae leaned toward me, her voice low. "Over the months, I've gotten to know many of these folks," she said. "They were once bankers, secretaries, school teachers, and construction workers. Most of them lost their jobs. Some lost their homes. Don't pity them, Angela. They wouldn't want that."

As it turned out, there was a little soup left in the pot, enough for us eat. We sat at a table and visited with the people. I discovered Mae was right. Some of them had held respectable jobs at one time. Through no fault of their own, they had gone from affluent to merely comfortable to indigent, in only a few months. The realization hit me like a hammer. This was the kind of hardship my husband was trying to avoid. He wasn't off on some wild adventure. He was laboring in a forest camp for one purpose, to keep me safe. Had Fredo not left to take that job, we, too, might have been begging for a bowl of soup.

As the last of our "guests" filed out into the street, Andrew came up beside me.

"There but by the grace of God ... " he said. I nodded in agreement.

CHAPTER THIRTEEN

JACK

2008

With concerns for his mother heavy on his heart, Jack gets out of bed, slips into a bathrobe and saunters into the kitchen. The aroma of fresh-brewed coffee draws him to the carafe on the counter. He grabs a cup off the rack and pours the steamy liquid, then adds a shot of cream.

Amy's sitting at the table reading the morning newspaper. He sweeps his eyes over her honey-colored hair, her peaches-and-cream complexion, her turned-up nose, features that, along with her easy-going way, helped her hold onto her youthful innocence. She's the mother of a grown son, but Jack still looks at her and sees the girl he fell in love with thirty-five years ago. She raises her head and smiles at him.

He takes a careful sip of the hot coffee, then nods toward the newspaper spread open on the table. "Anything important happening?"

She shakes her head. "The usual. The economy's gone stagnant. The auto industry may not survive. Locally, a shelter has started handing out toilet paper and diapers. And the Salvation Army has put out a request for food. That's what this world's come to, Jack."

"Why read that stuff? It'll only depress you." He takes a seat across from her and nurses his coffee.

"Actually, I skimmed past all the negative news and now I'm looking through the employment ads." She turns the page.

"Really? Looking for a job?"

"Yes. I mean no. I mean, not for me. For Fred." She looks up, her brow furrows. "I'm afraid there's not much."

"He'd probably do better with an Internet search."

"Yeah, I guess you're right." She folds up the paper and sips her coffee. Her hazel eyes peer at him from behind the vapor rising from her cup. She appears puzzled, but says nothing.

"I've been thinking, Amy. Should we go to Florida?"

She stares back at him, then surprises him with a nod.

"Really? Is that a yes? You didn't want to go yesterday. What changed your mind?"

She sets down her cup and leans across the table toward him, like she's about to share a secret. "With Fred and Marcie here—and their kids—I can use a break." She sighs. "Maybe they can use one, too."

"I see." Jack nods his understanding and swallows more coffee. "After you went to bed last night, I got a text from Dorothy. She says Mom isn't doing well. The paralysis isn't subsiding, and she's starting to show signs of dementia." He shrugs. "My sister does tend to exaggerate, but—"

Amy's shaking her head. "When I called, last week, Dorothy told me the same thing. She said your mom forgets where she puts things." Amy releases a ripple of giggles. "Your sister found your mom's hairbrush in the freezer. And the poor girl couldn't locate her purse for a couple of days. Dorothy found it under your mother's bed."

Jack shakes his head and snickers. "I guess we should've expected this. She *is* ninety-four."

"Come on. My parents are in their nineties too. They both still drive, and Mom cooks and does her own housework."

Jack cocks his head. "I guess everybody's different."

Amy takes her cup to the counter for a refill. On her way back to her chair she pauses next to Jack and leans in for a hug. He breathes in the scent of her apple shampoo.

"There's more, Jack," she says.

"Yeah?"

"Dorothy said your mom dwells on the past, that she rambles on about your dad and their lives back in New York, some guy named Giuseppe, her girlfriend, Katie, and a lot of other people she used to know. Sometimes, your mom goes back sixty or seventy years and describes things in detail. Yet, she can't remember what happened yesterday. Your sister thinks she may be getting Alzheimer's."

Jack shakes his head. "I'm not sure I agree with her diagnosis. Alzheimer's? My mom sounds fine on the phone. Whenever I call, she knows right away it's me. Lots of people reminisce about the old days. There's nothing wrong in that. I'm more concerned about how the two of them are getting along. Dorothy can be a little overbearing, you know."

Amy rests her hand on his arm. "If we go to Florida, you know what it'll mean, don't you?"

"What?"

"You'll have to deal with your sister."

"I know. I really don't want to get into a debate with her, but—" For a second he's a twelve-year-old boy and Dorothy has dumped his favorite baseball mitt in the trash, simply because she didn't like something he said.

"But what?" Amy's question jolts him back.

"Well, Mom's collected a lot of things that have sentimental value to her. Dorothy may be forcing her to get rid of things she'd rather keep. At ninety-four, my mother won't survive a battle with that strong-willed woman. Heck, at sixty, I wouldn't stand a chance."

"So ... do we stay here and put up with the noisy grandkids, or do we head for Florida and face a different kind of trauma?"

Jack breathes a sigh of surrender. "Well, Dorothy *has* asked me to come. Begged me, actually. She said Barry can use some help moving the furniture out. There's also Dad's tool shed. From what Dorothy tells me, it's full of a lot of useless junk. It wouldn't be right if I left all the work to the two of them." He sips his coffee. "Maybe my presence alone might set my mom at ease."

Amy takes her seat and settles back. "Sounds like a major project."

"By the way ... " Jack lets out a hardy chuckle. "You won't believe what Dorothy found in the spare bedroom yesterday."

"What did she find?" Amy tilts her head; her eyes light up with interest.

"Several shoeboxes full of—guess what Money. Lots of it. She said there must be thousands of dollars in there."

Amy's mouth drops open.

"Can you imagine?" he says. "Apparently, my folks didn't use a bank for years. Who knew?"

"So, there's a ton of stuff to clear out, plus shoeboxes full of money?"

He nods. "It's not unusual behavior for people who lived through the Great Depression. They're afraid they might have to do without, like before, when things got really tough. So they save everything, even worthless junk. It's like they're trying to stay alive anyway they can."

"Yeah, I've known people like that. It's weird."

"Yes, and, to them, it's reality. In my work at the mental health clinic I sometimes see patients who struggle with that kind of anxiety. Some of them are collectors. Some are hoarders. Some are downright slobs. Meanwhile, their kids don't understand them."

"Is there a cure? I mean, how do you help someone like that?"

"I don't. That's not my area of expertise. I deal with family issues, like divorce and extended families and troubled teenagers. Those older folks are a whole other animal."

"So, what do you do?"

"I pass them to Bob Dixon. He's done a lot of research on the subject. It's funny, but looking back, I should have known my folks were hoarders the day I went looking for my yearbook in their attic and found the place cluttered with a bunch of worthless stuff—vintage clothing, broken furniture, lamps that didn't work, plus stacks and stacks of old newspapers and magazines. Downstairs, their house was always immaculate. I had no idea my parents had saved so much trash."

"Maybe hoarders is the wrong word for them. Maybe they were packrats."

"Right. But, in either case—hoarder or packrat—Bob has a theory about it. He calls it the Great Depression Syndrome."

"Really?" She props her elbows on the edge of the table and leans toward him, her coffee cup clasped in both hands. "Sounds interesting."

"Bob's done a lot of research. He's interviewed multiple individuals and compiled a huge database of his cases. He adds detailed notations—the age of the patient, the places where he or she lived in the past, and, most importantly, what their lives were like during the 1930s and '40s. Of course, some of the personal details also came from their children. Bob also made a separate file logging historical data and statistics. It's a pretty informative study."

"The Great Depression Syndrome, huh? Maybe he should put your mom in his database."

Jack chuckles. "My mom? Treat her like a guinea pig at this stage of her life? I don't think so." He drains his coffee. "Now that I think about it, she never threw anything away, not even when my dad's business took off and they lived well. She still kept on patching the knees on my jeans until they nearly fell apart. And, would you believe it? She cut my hair with kitchen sheers until I graduated from high school."

Amy laughs until tears come to her eyes. "Oh, Jack. You must have looked like one of those scruffy little rascals in the movies."

"Yeah, funny for you, but *I* lived it. My mother was one resourceful woman."

"You're a mental health counselor, what do *you* make of it all?"

"I have no idea. For now, I only want to be her son."

Amy nods her understanding. "Can you imagine how hard things must have been back then? To raise a family, all the while wondering if your next paycheck could be your last? It's kind of like what our Freddie and Marcie are going through right now—you know, with three kids, no job, and now losing their home."

"It's not quite like what happened with Mom and Dad. But, yes, they're experiencing a lot of the same challenges. I hope *they* don't turn into hoarders—at least not while they're living here."

"Well, we don't have to worry about the kids right now. But we do need to think about your mom. How can we help her? I mean, we can't bring her back here to live, not with young Fred and his family crowded in with us. Where would we put her?"

"I don't know. I love her, Amy. She's my mother, and even though she never said it, I believe I was her favorite. We had a bond ... " His mind momentarily drifts back to the young woman in the housedress, the scent of lemons on her hands, the feel of strong arms lifting him onto her lap. Only yesterday he was five years old.

Amy inhales deeply and lets out a long, slow breath. "Remember what happened the last time we visited? Not at your dad's funeral, but two years ago when you attended the conference in Orlando."

"Right. You stayed with my mother for a few days."

Amy wrinkles her nose. "She wanted to go grocery shopping. *Every day.* We brought home a ton of meat. I couldn't find room in the freezer, she already had jammed too much food in there. I was wondering how we were going to cook everything, when your mom nudged past me and crammed the new purchases inside and forced the door shut. I never saw anything like it before."

"You have to understand, my dad was a poor immigrant. My parents didn't have the same kind of life your folks had. Your parents grew up with the country club set. They never had to wonder where their next dollar was coming from."

She reaches across the table and takes his hand. "You're right, Jack. Even during the depression, Daddy's business flourished. From what my mother says, he ran a Hollywood nightclub that catered to the elite—you know, politicians, showgirls, movie stars. My parents never had to save anything. Once something wore out, they simply threw it away. I was born into an affluent home. They paid for my college, bought me a car, and—well—you know what they did for our wedding."

He recalls the envelope her parents tucked in his hand after the ceremony. It held enough Grover Clevelands for a sizeable down-payment on a house. "They were quite generous," he says.

Amy withdraws her hand, pushes back from the table, and walks to the kitchen sink. She leaves her cup there and pauses. "You know," she says, turning. "The Bible addresses situations like this. We're supposed to take care of our own, aren't we? Particularly widows and orphans?"

"Yeah, I guess so."

She starts for the door to the hall. "Look, Jack. We've taken in young Fred and his family. With the loss of his job, and now their house going into foreclosure, they're going to need a little more time to figure things out. You haven't taken a real vacation in four years. Why don't you let one of your colleagues handle your clients? We can head east for a couple of weeks, spend time with your mother, help clean up the house, and maybe catch a day or two at the beach or at one of the theme parks."

"Is that what *you* want to do?"

"I know you, Jack. You'll be hard to live with if we don't go."

"Yeah, Dorothy will make sure I feel guilty." He strokes his chin and considers Amy's suggestion. His heart swells with love for her. Always thinking of others.

"Fred and his family might appreciate some time alone," he says.

Amy nods. "I think our leaving will ease the tension around here. It's no fun having so many people crowded together in one house. And two women in one kitchen—oh, my goodness. Don't get me wrong, I love Marcie, but ... And the grandkids are precious angels, but I'm getting too old for all the noise those youngsters make." She sighs. "We can use a break, and so can they."

Jack stares out the window. "The bougainvillea are in full bloom.

"Freddie's kept up with the lawn work," he says, more to himself than to Amy. "He mowed yesterday. The oranges are still green. They're not ready for picking yet."

He turns back toward Amy. She raises her brows in anticipation, then glances at the kitchen wall clock. "The kids will be getting up soon. What shall we tell them? Are we going to Florida or not?"

CHAPTER FOURTEEN

THE BRONX

1938

Fredo had been away for several months, and I had no idea when he'd be home. Every couple of weeks, I received a note from him and some cash. In a short time, we had a nice bundle stashed away in the shoeboxes under our sofa-bed.

Winter struck with coldhearted fury. Every time Ronnie opened the door to the soup kitchen, we got a blast of bitterness. Our "guests" came in shivering and blowing warm breath on their frozen fingers. We served hot soup and black coffee every day.

Andrew and Ronnie stayed warm in the kitchen, but inside the dining room icicles dripped from the sills and the air was icy cold. Mae ladled out the soup with gloves on her hands, and Ariella and I never took off our coats. Old Jake stayed at home with no plans to come back until March or April.

The people were shabbily dressed. They had no gloves or hats to keep their extremities warm. Children huddled inside their parents' coats for warmth, and the old folks shivered inside multiple layers of cotton. They looked like ice sculptures, with lines of worry etched on their faces. They scooted close together around the tables and rubbed their hands together over the steam rising from their soup bowls.

I made a mental note to ask Katie and her mom if they'd

knit some hats and scarves from their leftover yarn. I had no doubt they would want to contribute something.

I took Mae aside. "What will they do for heavier coats?" I said. "The weather's going to get worse before it gets better."

She shrugged. "I'll mention the need to the churches that support us. Then, we'll just have to pray for donations."

Pray? Mae had the same answer for everything. *Pray for a little meat to flavor our stew. Pray for someone to come in and fix our broken chairs. Pray for financial donations from the rich who drive by in their big cars every day.*

She placed a hand on my shoulder. "Angela, stop worrying. We'll do what we can, but sometimes we have to wait for the miracle."

"Wait?" I shook my head. "Are you going to ask these people to wait?"

"All I know is, God sometimes shows up at the last minute, if we keep the faith."

I wasn't sure faith and prayers worked. Had I ever seen a miracle? No. My brother lost his eye in a tragic accident at work. My parents never became rich like they hoped when they came to America. My husband had been snatched away from me in the prime of our marriage. Where was my miracle? For that matter, where was the miracle for the people who came to God's Kitchen?

I glanced around the room, astounded by the transformation that was taking place. As stomachs filled with hot soup, faces took on a glow, eyes gave off a sparkle that wasn't there when the people walked in. The room came alive as stories flew back and forth across the tables. It could have been a family reunion. Though their histories differed, the people shared one thing in common—the depression had shattered their hopes and dreams. But this brief time of fellowship was like a therapy session for some, and encouragement for others.

Like the day Donald Kiefer burst through the door. He'd been a regular long before the day I started helping there. "I've found a job," he announced, his face beaming. "Now I can send for my family. We can be together again."

Mae invited him to sit and eat, but he shook his head. "You've taken care of me long enough. Help someone else. I can make it on my own now."

A few days later, someone brought in a homeless friend. The newcomer took Donald's usual seat at the table, and the cycle continued. One left and another came in. After a while I started to get used to the pattern.

Even in the wake of success stories, bad news fell on us now and then. One frigid morning, we learned that another one of our regulars had spent the entire night in an alley, shivering beneath layers of crumpled up newspapers. The police found him that morning, frozen to death. Ariella and I took turns crying for the rest of the day. No sooner did she stop sobbing, than I let my tears flow.

Mae kept assuring us that we couldn't rescue them all.

"We can merely feed them and wish them well," she said. "Once they fill their stomachs, we have to send them back out into the cold and place them in God's care."

I didn't want to tell Mae this, but I was growing a little tired about hearing that phrase. So far, I hadn't observed any miraculous relief, not for myself and certainly not for the poor people who came through that door.

After the last of our diners left, Ariella entertained us with stories about her life back in Germany. Her dark eyes glistened as she spoke of parties she'd attended and her girlfriends' wedding plans. Though Ronnie was busy sweeping the floor, I caught him glancing in her direction, a pathetic yearning in his eyes.

As for Andrew and Mae, they often escaped to their own little world. Once, I walked into the kitchen and caught them kissing. They quickly went back to work. Often, when Mae was struggling with a tray of sandwiches, Andrew would drop whatever he was doing and he'd whisk the tray out of her hands. After placing it on the serving table, he'd give his wife a pat on the behind, and then, whistling a tune, he'd go back to cutting up vegetables in the kitchen. Their little acts of intimacy made me miss Fredo all the more.

The place echoed with different sounds. Pots and pans rattled in the kitchen, water splashed in the sink, and chairs scraped against the wooden floor as they were shoved back in place. In the midst of all the clatter, Mae sang Christian hymns. Then, at the end of each day, we gathered in a circle for prayer. Afterward, Andrew donned a pair of overalls and headed out to his part-time job at the railroad yard. Ronnie found a place in the corner where he could do his homework. And, Ariella and I went to our respective homes.

Then, one morning, the bottom dropped out of our ministry. I was busy spreading tablecloths on the serving tables, when Mae came out of the kitchen, her eyes red, her cheeks stained with tears. She pulled a handkerchief out of her apron pocket and dropped into a chair, blotting her face.

I stopped what I was doing and hurried to her side. "What's the matter, Mae?"

She raised her head and gazed tearfully into my eyes.

"Please, tell me what's wrong. Let me help."

She mopped her tears and blew her nose. "There's nothing

you can do, darling," she said, shaking her head. "Our main donor, a local church, has disbanded. I received their last donation today. Come next week, our supply of food will be gone."

"Next week?" I searched her face. "How long have you known?"

She let out a sigh. "They alerted me a month ago, said it was inevitable, and they were very sorry."

"Why didn't you say something to the rest of us?"

She shrugged. "I didn't want to worry everyone. Andrew knew, of course. We thought we'd be able to find another donor. We prayed. We checked with other churches. They either couldn't spare the money or they have their own feeding ministries."

I rubbed her back. "Oh, Mae. This is terrible. Whatever will we do?"

She forced a smile and fingered the gold cross hanging from a chain around her neck. "We'll pray, of course. And, we'll keep serving until we run out of food. I have to keep believing the Lord will rescue us."

I wrapped my arms around her and we wept together. Ariella came over. Mae told her what had happened, and the three of us formed a huddle and cried. If things didn't change in a few weeks, Andrew would have to shut down God's Kitchen. Then where would all the needy people go for a hot meal?

That night I pulled one of the shoeboxes out from under the sofa-bed. With tears running down my cheeks, I removed the cash and stuffed it in my coat pocket. Then I slid the empty shoebox back under the bed.

The next day, I handed my donation to Mae. Hopefully, the extra cash would be enough to keep the soup kitchen going for a few more weeks. She blubbered her gratitude, ran into the kitchen to tell Andrew, then grabbed her purse and rushed out the door.

I sank into a chair and chewed my bottom lip. I had made the decision without writing my husband to ask his permission. I had to believe Fredo would support my impulse.

That evening, I wrote and, with sincere apology, I told him what I had done. I had to wait nearly two weeks for the mail to run its course. Instead of ranting about my misuse of our funds, my dear husband sent me another forty dollars and a loving note.

"Mio amore, Angelina. What you do is good thing. God help me, give me job. I help you. Now you help the poor."

I breathed a sigh of relief and read the rest of his letter.

"New York camp cold," Fredo wrote. *"We live in barracks, like soldiers, no heat. Eat in big tent. Werk all day. Have fun, do rassling games. Pietro win all time. Sum young boys here. They come by hop train, say they werk for place to sleep and food. My friends and me, we give them little money. At night, we sit at campfire, tell stories. Job change every day. Dig dichs, plant trees, make dams, move big rocks. Hands sore, feet tire, but new big mussels for hug you with. John help me write letter, fix my spells. Mio amore, I send much denaro. You pay rent, get food. Help soup people. Wait for me. I home soon."*

I sat at the kitchen table and gazed out the window at a massive web of stars. A full moon cast it's glow on the letter in my hand. I read Fredo's words two more times, a stream of tears running down my face. A familiar song ran through my head and I mouthed the words—"By the light of the silvery moon ... " A sob rose to my throat. I pulled a handkerchief from my pocket and mopped my cheek, then I drew a long breath and resumed my singing. "To my honey I'll croon love's tu—"

The loneliness was more than I could bear. I collapsed on our sofa bed, buried my face in Fredo's pillow and cried myself to sleep.

And so, like my man told me, I paid the rent, bought a few things for my pantry, and set aside the rest for the soup kitchen. For a while, nothing went into our shoeboxes.

In the meantime, Mae and Ronnie solicited coats and blankets from a nearby Salvation Army center. Katie and her mom dropped off a huge pile of knitted hats and gloves in variegated colors. And, a donation of men's clothing came in from a rich guy whose shirts Katie ironed.

I'll never forget the day we distributed those items. We piled them on a table in the corner. I expected our guests to rush over and grab and pull like people do during a department store basement sale. But these folks didn't crowd each other. The men stepped aside and allowed the women to approach the table first. The mothers made sure the children, including the older teenagers, had warm coats. Two women reached for the same garment. They both let it go so the other one could have it.

I was so moved by this show of unselfishness, I had to disappear inside the kitchen. I found a corner and wept into a handkerchief. I hadn't grieved about my husband for weeks. Yet, here I was, shedding tears over a bunch of strangers. Then, the shock hit me. These weren't strangers at all. I had gotten to know these people like my own family. Race and gender didn't matter. We were a mixed group—young, old, black, white—there was even a Chinese family and a couple of newly-weds from India.

One afternoon a black couple wandered into God's Kitchen with seven children in tow. The kids' clothes weren't fit for a rag bag, and they had a gaunt look, sunken cheeks and hollow eyes, much like the photos I'd seen of African children who suffer from malnutrition.

Without hesitation, those who were already seated slid over and made room so the family could sit together. I placed bowls of soup in front of the children and gazed at their expressionless faces. Would they ever smile and play again like kids are supposed to? I wanted to know their story. I looked to their mother. Between sips of hot soup, she spoke about the trial that ended her husband's job and swept them from their home.

"My husband, he ain't had work in six months." Her voice was thick with despair. "We're tired o' eatin' outa garbage cans. We're fed up with driftin' from place to place."

I'd finished my work, so I pulled up a chair beside her. "What kind of work does he do?"

"Handyman. My Cappy can fix almost anythin'. He's real talented that way. For a while, he was workin' at a school. They up and fired him and brung in somebody else."

"I'm so sorry." A thousand thoughts ran through my head, but I couldn't think of anything else to say. How do you tell a mother she may not be able to feed her children tomorrow? Or buy them decent clothes? Or put a roof over their heads?

I glanced at Mae behind the serving table. She picked up my silent plea, set down the ladle, and came over to us.

"I couldn't help but overhear," she said. "Tell ya' what. We can use an extra hand around here. Temporarily, of course."

My mouth dropped. Mae didn't have the money to hire a handyman. The little bit that came in from a local church, plus what I gave her each month, provided barely enough food for the kitchen. Mae ignored my puzzled stare and set her eyes on Cappy.

"A few of our chairs need fixin' and one of the burners on our stove stopped working." Mae smiled as though she had a bankroll in her pocket. "It'll take you maybe two mornings. I can't pay much, but you and your family can stay and eat with us."

How on earth did Mae expect to pay the man? I caught her fingering the gold cross that hung around her neck. My insides tightened up in a knot. Then I looked at Cappy and I understood. His broad grin temporarily erased the scar that trailed from his left eye to the corner of his mouth. There was no telling what kind of trouble he'd gotten himself into. His moist eyes and trembling lip revealed a much gentler man.

He looked at Mae and pressed his hand to his heart. "Thank ya', Ma'am. Anythin' you provide will be more'n enough."

Cappy's wife started blubbering so hard, she couldn't finish her soup. Cappy rubbed her back with one hand. With the other, he swept up his littlest child and propped her on his knee. "This my Tanya—my angel," he gushed, and the puddle in his eyes confirmed his deep love for the child.

In fact, the entire family huddled so close together even a crowbar wouldn't have been able to pull them apart. They owned no material wealth, yet I found myself envying them and the unity they had. Despite all that had happened, they'd managed to stay together.

With Fredo so far away, I didn't have the chance to experience what this family had found. I would have willingly given up every dollar my husband sent home if I could have had him by my side. Some things are more important than money.

Cappy and his family rose from the table, looking much like a dance troupe from an *Oliver Twist* musical, linked together and flowing toward the door as one.

"Come back in the morning and we'll get you started," Mae called after him. "And bring your family."

"Bless ya', Ma'am. I won't let ya' down," he said, an air of pride filling his voice.

I thought of my Papa and how his self-worth had vanished when he stopped working. It was almost like he died before his time. I figured it must have been like that for Cappy too. Such a proud man needed to know he could support his family.

The next morning, Cappy started nailing slats on the broken chairs. Then he tackled the faulty stove burner. Within an hour he had flames coming out of it, and Andrew was able to fire up an extra pot of soup.

While Cappy dove into his work, I picked up little Tanya and cuddled her against my chest. She was so frail, it was like grabbing a pile of doggie bones. I hurried to the kitchen and swiped an extra piece of bread for her. She gnawed on it and snuggled under my chin. She wrapped her arm around my neck and leaned back so she could study my face. Her dark eyes softened, then glistened beneath a blanket of lashes. I smiled and pulled her close. Would I be able to love a child of my own as much as I loved that pathetic little one at that very moment? I could only hope.

Three days later, Cappy finished his work. He gobbled down a sandwich, then he gathered his family together and strode from the building with a pocketful of cash and a satisfied grin on his face.

Mae's necklace was gone. So was her wedding ring. I didn't bother to ask her what had become of them. The pawn shop owner on the next block probably had them. They did what banks couldn't do back then—offer people money for their jewelry.

That evening, I trudged up the stairs to my empty apartment, silently berating myself for complaining over little things, when I had watched Mae sacrifice her most precious possessions for a man who had nothing.

At that moment, I caught sight of the corner of an envelope under my door. I fumbled with my key and rushed inside, ditched my coat and purse, and tore open Fredo's letter. My spirits lifted, I settled on the sofa-bed and began to read.

CCC group come today, so now we crowd together. Pietro afraid we be sent home. I no think it happen. There plenty werk for all. We dig holes. We fill holes. We cut trees. We plant trees. At night my back hert. Next morning, up before sun rize. Same thing next day. Need my wife. Miss you cooking, mio amore. I send money. Help soup place...

Fredo wrote a little more about his work and the possibility they might be transferred to another location. Nothing had been decided yet, but he wanted me to be ready, in case the move happened quickly.

Maybe chance I no able write for while. I try, but boss have charge.

Even before I got to the last line the tears blurred my vision. I missed my husband more than anything in the world. Though Katie had assured me my work at the soup kitchen would help to fill the void, by the time I got home, a terrible sadness overcame me. I felt like I had two different people inside me. One was actively involved in ministry. The other was a grieving widow, longing for the return of her husband.

Sometimes Fredo's letters left me laughing out loud. He wrote funny stories about Pietro and John and their silly antics. Once, the three of them put together a little skit to entertain the other men in the camp. One of the bosses took a photo, which Fredo slipped in the envelope before mailing it. In the picture, Pietro towered over the other two. He was twice the size of Fredo. The big oaf hiked up his pants and wrapped a blanket around his middle, then tied a handkerchief around his head. He was the ugliest woman I'd ever seen. In the photo, he was making eyes at my little Italian husband, while, John, as the rejected suitor, stood behind them with his hands on his hips.

Those three were an odd bunch. Pietro drew trouble like a magnet. John had positive goals and a strong religious faith. Then there was Fredo, a meek, yet confident man of integrity. My husband didn't fit in with either of them. Yet, he joked about Pietro's antics, and he praised John for his wisdom. Somehow, they had banded together to form an inseparable trio. They were Alexandre Dumas' *Three Musketeers*. They were Robin Hood and his Merry Men. They were my beloved and his two *amici*.

The truth was, they weren't swashbuckling heroes at all. They were ordinary men roughing it in the woods and, apparently, having a grand old time.

The one thing Fredo and Pietro had in common was that they both came from the old country. But, while Fredo lived in a backwoods village and labored in the vineyards, Pietro had grown up in a large farmhouse in Tuscany. His father owned a flourishing wine production business. Though Pietro had servants and the promise of a huge inheritance, when he turned eighteen he defied his father and left home, penniless, for America. He met Fredo on the ship and they immediately sealed a friendship.

John came from an upper-class Irish family. His father ran a law office in Boston. John put in two years of college before coming to New York. Unlike Pietro, he didn't walk away from his wealth. Not totally. He told his parents he wanted a taste of adventure before he returned to college. They talked it over, and, big surprise, his father supported his decision. He figured it would be a good learning experience for his son.

Now John had gone off to a rundown forest camp with two rag-a-muffin Italian immigrants. Hopefully, his father wouldn't object.

Pietro kept Fredo and John in high spirits during their time at the forest camp. But, his impulsive nature troubled me, and my worst fears surfaced the day I opened Fredo's letter and read that Pietro had climbed a fifty-foot tree during a windstorm. He wanted to lop off the upper branches. Instead, he flipped over and hung upside-down, dangling by a rope over a pile of rocks.

Fredo wrote about it like it was another one of their comedy acts. *"John and me, we clime up so get our buddy. I reach him first, pull him clos to me. John clime hyer and cut rope, and Pietro drop down like a stoopid munkey. We have big laf over it."*

The camp boss threatened to send Pietro home, but John stepped up and spoke on his behalf. Afterward, John lectured Pietro for putting the three of them in danger and almost ending their forest career.

"Pietro say John big sissy," Fredo wrote. *"He tell him, you college boy. You rich kid. You talk so perfect, but don't do nothing. I tell Pietro he shud be nice."*

While Pietro brought fun and games to their campsite, John showed my husband what a person could accomplish if he studied hard and set a goal for himself. He didn't only talk about it. He worked hard in the camp. And, he helped Fredo with his English. Thanks to John, the letters kept coming every month, and Fredo's spelling started to improve.

Days passed. Weeks. Then months. The snow melted. The streets rumbled with traffic again. People shed their coats. Old Jake returned to his seat at the head of the table.

Another letter from Fredo left me in tears. *"Mio amore, I transfer Ohio. Snow melt. Rain come. They say flood soon. Need werkers. We go with CCC to place near city call Sinsinati. My job—same—move dirt—plant trees, dig holes. This time to keep river from houses. People maybe leave homes if polizia say go. If much snow melt, bigger flood. They give us raincoats, boots, gluvs. Ready for big job. I miss you, my wife.*

Disappointment swept over me. Fredo wasn't coming home after all. But Cincinnati? I shuddered at the thought of him laboring under those sickening conditions. He included another photo of himself and his two buddies. They looked like soldiers in their green work pants, khaki shirts, and caps. They had struck another comical pose, all three of them with broad grins on their faces, their arms and legs pointing in different directions. They looked like a bunch of Boy Scouts at an overnight camp.

"More later, mio amore." I didn't hear from him for several weeks.

CHAPTER FIFTEEN

ANGELA

SEPTEMBER 2008

"Mother, why are you crying?" Dorothy's brow is lined with genuine concern.

I touch my cheek, surprised to find moisture there.

"No reason. Just thinking."

"Look what I found in your spare bedroom closet. Your embroidery satchel. There's lots of floss, plus two pillowcases and several handkerchiefs you never finished."

My daughter plunges her hand inside the cloth bag and pulls out a web of colored threads. "Why don't you work on one of your projects? It will give you something to do while you're sitting here."

I tilt my head to one side and inspect the colored yarn in my daughter's hands.

"I don't know if I can do much. Not with my hand like this."

"Here." She searches inside the bag and brings out a handkerchief, partially decorated with pink flowers. "I'll attach this fabric to a hoop. You can use your weak hand to hold it steady and pull the stitches through with your good hand."

I shake my head.

"Come on, Mother. Pick a color. Pink for the flower, or green for the stem? I'll thread a few needles and stick them to a pin cushion."

I let out a sigh. Dorothy lays the handkerchief on my lap, and as I get a closer look at the pattern I start to get interested.

"Let's start with the stems and leaves." She says and pulls a forest green floss from the pack. "There you are. You do remember how to make those stitches, don't you?"

I nod and accept the needle she's holding out to me. Dorothy sets my sewing satchel on the floor beside my chair.

"There. Call me if you need anything." She hurries off down the hall with a little skip in her step.

I turn my attention to the project on my lap. With a little effort I slide my left hand under the hoop. With my right hand, I begin a series of straight stitches for the stem, then I do several lazy daises for a leaf. Surprise. I haven't forgotten the way Katie's mother taught me many years ago. I guess it's like riding a bicycle.

I hear my daughter humming in the spare room. Maybe I should finish this one for her. I chuckle. It'll be like stitching up the rift between us.

This isn't the first time Dorothy and I butted heads. We've had plenty of run-ins. Maybe it's because we're so much alike. Stubborn. Determined. Pessimistic even. What's more, we like to make up our own minds about things and we aren't open to someone else's opinion.

The last time we collided we were planning Fredo's memorial service. How silly for a mother and daughter to argue over what kind of music to have when it should have been *my* decision. I knew better than anyone what kind of songs my husband wanted at his service. We'd talked about it often enough during those last weeks.

But, when I suggested "The Battle Hymn of the Republic"

and the Italian anthem, "The March of the House of Savoy," Dorothy threw up her hands.

"Those songs are inappropriate for a funeral. They're too—patriotic."

I tried to tell her that's what her father was, a patriot, but she wouldn't listen. So I reminded her about his last wish, spoken from his deathbed.

"Your father doesn't want a funeral. He wants a celebration of life."

"I don't care what you call it, Mother, we're not going to embarrass ourselves—or Daddy—with parade music."

She showed me her own list, which included the most depressing hymns, and she insisted they be played on an organ. Fredo didn't want everyone bawling their eyes out. I crossed my arms and stood my ground.

"Your father didn't want everybody wailing and carrying on. He said he wanted a party and we're going to give him one."

And so it went, back and forth. Dorothy had her opinion. And I had mine. My other two children didn't get involved. In the end, I lost, of course. Dorothy planned the whole affair—which casket to buy, what clothes my husband would wear, the eulogy, the hymns, the Bible passage she wanted read, right down to the refreshments afterward.

She did, however, agree to ask Delores Evans to sing the "Ave Maria." Delores' beautiful soprano voice brought me to tears. It was the only part of the service I honestly enjoyed. I think it probably was Fredo's favorite part too.

I take a few stitches and breathe a sigh. I've actually started to form a flower stem. I never could have accomplished something this delicate if not for those afternoons I spent at Colleen's sewing shop. I'll never forget the day Katie's mother handed me a couple of squares of cloth and a clump of floss. She sat me down at a table, leaned over my shoulder, and guided me in my first design, a pink rosebud with a long green stem, just like the one I'm sewing now.

There in Colleen's tiny shop, far from Ohio's backwoods, far from the love of my life, I was able to lose myself in a new hobby. With the whir of Colleen's sewing machine in the background and Katie humming an Irish tune, I made a pile of handkerchiefs, and by the time Christmas rolled around, I had a gift for each of the ladies who came into the soup kitchen.

Even now, this simple activity has taken my mind off of what's happening to my house. I'm not looking forward to making the move to Dorothy's place. That house is too big and drafty. I would get lost in that kitchen of hers. My little galley kitchen suits me just fine. I can stand at the sink and turn around to get something out of the fridge. Or I can take a step and stir something on the stove.

I admit, I don't do much cooking anymore, not since Fredo went on a special diet. Afterward, I stuck with canned soup and packaged meals. Maybe someday I'll get the urge to whip up something special, like I used to.

I set aside my sewing, reach for my walker, and crawl to the kitchen for a drink of water. As I round the corner, I freeze. The cupboard doors stand open exposing bare shelves. The counters have been swept clean. My toaster, my hot plate, and my microwave oven have disappeared, probably into one of those boxes over there. My kitchen walls have been stripped bare. Gone are my Christmas plates, my clock with all the different bird whistles, and the large wooden fork and spoon Fredo and I lugged from one house to the next. The empty walls confirm the truth. I'm almost ready to move.

A glass sits by the sink. With one hand on my walker and the other holding the glass, I sidle over to the refrigerator and press the glass against the water lever. The splash of liquid sets me to smiling, and I'm taken back to the day Fredo bought me my first side-by-side refrigerator with the door butler. He beamed as he pushed the buttons. "Look here—ice-a come out. An' water. See, Angelina? We rich people now."

I'm about to head back to my chair in the living room when Dorothy walks in with two stacks of letters in her hands. It's all I can do to set the glass on the table and grab the back of a chair. I stare at the yellowed envelopes bound together with red yarn. For years they've lain tucked away in my cedar chest.

Dorothy's got a twinkle in her eye. "Daddy wrote these, didn't he?"

My own eyes blur with tears. "Please, Dorothy, don't throw my letters in the trash."

My daughter gives me a rare smile and sets the two bundles on the kitchen table. She slips one of the letters from the pack, then looks at me. "May I?"

I nod. Dorothy pulls the letter out and skims the page. She chuckles, glances up at me, and continues reading. A tear oozes from the inside corner of her eye.

"What a treasure," she says. "Of course, I won't throw them away, Mother."

"Your father wrote those letters to me when we were apart for a long time."

"I'll put them in your cedar chest along with some of your other things. You can take the chest with you wherever you go. See? You'll always have Daddy with you."

I'm stunned by Dorothy's soft tone. For now, she leaves the letters on the kitchen table and returns to her work in the back of the house. I settle into a chair and pull one of the bundles closer. I untie the ribbon. The letters tumble onto the table. One of them is a wire. No envelope, just a slip of paper. Fredo didn't send that telegram. It was from John.

CHAPTER SIXTEEN

THE BRONX

1939

After Fredo and his buddies transferred to Ohio, the letters stopped coming for a long while. News reports said there'd been a lot of flooding along the river. Thousands had to evacuate their homes. The river surged past eighty feet. Downtown stores went underwater. The rain poured, and the snow melted. Together they caused an awful flood. At least ten people died during those first days.

My husband was in the midst of all that misery. What was he going to do over there? Dig more holes? Pile more dirt along the river? Chop down another tree?

I curled up on the sofa-bed with a book and tried to get my mind off the situation in Ohio. I was fretting over something I couldn't see but could only imagine.

I was well into the second chapter of *David Copperfield* when Giuseppe came to my door. "Telephone, Angela," he said.

Giuseppe never came to my door to tell me I had a phone call. He always yelled the message from the bottom of the stairwell. This time, his voice shook. Then I shook too. Something bad had happened.

I tossed aside the book and flew from the sofa-bed. I beat Giuseppe down the stairs and grabbed the phone that was dangling from a wire. I expected to hear Fredo's broken English. The smooth, higher tone belonged to John.

Dear God, I whispered. *Please, let Fredo be all right.*

My hands trembling, I pressed the phone to my ear. I strained to hear what John was saying amidst the static and a terrible whooshing sound.

"Angela? Are you there?" He was shouting, like he was in a tunnel.

"Yes, Yes, John. Where's Fredo?" I raised my own voice to match his.

"I'm sorry, Angela. Fredo is missing. Pietro too." There was more noisy static and another loud whoosh.

"What? What did you say?"

"I said, Fredo is missing."

"My God, John, what happened?"

"This morning, a group of men were working along the riverbank. Fredo and Pietro were with them. You know Pietro. He thinks nothing bad will happen to him. He was fooling around and got too close to the edge. The soil crumbled under his feet and he slid into the river."

"That's terrible. But what about Fredo? Where's my husband?"

"Fredo jumped in after him."

"No. Please, no."

"I'm sorry, Angela, they both were swept away."

An icy chill ran through me. I shut my eyes. "No, John. Please don't tell me that."

"Listen, Angela. I'm confident we're going to find them. They're probably lolling around on some riverbank, laughing their heads off."

"What are the men doing to find them? Have they searched? Should I come down there?"

"No, Angie. Stay put. I promise, I'm going to try to find them. A search party already went out. I'm set to go with the next one. I just wanted to call you first."

His voice faded, like he'd stepped away from the phone and was talking to someone else. Then, he was back. "The truck's waiting. I gotta go, Angela. I'll notify you as soon as we know something. I won't be able to call again. They're telling us the phones will be tied up, emergency calls only. I'll stay in touch, but I'll have to send a wire next time. Watch for it, Angela. Stay strong and pray."

Did I let the phone drop, or did I replace it in the cradle? Did I make it up the stairs under my own power, or did Giuseppe help me? The next thing I knew, I was on my knees on the floor of my apartment, bent over in a heap, retching and sobbing until I thought my heart would burst. My husband was missing. I might never see him again.

Then I shifted from overwhelming agony to intense rage. The accident was Pietro's fault. That idiot had pulled another one of his stunts, and my husband had risked his life to save him. I secretly wished the men would find Fredo and not his friend.

For the next hour, I wavered between ranting and wailing. Tears flowed. I cried out to God. I cursed Pietro. I wept and sobbed and ultimately slumped into a whimpering ball of misery.

When I raised my head, my apartment lay in shadows. I didn't bother to light a lamp. Still in my clothes, I crawled into bed, buried my face in Fredo's pillow, and cried myself to sleep.

The next morning, I turned on the radio, hoping for news about the flood. The reporter said the entire river valley had been consumed by oil fires and explosions. The flooding hadn't subsided. Water covered city streets up to twenty feet deep. Most of the residents had sought shelter in other towns. He never mentioned the missing men.

I could sit in the apartment all day, listen to the news until I went nuts, and wait for word from John. Or, I could help out at God's Kitchen and get my mind off my own troubles. I quickly dressed and left the apartment.

As we set the tables, I told Mae what had happened. She immediately rounded us up for prayer. Afterward, I tried to concentrate on the folks we were serving, but my mind kept drifting to the raging river. I pictured my husband being swept away, helpless. Tears came often that day.

The usual faces came through the door. I mentioned to Mae that Cappy and his brood hadn't come in for several days.

"I'm worried about little Tanya," I said. "She wouldn't eat the last time they were here."

"I know," Mae said. "I'm concerned for the whole family. I had more work for Cappy to do, but I have no way to get in touch with him."

I needed to get outside, before Mae offered to say another of her impotent prayers. With so many falling by the wayside, my already crumbling faith took another blow and I no longer believed God cared.

"Tell me where they live. I'll go and check on them."

Mae stared wide-eyed at me. Other guests had come and gone. We never went searching for any of them. But this was different. Mae had grown close to Cappy. And I'd gotten attached to the little one.

"Give me their address," I said.

Mae hesitated. "I don't know. They live in a rundown

housing complex in East Harlem. It's not the best part of town."

"Please, I need to have something to do, anything to keep my mind off of Fredo."

Shaking her head, Mae wrote out the address along with directions. "Be careful," she said. "I don't want anything to happen to you." Then she paused and glanced at her son who was cleaning the floor across the room. "Wait a minute," she said. "Ronnie, come here."

The boy finished sweeping crumbs into a dustpan, then leaned the broom in the corner and came toward us. Mae told him where I was going. He nodded with enthusiasm.

"Don't worry, Mom, I'll take care of Angela."

Inwardly, I smiled. A skinny teenager had promised to protect me. Somehow, that wasn't at all comforting, but I accepted his offer. I really didn't feel like going into the unknown alone.

The trip took forty-five minutes by bus. I stared out the window as busy stores gave way to empty shells. We left behind brownstone structures and well-dressed people walking the sidewalks. East Harlem was a mix of neon-lit nightclubs on the main drag and side streets with dilapidated buildings, their windows boarded up against the cold. Laundry dangled from ropes strung across alleys. Wet newspapers and garbage littered the streets.

We reached a bus stop at what must have been the darkest and dirtiest corner of that part of town. I shuddered at the sight of a long block of crumbling row houses, their doorways opening onto a common alley.

I checked Mae's directions. "This is it," I said to Ronnie.

I took a deep breath and forced myself to step off the bus.

Ronnie stayed close behind me. We approached the tenement. A dark-skinned woman squatted on a front step, a cigarette butt between her teeth, her face riddled with acne. I winced against the odor of urine rising from the pavement.

"I'm looking for a man named Cappy," I said. " Do you know him?"

The hard look in her eyes sent a chill through me. She pointed toward the third door, a black opening that led to a dimly lit passage. I hesitated.

"Let's go," Ronnie said. He nudged my elbow.

I stepped inside and gasped from the stench. At the end of the hall stood a toilet, boxed in by three walls.

"What in the world?" I looked at Ronnie.

"I guess everybody in the building must use it," he said. He shrugged. "Relax, Angela. These folks don't know any different. They'd rather live like this instead of on the streets."

"That's disgusting."

"I know. Try and tell their landlord that."

I turned my attention to the slip of paper with Mae's directions.

"It's on the second floor," I whispered, though there was no reason to speak softly. Ronnie and I were alone in the hall. There wasn't another soul around.

"We need to find Cappy, don't we?" Ronnie had a touch of impatience in his voice.

As for me, I would have turned around right there and left if he hadn't been with me. But then, we'd never find out what happened to the man. With a burst of courage, I climbed the uneven boards to the next level. At the top was another open door. The number of Cappy's apartment was handwritten on the doorframe in black ink. I took a breath and moved inside. The darkness seemed to go on forever. My eyes gradually adjusted to the dark.

A rustle of cloth drew my attention to the far corner.

"Cappy?" I called out.

No one answered.

"Cappy?" I repeated.

Something scampered past me. I jumped back, nearly slamming into Ronnie.

"It's just a rat," he said with a chuckle.

"A rat? Maybe we'd better leave. Anyway, I don't think anyone's here."

I started to back away when a large, cloaked figure rose from the corner. He stepped toward us and dropped his coat to the floor. I reached behind me for Ronnie's arm. He drew close. "It's okay, Angela," he whispered.

"We-we're looking for Cappy and his family," I said as politely as I could.

I hoped the big guy hadn't sensed my fear. Animals did that. They seemed to have an innate sense for such things. But a human? Maybe someone who lived like an animal also had the ability. I wasn't taking any chances. I took another step back and ended up in the doorway. Ronnie did too.

"Cappy gone," the man growled. Invisible needles pricked the back of my neck and a cold chill travelled down my arms. "His youngest died ta' other day. He done took ta' rest o' dem to Florida."

My anxiety gave way to heartache. "The little one died?" I mumbled her name. "Tanya? How?"

The man took another step toward us. "Don' know. She bad sick. Maybe consumption."

Ronnie stepped in front of me and straightened his

shoulders. "You're sure they're gone?" he said, his voice surprisingly strong for such a skinny guy.

"That what I say." The man moved closer, his eyes on my purse.

I stumbled back onto the landing. "Th-thank you," I said.

Then, I turned and fled down the stairs, stumbling several times before I reached the bottom. Ronnie was on my heels. Like he'd promised, the boy had never left my side. I don't know what might have happened to me had he not been there. I looked at him with fresh eyes. He was several years younger than I, but he had accepted the role of protector. Mae truly should be proud of him.

My heart didn't stop pounding until we were on the bus heading back to Brooklyn. During the ride I broke down.

"What's wrong?" Ronnie asked. "Why are you crying? We found out what we needed to know, didn't we? Cappy went to Florida."

"Tanya's dead," I sobbed. "Cappy's little angel is gone."

Ronnie placed a comforting hand on my shoulder. "Shhh," he murmured. "She's with Jesus now."

I couldn't believe he'd said that. A beautiful, little child was dead and all he could say was, "She's with Jesus." I found no comfort in those words. The kid was the exact replica of his mother.

I blotted my tears with a hanky and stared at him, my watery eyes spilling over with more tears. "That place. No one should have to live like that. It's a filthy hole in the wall. No one deserves that kind of existence, especially not an innocent child."

He nodded, and though there was compassion in his eyes, he spoke with firmness. "I agree, Angela. But, it wasn't Cappy's fault."

"I'm not blaming Cappy. I'm blaming a society that doesn't care. I'm blaming a government that doesn't help people rise above their circumstances. Good people. Like Cappy and his wife." I spun toward him in my seat. "Tell me this, Ronnie, what's become of all the promises we heard during the presidential campaign? Where are all the programs? Where's Roosevelt? Sitting in the White House with a steak on his table?"

Heads turned in our direction. I'd gotten louder than I had intended. But, I really didn't care. Maybe those other people on the bus needed to hear the truth.

"Where are all the jobs?" I went on, ignoring the stares. I lowered my voice then. "Cappy lost his job through no fault of his own. If the President had kept his word, Cappy would have been able to provide a decent home for his family. And—and, my Fredo would be home instead of swept away by some river in Ohio."

Ronnie didn't say a word. Smart kid. Nothing he said could soothe the monster inside me. By the time we got to the soup kitchen, I was so worked up, I didn't go inside. I asked Ronnie to tell his mother what we'd discovered. Then, I hopped on another bus and headed straight for home.

When I got to the apartment, I tore off my clothes and left them on the floor by the door. I took a sponge bath and washed my hair in the bathroom sink. The itching subsided and I sat in the dark and stared out the window. Once again, I released a flood of tears. Not only for myself and Fredo, but for those poor people who lived in the back streets of East Harlem.

I considered my own situation. I had food in my pantry and a roof over my head, plus friends who cared about me. And, somewhere, miles away, my husband had been claimed by a violent river. I gazed into the sky at the starry expanse and wondered if Fredo might be sitting on a riverbank looking at the same moon.

I wanted to believe in Mae's God, but I was riddled with confusion. Why hadn't her God used his power to help Cappy? Why had he let little Tanya die? And what about Fredo? Did Mae's all-powerful God really care? Mae says he does. She told me God had experienced a far worse agony than I was going through. And he'd done it for us. For me.

CHAPTER SEVENTEEN

THE BRONX

1939

I dragged myself to the soup kitchen the next morning. I couldn't face Ronnie again, not after my behavior on the bus. And Mae? She'd been trying to instill hope in me, and I had refused to believe as she did.

To my surprise, they both greeted me with open arms and never mentioned my behavior of the day before. Their unconditional kindness had me looking at them with inquisitive eyes. I'd never experienced that kind of acceptance before. If I'd acted like an idiot in front of my brothers, they never would have let me forget it. But not these people. They looked the other way when I messed up.

Two days later, when I returned to my apartment, I found the awaited telegram wedged under my door. I tore it open and began to read its ten precious words. *Phone down. Men found safe downriver. Home soon. John. Stop.*

I choked out a sob. My head swirled with questions. He hadn't told me if Fredo was all right. He didn't say when my husband would be home. And why had John sent the wire and not Fredo?

Elated, I grabbed my purse off the floor and headed back outside. Long shadows spilled across the pavement. I didn't care. I needed to see my best friend. I could have phoned her, but this was too important. I had to see her face when I told her the news. Fredo was coming home. So was John.

I burst through the door of Colleen's shop. Katie was at the ironing board. She stared at me, shocked that I would come there at closing time.

"Fredo's alive. He's alive." I choked out my news, then I broke into sobs.

Katie dropped the shirt she was ironing and let out a happy shriek. She danced toward me, her red curls bouncing like flames in the waning light. Flinging her arms around my shoulders, she called out to the back room. "Mum! Come out. Angela's here."

Colleen appeared in the doorway, her eyebrows raised and her mouth open. She had a towel in one hand and a large spoon in the other.

"What is it, child? Good news about your husband, I hope."

I read John's telegram to them.

Colleen chuckled. "My dear, you must be so happy. Sure, and you should stay awhile and eat with us. We can talk a little more over dinner."

I had hoped they'd invite me to eat with them. My excitement was so high, I didn't feel like cooking and certainly didn't want to eat alone.

Katie took me by the arm and led me into the tiny kitchen. Colleen hurried to the stove, lifted the lid off a large iron pot and ladled out three portions of carrots and potatoes in a watery gravy.

"So sorry, there's no meat, this time," Colleen apologized over her shoulder.

"I don't care," I squealed. "Do you think I care about meat at a time like this?"

"I'm sure you don't," Colleen said, laughing.

While we ate I talked about my plans for when Fredo came home. My joy must have been contagious. The two of them wept happy tears and laughed with me.

Before I left, I told them about my trip to Harlem and the dire living conditions I discovered there. "I wish I could have helped Cappy and his family. And—and, that poor child. She's gone. Tanya didn't even have the chance to live or to play like other kids. She knew only poverty her entire life."

Colleen shook her head. "No matter how bad things get, there's always someone worse off, isn't there? I suppose 'tis better to thank the Lord for all he provides, instead of pining away for what ye don't have."

I couldn't disagree with her. I had received good news about my husband. I should be thankful.

"When Fredo comes home, I want to greet him with a happy heart and a smile on my face," I said. "He doesn't need to start life over with a grumbling wife."

"Amen to that," Colleen said.

Fortified for the chilly trip home, I left Colleen's shop with a spring in my step. The love I received in that tiny kitchen had warmed my heart even more than the hot soup.

I stepped out into the darkening city. There were fewer streetlamps in that part of town. I picked up my step and hurried to the bus stop. As I walked, I pulled out a nickel. I was alone—or so I thought. A dark shadow suddenly engulfed me. I caught the sickening sweet odor of bootleg whiskey and the stench of perspiration. Strong hands gripped my arms. I struggled to break free, spun towards my attacker, and tried to push him away. He shoved me to the pavement and held me there.

I flailed my arms and legs, kicked him in the knee, and pushed against his chest with my palms. I felt his hot breath on my face. Then, without warning, he released me, scrambled to his feet, and fled. Groaning, I pushed myself upright. I felt around the pavement. My hand touched the nickel I'd been holding for bus fare. But my purse was gone.

I struggled to my feet and screamed, "Thief!" A couple of men across the street turned their heads in my direction then resumed walking. No one came to my rescue. The robber had already disappeared into the night.

I looked down at my torn stockings. Both my knees had bits of gravel imbedded in them and blood oozed from the scrapes. The bus was coming, so I pulled my skirt down over my injuries and brushed the wrinkles out of my clothes. I didn't have time to do anything about my hair, or the dirt on my hands. As the door hissed open, the driver eyed me with puzzlement. I didn't say anything, just dropped the nickel in the slot and found a seat.

I wept during the entire ride. When I got to the apartment, I searched under the mat for my spare key. I'd never had a reason to use it before. After Fredo left for the forest camp, I hoped he'd surprise me one day by being there when I came home.

Once inside, I pulled off my coat and hurried to the bathroom. I washed the grit off the bloody scrapes on both knees and cleansed the palms of my hands. Inside the medicine cabinet I found a bottle of Iodine and a roll of gauze. The whole while I doctored my wounds I thought about my purse and its contents—the key to my apartment, some loose change, a soiled handkerchief—and John's telegram, with my address on it. The robber only had to look at that telegram to know where I lived. And, if he read the wire, he also would know my husband was far from home.

I couldn't sleep all night, afraid the robber would come to my apartment and attack me again. The next morning, I asked Giuseppe to change the lock on my door. Then, I went out and bought a flashlight and a purse.

Once I had a new lock, I breathed easier. Three days passed with no further incident. On Friday, we had an extra long line at the soup kitchen. We didn't finish cleaning up until four in the afternoon. With so many more people out of work, Andrew and Mae decided to hold a spontaneous prayer meeting. Mae kindly mentioned my attack, and, no surprise, the woman also prayed for my attacker. I had a hard time saying Amen to that one.

Dusk had fallen when I left for home. Ronnie walked me to the bus stop. I had a new lock on my door, so I wasn't worried. I made the trip, confident that I was safe, climbed the stairwell, reached the second floor, and started to turn the key in the lock. At that instant, someone burst from the shadows and grabbed my arm. The smell of bootleg whiskey and perspiration took me back to the dimly lit bus stop. Once again, I'd met the same attacker.

Just like before, his strong hands grabbed my arms. He forced me inside the apartment and wrestled me to the floor. I slipped out of his grip and scooted back against the bureau. A scream rose from my throat, though no one was there to hear. Giuseppe would have gone home hours ago.

A hand went over my mouth. His other hand pressed my shoulder to the floor. I looked up into bloodshot eyes, shocked to see a teenager staring back at me, his face contorted in desperation. The guy couldn't have been much older than Ronnie Barton.

"You have money?" He sounded like he had gravel in his throat.

"No, I don't. You took everything when you stole my purse."

His eyebrows went up. "You recognize me?"

"Of course, how could I forget your smell?"

He struck my right cheek. My face stung. I clenched my teeth, determined not to cry.

"Look," he said, his voice hoarse. "I won't hurt you if you tell me where you keep your money."

"I'm telling you, I don't have any."

"Liar!" He shook my shoulders. "Where do you keep your cash? Under the mattress? In the ice box? Where?"

He drew back his fist to strike me again. I winced and waited for the blow. It never came. Instead, my attacker lurched backward as if some force had yanked him off of me. He sailed across the room. His back struck the stove, and he sprawled in a heap on the floor. He let out a shriek and lunged to his feet. I scooted backward, out of the way, and searched the floor for a weapon. Anything. My hand came to rest on one of Fredo's shoes.

A shadowy form came between us. There was a scuffle, a series of loud punches, and the robber fell to the floor again. This time, he stayed there.

From the doorway came Giuseppe's voice. "I call *polizia*. They come soon," he said. His bulky shadow hovered in the opening.

My entire body was shaking. A hand reached down and gently eased me to my feet, then guided me to the sofa-bed and helped me settle there. Giuseppe hit the light switch, and I looked into the face of my rescuer.

"Fredo!"

"*Mio amore,*" he murmured. "No worry. I home. I take care you, like I promise."

"Oh, Fredo, Fredo, Fredo." I fell into my husband's arms, weeping and smiling and sobbing and laughing. My love had returned at the exact moment I needed him. What was it Mae had said about God being the God of the last minute? Maybe she wasn't so far off. He'd brought Fredo home to me not a minute too late.

The burglar lay unconscious on the floor. Giuseppe blocked the open doorway, his arms crossed and a grin on his face.

I shook my head in awe. "Giuseppe, I thought you went home hours ago."

"I work late, in back of store. Fredo come, say you no home. So we talk. You friend—" he nodded toward my attacker. "He make lots o' noise. We hear all the slamming and pounding, so I drop what I do, an' we come up."

I bit my lower lip. My eyes burned with fresh tears. "Thank you, Giuseppe. Thank you for working late." I turned toward Fredo. "And you? I'm so happy you're home. I missed you, Fredo. You saved my life. You're my hero. My prince."

"Oh no, Angelina. I no special. Joost-a you husband, that's all."

I laughed and tucked my face against his neck. He wrapped both arms around me. At that moment I realized I hadn't felt safe in nearly a year.

The police showed up about ten minutes later and took the robber away. He no longer had my purse, but its contents were still in his pocket, so I was able to get nearly everything back. When the officer dragged him to his feet, I got a good look at him and was overcome with pity for the young man. What kind of future did he have? Jail, most likely. And, when he got out, perhaps another type of imprisonment, bound to the alcohol he so desperately needed, like so many others, trapped there by a failed society.

As for me? I had my husband back, and that's all that mattered. I clung to Fredo that night and hoped he wouldn't leave me ever again. As far as I was concerned, we could lose everything. I wouldn't care, as long as we were together.

CHAPTER EIGHTEEN

PATRICIA

2008

"What do you mean, they're closing your store?"

Patricia ignores Billy's screwed up face and drops an armful of paper sacks on the dinette table in the kitchen.

"That's what I said." She removes her jacket and drapes it over the back of a chair. Then she grabs the paper sacks and starts dumping their contents on the two placemats. "It's not just a rumor anymore. They've started with a sweep of middle management—me included—to be followed by more layoffs down the line."

He approaches the table. "What's this?" He checks the logo on one of the bags. "McDonalds? Are you kidding me? What happened to Lorenzo's? Or Wong's Chinese?" His voice rings with incredulity. "Are you saying we won't eat in style anymore?"

She stares him in the eye. "Get used to it. Come next week, I'm out of a job."

He wrinkles his brow, looking an awful lot like a chastised puppy. Her heart softens for the moment. Billy can't help what he's become. She created the monster. She coddled him, and spoiled him, and treated him like what he was. A gigolo.

She drops into her chair and unwraps a burger. He marches to the refrigerator and returns with a bottle of Stella Artois.

"Guess it's beer instead of wine from now on, huh?"

"Maybe not even beer. At least, not the expensive brands."

He stops short of the table and frowns.

"Don't you understand, Billy? We could lose everything. We need to make serious plans for the future, which means we may have to do without any luxuries for a while."

With a grumble, he plunks into the chair across from her, gulps his beer, then sets the bottle aside. "Okay," he says, as he rifles through the bags. "So, they're letting you go. What'r ya' gonna do? Give up?" He tears open a pouch of fries and shoves a handful in his mouth.

"No, I won't give up. But I need to organize my people for a close-out sale. Then, I'll ship what's left of my stock to other stores. Of course, I won't order any more merchan—"

"What? You're about to lose your job and you're thinking about work? They're giving you the shaft. You should give it right back to them. Walk out and let them deal with it."

She stares at him as though seeing him for the first time. Somehow, their relationship had evolved from two lovers to parent and child to breadwinner and spoiled brat.

She takes a bite of her sandwich and swallows it along with the nasty remark on her tongue. "I don't operate that way, Billy," she says, struggling to keep her voice calm.

He shrugs. "All I'm sayin' is, you've put in twenty-five years at that place. You built your department from nothing. Now they're dropping you. It's not fair."

"Yes, but they're giving me a decent severance package. If I walk out now, I can kiss that money good-bye."

"Rats."

She gives in to a soft chuckle. "Look, Billy, there's nothing I can do but finish the job I started." She leans back in her chair. "Do you know what hurts the most? They're giving the younger employees an opportunity to transfer to another store. As for us older folks—

"That can't be legal." Billy's scowling now. "You ought-a call a lawyer."

She shakes her head. "It wouldn't do any good. They'll find a loophole. They'll say I haven't pulled my weight or that I failed to do my job—anything that will keep me from suing."

Billy rips open another bag and pulls out a Big Mac. "Maybe it's time you retired."

"What? You want me to *retire*?" Patricia has been avoiding the word since she became eligible a year ago. Somehow, the word "retirement" has a fatalistic ring. It signals the end of an era, maybe even the end of a life.

She locks eyes with him. "Why do you want me to retire? What will I do—sit in a rocking chair, quilting?"

"We could spend more time together." He grins and a trickle of sauce oozes from the corner of his mouth. "We could travel, take a world cruise, live in Europe for a while. I mean, it's not such a bad thing, is it? To retire?"

She shakes her head and releases a sigh. "You don't understand. Old people retire. I don't feel old. I don't look old. And, you have to admit, I don't *act* old."

"Look at *me*." He cocks his head. "I retired ten years ago. I'm still the same person, but I'm in control of my life now."

She finishes her sandwich in silence. Billy may have a point. Some days she comes home from work totally exhausted and wishing she could quit her job. But, the feeling is generally short-lived. Once she's had a vacation, or even a do-nothing weekend, she's anxious to get back on the floor again. There's something exhilarating about making decisions no one else can make.

"So, what's gonna happen to us?" He swallows the last of his beer.

Patricia looks into his puppy-dog eyes. "Get ready for the *real* shocker," she says. "With the loss of my job, we're also about to lose our lavish lifestyle. No more nights out on the town. No more skiing trips to Colorado. No more California beaches. What's more, I won't even have enough income to keep up this place." She sweeps her hand in a half-circle. "Except for my IRA, every cent I made went into decorating this condo, plus clothes, and jewelry—and you, Billy—you and all your stuff."

He releases a shaky laugh. "Come on, baby, things can't be that bad. How can somebody have everything one day and lose it all the next?"

She rises slightly and leans toward him. "First of all, don't call me baby. Second of all, things are going to change around here." She stands to her feet and hovers over him. "Next week, I'll be searching for another job. If I don't find one, we'll be looking for a cheaper place to live." She walks toward the refrigerator and grabs a bottled water, then leans against the counter, a move that forces him to turn around and face her.

"Here's what's going to happen, Billy. I've decided not to pay next month's mortgage. I'm going to let the place go into foreclosure. Then we're going to start making plans to move out of here. I can't—"

"Whatta ya mean, move?"

"Don't you understand? We can't afford this condo. The taxes alone will kill us."

Billy's mouth drops open.

"Don't look at me like that. I sank a ton of money into that BMW you wanted. You couldn't take cabs like the rest of us, had to have a fancy car to show off to all your friends."

"I love that car."

"Well, it's gonna have to go. I can't afford to pay for maintenance or for the garage I had to rent." She pauses to let her decision sink in. He doesn't move, but appears frozen with his index finger pressing against his chin, like he's posing for a magazine ad.

She shakes off the image. "I've been running the numbers, and I've made a list of what I can afford to keep and what I can't. Your car is at the top of the elimination list. So is this condo and a lot of other luxuries we've gotten used to. No more expensive wines, no more restaurant dinners, and no more cigarettes." She shrugs. "It's time I quit smoking anyway."

She walks past him to the living room and sinks into the white, leather loveseat. The furniture will probably have to go too. Billy follows from the kitchen and stands in front of her, his arms crossed, a web of lines on his forehead.

"I can't do this alone, Billy. You're gonna have to get a job. Unless you help me financially, we'll lose everything."

They stare daggers at each other, like two dogs squaring off for a fight. She searches his face and waits for some kind of response. Does he stand with her or against her?

"Right," he says at last. A sarcastic smile curls one corner of his mouth. "Get real, Patricia. How am I supposed to pitch in? They haven't called me on a photo shoot in ten years."

She shakes her head. "You don't have to go back to modeling. You could get a *real* job."

"Hah! I dropped out of high school for a career in modeling.

It's all I know. Just what kind of a *real* job do you suggest?"

She cocks her head to one side and sizes him up. "With your background, you've learned a lot about fashion. You have a great eye for color and style. And you have a terrific personality. Why don't you go to work in sales? Men's clothing, perhaps. Or you can sell cars, like the albatross that sits in our garage most of the time."

He shakes his head and scowls. "That kind of work pays on commission. There's no guarantee I'll earn anything at all selling cars."

"You will if you work hard."

"I don't know ..."

"Billy, you're gonna have to get off your lazy rear end and help out for a change."

He narrows his eyes, huffs out an unintelligible response, then spins away and stalks off to the bedroom. Moments later, he returns wearing his brown leather jacket—a Brunello Cucinelli, the one she bought him for his birthday last year. He yanks the zipper closed with a snap of his wrist.

"You sit there, Patti, and think about what you just said. If our staying together depends on my getting a two-bit job, I don't think I can stick around. You're asking way too much."

She lurches to the edge of her seat. "What exactly do you mean? Until now, our relationship has involved me working and you sitting around the apartment or out partying with your friends—most of whom I don't even know—or care to."

He snorts, an absolutely disgraceful sound. "Don't count on me to support you in your old age," he says with a smirk.

She leaps to her feet. "Why you miserable ingrate. You—"

"It's not my fault you got canned. I don't have to pay for your mistakes." He points a finger at her. "Now that you've failed, you expect me to take over. Well, I've got news for you, sweetheart, I won't do it."

"Then *leave*. But if you do, you'd better take your stuff with you. I'm done babysitting a grown man. If you want to go—go. And don't come back."

He stomps back down the hall and into the bedroom. Patricia walks over to the wall of windows. Darkness has fallen on her domain. Her world is quickly slipping away from her. She hasn't shed a tear in five years. Not since Daddy's funeral. Yet at this moment, she chokes up, and though a well of emotions is bottled up inside her, tears don't come.

Ten minutes later, Billy emerges carrying two large suitcases. She turns to face him.

"I had to borrow your luggage," he says. His fiery eyes dare her to object. "I've packed all my clothes. You won't find a stitch of my things in your closet."

She remains rigid, doesn't try to stop him. He breezes past her and stomps out, leaving the door wide open. Sapped of energy, she walks slowly to the door and shuts it with a soft click.

A day passes. Then two days. Billy hasn't returned, hasn't called, hasn't even sent her a text message. Patricia takes a quick inventory of her belongings and starts phoning her friends.

"I'm selling everything," she tells them with a forced chuckle. "Sort of like the movie stars do when they upgrade. But in this case, I'm downgrading. C'mon over tomorrow. Pick out what you want. I'll give you a good price."

With a heavy heart, she places her fine china and crystal

on the dining room table, sets out her gold-plated flatware, all her cutlery and pans. She lays most of her wardrobe on her bed, arranges her jewelry on top of a dresser, and sets curios on the coffee table in the living room.

The following day, Patricia's "friends" file in, some in pairs, some alone. They hug her, give air kisses, murmur their regrets, and head straight for the bedroom. They emerge with their arms laden with silks, satins, and furs, their fists grasping necklaces, earrings, and bracelets. They pay a paltry amount, utter their condolences, and sail out the door. She knows she'll never see them again.

Patricia perches on the arm of a chair and watches the parade. Not one of her dear friends has asked if she can do anything to help. They've extended no invitations to dinner. No offers to assist in the cleaning of the condo. They hand her what they think her "used and damaged" items are worth, and they leave without a backward glance. When the last of them departs, she bolts the door, and walks from one room to another, noting what few items remain.

Still unable to cry, she allows a surge of bitterness to take over. Her so-called friends and her young lover have deserted her. She feels like a female version of Job in the Bible. The only difference was, Job was called righteous. She didn't feel righteous. What's more, Job's friends came back to accuse him. Her friends didn't hang around at all.

She picks up the local newspaper and flips to the want ads. Except for the medical field nothing grabs her attention. She tosses the paper aside, goes into her bedroom, and pulls her tablet out of its case. Settling on the bed, she scoots back against a pile of pillows and begins an Internet search. An hour passes. She's come up with no job possibilities. Nearly eleven million people are out of work, and she's one of them.

"I'm nothing but a big, fat failure," she mumbles. "What am I supposed to do?" She's reminded of Job again. How did that verse go? *The Lord gave and the Lord hath taken away; blessed be the name of the Lord.* Even when he lost everything, including his health, Job still praised the Lord. What kind of person would do that?

She slides out of bed and starts rummaging around in her closet. That book was in here somewhere. There, on the top shelf behind a stack of bed linens. Daddy's Bible. After the funeral, when they cleaned out her father's dresser drawers, she spotted his Bible and asked Mother if she could have it. Though she hasn't picked it up in five years, owning it made her feel close to him. It's how she remembered Daddy—seated in his easy chair with the book opened on his lap, lost in its pages.

She returns to her bed, opens the Bible, and searches for the Book of Job. She flips to the last chapter and reads the poor man's final testimony. *I abhor myself, and repent in dust and ashes.*

Repent. The word drives a knife into her heart. She's never repented about anything. Not her divorce. Not her self-centeredness. Not even her affair with Billy. She's broken several of the Ten Commandments, and she never repented of any of them.

Now a surge of guilt washes over her. *I messed up big time. If I had any dust and ashes, I'd dump them on my head right now.*

She touches her cheek, surprised to find it wet with tears. She slides off the bed and onto her knees, taking her father's Bible with her.

Dear God, what's happened to me? When I was a little girl, I knew you. I went to church. I said bedtime prayers. Then, I walked away. Why didn't you stop me?

"Forgive me," she says aloud. "Tell me what to do, and I'll do it."

Go home. The voice startles her. It isn't audible. It came from somewhere inside.

"Go home?" she says. "I can't. I'd be going home a failure. My family doesn't know me anymore. Dorothy hates me. Jack avoids me. And my mom? Even if I stood right in front of her, I doubt she'd recognize me."

Go home.

"Oh, God. Not now. I need to find another job. Maybe in New York City. Or I can go to Canada. Or to some small town where I can retire and live comfortably in a tiny apartment, maybe do some volunteer work. But please, don't ask me to go back to Florida."

Silence, this time. No inner voice. No further commands. Only silence.

CHAPTER NINETEEN

ANGELA

SEPTEMBER 2008

"It's getting dark. Time to go."

Dorothy's voice draws my attention away from the mail strewn across my table. So many letters. Most of them written by my beloved Fredo when we were apart. A few from Mae after we moved to Florida. Several from my best friend, Katie. As I read through them, a painful emptiness returns with unexpected force. I would have been helpless without those people who came up beside me during the difficult times.

"Mother?" Dorothy has rested her hand on my shoulder. "Are you okay?"

"Huh? Yes, dear. I'm okay."

"We need to go to my house now. Barry's got dinner ready."

"Okay. Dinner. Fine."

"I think you should sleep in our spare bedroom tonight. If you stay in this house, you might trip and fall on your way to the bathroom. You have so much stuff, I've had to pile your things everywhere."

I think about my own bed and how I'd like to spend the night in it. But, I'm tired. And hungry. And too weak to argue. I guess one night at Dorothy's won't hurt.

My daughter helps me down the stairs and into her car. As we pull out of my driveway, I turn my head for a last look at my home. Then I switch to the rear-facing mirror outside my window. My house grows smaller in the distance.

If only I were young and strong. I'd run away, like a teenager who's been grounded. Just slip out the bedroom window and take off. Sadly, *my* grounding isn't for one night or a single weekend. It's permanent. I feel like I'm being punished for staying alive longer than I should have.

We enter Dorothy's kitchen and my taste buds come alive to the aroma of roast chicken. Barry's standing at the stove, tossing toasted almonds into a pan of green beans. He turns around to nod a welcome. Dark circles rest beneath his eyes and I can't help but wonder if more trouble has come to the big oaf. I make a silent vow to try to get along with him. After all, I'm going to be living under his roof, whether I like it or not.

We eat dinner over idle chatter. Dorothy fills her husband in on the latest find—a stack of old photo albums.

"Mother should have a grand time going through them," she says, patting my hand.

Then Barry hits us with the bombshell. "I'm gonna have to sell the rest of my General Electric shares. After that, I'll have no stock left. None at all."

"What?" Dorothy's mouth has dropped and she's suspended her fork over her plate. She looks frozen, like one of those ice sculptures at a wedding, only not a very attractive one.

"You heard me," he says with a frown. "I'm letting go of the last of my stock holdings. Anyway, those pieces of paper aren't worth much anymore."

"But they might increase in value—someday. Can't we get the cash somewhere else? What about the CD you purchased a decade ago?"

"Don't you remember? That money went toward our granddaughter's college bill."

"What about your IRA?"

"Get serious, Dorothy. Cash in my retirement account? Are you kidding? If we can hold on for a few more years, that fund will keep us going in our old age."

Old age? If Barry's approaching old age, what am I looking forward to?

Dorothy cocks her head. "Have you shown any houses lately?"

"A couple. I got an offer on one. But, even if I write up a contract, it'll take a good month or two to get to closing. We're already one month behind on our mortgage. The end of September will make two. Those stocks can bring us up to date and even pay a few months in advance."

Dorothy raises a hand. "Hold off for another week. When I finish taking care of my mother's place, I'm going to search for a job—"

Barry snickers. "Haven't you read the newspapers lately? The unemployment rate has climbed to fourteen percent here in Florida. It's one of the highest in the nation. So tell me, with jobs so scarce, who's gonna hire a 66-year-old woman?"

"Barry, I'm not over the hill yet. Surely, there's *something* I can do."

"Yeah, get ready to flip burgers."

Dorothy scowls at him. She grinds a piece of chicken between her teeth.

"Look," Barry says. "I'm doing what I can to keep us afloat. I have to sell the rest of my stocks."

"There's something else ... " She glances at me, hesitates, then plunges ahead as if she doesn't care if I hear. "I found something in Mother's spare bedroom. You won't believe it, Barry."

So, Dorothy's had her mind on my shoeboxes. I stab a bean and stuff it in my mouth.

Barry's eyebrows go up. "What did you find? Anything that can help us out?"

"Mother and Daddy saved a lot of cash over the years. There must be several thousand dollars stashed away. With her permission—" She lowers her fork and turns toward me again, this time with her eyebrows raised, as though she's hoping for a response. "—we can use her cash to save our house. What do you say, Mother?"

I narrow my eyes and clamp my mouth shut. Dorothy sits back and mops her lips with a napkin. Her face muscles turn hard as stone. "Or, you can list her house on the market," she says, a threatening tone in her voice. "There's plenty of equity in it."

So, either my house goes or they use my shoebox money. Either way, I lose.

"In a few days, I'll have the place all cleaned up and showroom ready," Dorothy says with an air of confidence. "It should sell a lot faster than the homes we passed on the way over here. Most of them have *Foreclosure* signs out front. The properties are run down, the lawns need grooming, and the houses could stand a good paint job. Compared to them, Mother's house looks like a palace."

I look at the two of them. They're huddled over the table, their faces inches apart. They're whispering now, cutting me out of the conversation entirely. It's my house, but my opinion no longer matters.

I can't believe their behavior. Fredo and I went through

hard times, too, but we never sold someone else's property. My husband wouldn't have dreamed of making a profit at another person's expense. I push aside my half-eaten meal, reach for my walker, and amble off to the room they've set up for me—off the kitchen and next to the powder room. Their formal dining room has become a bedroom, kind of like my Papa did for Tomas and Benito in our tiny apartment in the Bronx. Papa added an entire wall, but all Barry had to do was install a door.

My daughter has come up beside me.

"Aren't you going to miss your dining room?" I say.

"Not really. We don't hold big dinner parties anymore. We don't need a dining room, but *you* need a bedroom."

I take a long look around. They've replaced their table and chairs and china hutch with a large bureau, a rocking chair, and what? A hospital bed? A multi-colored quilt lies on top with two matching pillows. A cross-stitched tapestry of fruit and flowers hangs on the wall, a lace curtain covers the window, and a vase of artificial poppies sits on the bureau. Did she call this a bedroom? It looks more like an old lady jail cell.

I must have fallen asleep the instant my head hit the pillow. Now I'm waking up to the smell of bacon frying in the kitchen. My stomach is calling out to me. I didn't eat much at supper last night. Might as well get moving and see what else my son-in-law's put on the table.

In a little while, Dorothy and I will return to my place. I expect it will look less like my home and more like the house of a stranger who's getting ready to move out.

Breakfast sets just fine on my tummy. Dorothy rushes us out and leaves Barry with the dishes.

When we finally pull into my driveway I spot a row of black trash bags. I count them. Seven. Seven bags filled with what my daughter considers garbage. I'd love to tear into those bags and put all my things back where they belong.

Once inside the house, Dorothy moves a few boxes aside and creates a path from the kitchen to the bathroom. All around are piles of clothing, stacks of books and magazines, and cartons filled to the brim with my belongings. It's a literal rummage sale. If my daughter's smart, she'll just open the doors and invite strangers in to pick through my stuff and buy whatever they want for a dollar.

I have to chuckle. Fredo and I went from almost nothing in 1935 to all of this. Now it's disappearing faster than I can blink.

Dorothy guides me to an empty chair in the kitchen. She fixes me a cup of tea. That seems to be our pattern lately. Sit her down out of the way and fill her up with tea.

I stare out the window. A boy is running through the park with a beautiful Golden Retriever close at his heels. They bring back a fond memory of Jack and his dog chasing each other around our suburban New York backyard. The vision slips away, and I'm left watching a young stranger romping with his pet.

Dorothy's somewhere in the back of the house. Her cell phone sends out a faint ring. I don't own a cell phone, never have. Modern technology simply passed me by. Nor do I use a computer. People talk about Facebook and texting and twittering. Such an impersonal form of interaction doesn't impress me in the least.

Dorothy said old lady Finley chats by email every day with her grandchildren. Well, I'm not old lady Finley, and my grandchildren don't even know I exist. Anyway, I have a perfectly good cordless phone. If anybody wants to talk to me, they know the number.

Dorothy rushes down the hall, her face aglow. "Mother, guess what? I got a text from Jack."

I perk up. "Jack?"

"He and Amy are coming to Florida. Isn't that great?"

"Jack is coming to Florida?"

"Yes. They're flying to Orlando tomorrow. They're going to hit a theme park. Then, they'll rent a car and drive here."

"Jack's coming?"

"Yes. Why do you keep saying that?"

"I-I'm surprised, that's all. What time will they arrive? Is it only Jack and Amy, or the kids too? Where will they stay? My house? Or yours?"

"Hold on, Mother." Dorothy's grin grows wider. "They'll be here late tomorrow, and no, young Fred and his family will not be coming. Jack and Amy will stay at my house. *My house.* With you and me and Barry."

I give Dorothy one of my best smiles. "We should go shopping. Jack likes barbecued ribs. Barry can do them on his grill. I have a great recipe for the sauce."

Dorothy's staring off somewhere beyond me. "We sure can use his help."

She hasn't heard a word I said. That girl hasn't seen her brother in two years, and what is she thinking about? Putting him to work.

"Jack and Barry can handle the big items," she says to no one in particular. "They'll have to move out the furniture, and the two of them can make quick work of Daddy's tool shed."

She walks out of the kitchen and down the hall, still mumbling.

I sip my tea and look out the window again. The boy and his dog have vanished. Sadly, so have my trips into the past. These days, those memories come and go.

I smile. I'm going to see my baby boy one more time before I die. When did Dorothy say he'd be here?

CHAPTER TWENTY

THE BRONX

1939-1940

Fredo had finally come home. We acted like newlyweds, though we'd both grown up some during our separation. We fell into a simple routine. I continued to help out in the soup kitchen. Fredo joined us when he wasn't out on the streets looking for a job. With half of the country's population out of work, most employers shied away from hiring foreigners, even naturalized citizens.

Thankfully, another church stepped up with donations for the soup kitchen, so Fredo and I were able to hang onto the small amount of cash we had left.

The line at the soup kitchen remained constant. By this time, I recognized the faces and had learned many of the names. I listened with interest to their stories.

Joe Fischer was a former banker. Before the depression, he had a big house in a high-class section of the city. When the banking industry started to fail, Joe's wife withdrew their savings, packed up their two kids and whatever else she could fit in their station wagon, and ran off to Nebraska to live with relatives. Joe went from manager, to teller, to bum on the streets.

Matthew Adams once owned a flourishing plastics company. Poor Matthew learned too late that his partner had embezzled thousands of dollars from their business. The members of the board were furious. With no way to prove his innocence, Matthew spent a year in jail. When he got out, he couldn't get another job. He sent his wife and kids to live with his in-laws, and he became a regular at the soup kitchen.

Maria Diaz lost her job as a waitress when the restaurant where she worked closed down. A single mother with a four-year-old son, she was given a place to sleep in the basement of a church in return for cleaning the sanctuary. With no one to care for her boy and little hope for employment, Maria came daily to God's Kitchen. She often left with an extra piece of bread stuffed in her pocket.

Whenever I sat down with our "guests" I listened to stories that pricked my heart. Though every situation was different, the end was always the same. Every day, I sat face-to-face with someone whose lot was much worse than my own situation.

Like a daily ritual, after the last of our people left the soup kitchen, Mae went straight to prayer. Except for Sunday mornings in church, I had never heard so much praying. Nor had I expected any results, until I met Mae. She acted as if she thought someone was actually listening.

Ronnie's dream of going to college became a reality when he received a scholarship to Penn State. Without it, he would have had to pay $700 a year for tuition. He also could avoid the dorm fees by moving in with an aunt who lived near the campus. Whenever Ronnie talked about going to college, his eyes lit up almost as bright as when Ariella walked in the room.

Meanwhile, Ariella was becoming more worried about the situation in Europe.

"The economy is worse in Germany than it is here," she said. "My cousin Rachel wrote that their currency is worthless. People have actually started burning their money to stay warm. Hitler promised change, but nothing positive has happened. His social welfare system was supposed to work like a charity, but it's had the opposite affect."

Other reports came to us through underground newspapers. Jews had to identify themselves to the *Gestapo*. They had to wear yellow armbands and could be imprisoned if found in the streets after seven o'clock at night. They could no longer shop in stores where they previously had done business. They couldn't eat in restaurants that had *verboten* signs in their windows.

"My relatives want to leave Germany," Ariella said. "They say Hitler's a monster. His soldiers have been rounding up Jews and forcing them into railroad cars. They're never heard from again."

She turned toward Mae, tears filling her eyes. "Rachel is frightened. Some of her friends have disappeared with no explanation. German soldiers have taken over their houses and apartments. My cousin warned me that she may not be able to write again."

Mae engulfed Ariella in her arms. "It would be best if your relatives leave soon, before things get worse."

"Yes," Ariella sobbed. "I hope they will pack up what they can and get out of there. My parents told them they have a place for them, if they can get to America."

Ariella brought updates nearly every week. Then, just as Rachel had predicted, the letters stopped coming.

One day, Ariella came into the soup kitchen, her eyes red from crying. We circled around her and begged her to tell us what had happened. She broke down sobbing till she could hardly speak. I feared something bad had happened to her cousin.

When Ariella raised her head, her face was flushed and damp with tears.

"What's troubling you, child?" Mae said. "Tell us. Let us help."

The girl wiped her eyes and took several deep breaths. "My boyfriend, Max, has enlisted in the Army Air Corps," she said, sobbing.

A hush settled over our circle. Ariella had never mentioned having a boyfriend. I glanced at Ronnie. He was looking at the floor, his face a deep red.

"We want to get married, but my parents won't allow it," Ariella said, her voice soft. "I suggested we elope before he leaves, but Max refused. He doesn't want to go against my parents."

Ronnie walked away and sat in a chair on the other side of the room. He put his face in his hands. Mae watched him go, then, pressing her lips together, she turned her attention back to Ariella.

"What do your parents have against Max?" Mae said.

"He's a Gentile. Worse—he's German."

Mae released a troubled sigh. "Oh, dear ..."

"He's not a Nazi," Ariella quickly added. "He doesn't approve of what Hitler's doing. He signed up with the Army Air Corps to prove whose side he is on. My parents don't care. No matter how much good Max does, he's not Jewish, and they won't approve of me marrying anyone who isn't."

Mae took Ariella's hand in both of hers. "Surely, in time, your parents will re—"

Ariella shook her head. Strands of hair fell across her face and stuck to her wet cheeks. She brushed them back. Then, with a flash of determination in her eyes, "I *refuse* to give up. My parents don't see any difference between the good German people and those who are persecuting the Jews. I'll defy them if I must."

"Now, now," Mae said, a warning in her voice. "Your parents are fine people. They'll soon understand that there are many good Germans. I've read stories about European Gentiles who have opened their homes to the Jews. They hide them in secret, risking their own lives. How can anyone think badly of a person who would do that?" Mae shook her head. "No, Ariella. You need to be patient. All you can do is encourage Max, and then ask the good Lord to bring him home safely. Isn't that your main concern right now? His safety?"

Ariella released a long sigh. "I suppose you're right. But he'll be leaving soon. I'm afraid I may never see him again. If America goes to war—"

"Dear child, you have to be ready. Our President has been meeting with Winston Churchill. Something's brewing. You may have no other choice but to wait and pray."

In a way, I could identify with Ariella's pain. After all, Fredo and I had been apart for nearly a year. Somehow, I had survived until he came home. Now it was Ariella's turn to wait. All I could do was wrap my arms around her and tell her I understood.

Now that Fredo was home, we had a different problem. He hadn't found a steady job. Neither had Pietro and John. The three of them settled for day work. They hopped on the back of a pickup truck and headed out to a construction site or to one of the large farms outside of town. Fredo came home exhausted at the end of each day, with only a few dollars in his pocket. He offered me a tired smile that failed to hide the disappointment in his eyes.

My husband's situation was different from that of the other two guys. Fredo had a wife. Pietro and John were single. They had no responsibilities except to buy food, a couple of beers, and a pack of cigarettes. The two of them shared a room in the back of a barber shop where they got free hair cuts and a break on their rent by sweeping up hair clippings and washing combs. They had no problem with standing in food lines or sleeping under the stars, if necessary.

So, from Monday to Thursday, Fredo either went with the day crew or pounded the streets looking for work. He set aside Fridays to help out at the soup kitchen.

"It make-a me feel good to help somebody who no have much," he said with a grin. "It only one day. Who knows? Maybe God bless the rest of my week."

Despite the economic dearth, the World's Fair opened on April 30, 1939. More than a thousand exhibitors from sixty countries participated. Roosevelt showed up on opening day. Even while he spoke to the crowd about "good will" among the nations, newspapers reported that a spark of hostility had ignited in Europe.

On opening day, Fredo pulled two dollars from our shoebox fund and we went to the fair. We blended into a crowd of two hundred thousand people moving in and out of the exhibits. Pietro and John had joined us, and I invited Katie along. To my surprise, Katie and John took an instant liking to each other. While touring the exhibits, they held hands and sometimes drifted away from us.

Why on earth hadn't I thought of matching them up

before? They made a perfect couple. Both were undeniably Irish. Their red hair and green eyes had me imagining what their kids might look like. John had brought along a Kodak box camera. He took a lot of pictures and made sure Katie was in all of them.

Fredo spoke excitedly about the innovations on display. Having grown up in a poor village in Italy, he said he would never have imagined such things as a youth. As for me, I was enthralled with Westinghouse's futuristic kitchen with its fancy appliances and time-saving gadgets. I couldn't imagine owning a machine that washed my dishes, or cooking food in half the time in a little box on my table. On top of all that, the big company also showcased a time capsule that wasn't supposed to be opened for five thousand years.

My husband paused for a long time in front of RCA's television prototype. The placard said twenty-thousand American homes already had one. Little did we know that one day Fredo and I would own three of those things.

Of course, the five of us were drawn to the rides. I didn't mind the roller coaster. I'd been on the one at Coney Island. But I balked at the foot of the Life Saver Parachute Jump. Its 250-foot tower promised a hair-raising plunge to the earth. Pietro boldly lunged ahead of us, and John and Katie trotted after him. Fredo raised his eyebrows and smiled at me. With the four of them egging me on, I finally gave in and boarded the ride. It turned out to be quite a thrill. I screamed only once, but it lasted for the entire drop.

The weather was sweltering that day, and the exhibits had poor ventilation. At one point, Katie said she felt faint. John rushed her out of the building and got her a Coke. For the rest of the day, he wouldn't leave her side. I watched them with envy. I missed those early days when Fredo and I looked at each other with moonstruck eyes. We had settled into married comfort, but I yearned for that sudden flip of the heart I used to feel whenever Fredo came into view.

After that first day at the fair, the four of us got together every weekend. Once in a while we went out for dinner or we took in a movie. For a quarter each, we got hooked on the Shirley Temple films. Then, *Gone With the Wind* made its debut. We paid double to see that one. Just like at the soup kitchen, a line circled around the block, but instead of soup, these people were looking for entertainment. Fredo paid an additional ten cents for a bag of popcorn and we snuggled shoulder-to-shoulder in our theater seats for the next four hours.

When a drive-in theater opened in New Jersey, John picked us up in a brand new Chevy convertible, a gift from his father, and we got our first taste of watching a movie while sitting in a car. Most of the time, though, we spent our evenings just sitting around our apartment, playing cards, listening to the radio, or reading library books. We didn't have a television set. We couldn't afford to go to a ballgame. But we made do with what we had.

Occasionally, Pietro got a date and joined us. I didn't care for the flashy girls he met at the neighborhood bars. While the rest of us played cards or sat around talking, Pietro and his current "true love" cooed and cuddled on our sofa-bed. At first, we turned our faces away and pretended their lovemaking didn't bother us. Finally, one evening, John and Fredo took Pietro aside and had a few words with him. He rarely came around after that. When he did, he came alone.

Apart from our evenings with John and Katie, Fredo and

I continued to help out at the soup kitchen. I went every day while he looked for work. Fredo stuck to his Friday commitment.

One Friday morning, Ariella showed up with a basket of the reddest, plumpest tomatoes we had seen in ages. Fredo came to life. He searched the kitchen shelves, found a few bulbs of garlic and a container of dried herbs. Within minutes the aroma of simmering tomatoes filled the dining hall. Mae and I mixed the last of our flour with water and a little salt and made a pasta dough. We cut it into spaghetti noodles, and after a period of drying, we plunged them into boiling water moments before the people streamed in from the street.

I'll never forget the proud smile on my husband's face when our guests drew him out of the kitchen with a hardy applause. He stood there, smiling wider than he had in weeks.

By the following month, the queue to the soup kitchen had doubled in length and circled around the block all the way to Colleen's sewing shop. A basket of tomatoes wouldn't have been enough to feed such a crowd. On more days than I'd like to admit, we ran out of food early and had to send away the folks at the end of the line. They had waited for more than an hour, but there was nothing we could do.

The newspaper reports added to my despair. They spoke about Hitler's rise to power and the growing unrest in Europe. German troops had invaded several smaller countries. Even while our President kept insisting we weren't going to war, he doubled the size of our Navy, and he created the selective service program. Men between the ages of twenty-one and thirty-six had to register for the draft. More than sixteen million guys signed up immediately. So did Pietro and John—and Fredo.

My brother Tomas was rejected because of his eye injury. Benny, who was listed as 1-A, quit college and joined the Navy. My mother cried for days when her *prezioso bambino* left for training.

Six months later, my younger brother headed for California and boarded a battleship bound for Hawaii.

Shortly after Benito sailed off, Papa had a massive heart attack. He died before Tommy could get him to the hospital.

Fredo and I rushed to Mama's side. When the doctor told her Papa didn't make it, she fell into a heap on the hospital floor and wailed in agony. None of my words of consolation were able to soothe her. As for me, I felt like I had lost my Papa many years before. From the time he stopped working, he fell into a state of despondency. He rarely spoke, and though he was there in bodily form, a part of him had already died.

After Papa's funeral, Tommy offered to move back in with Mama, along with his wife and three kids. Mama refused. She said her apartment was too small. Like many Italian women do after losing a lifelong relationship, she fell into a lengthy mourning period. Mama wore black for the rest of her life.

I went daily to Mama's apartment, hoping to lift her spirits. I found her sitting in the dark, fingering her rosary beads and mumbling to herself. I turned on the lights, helped her to the kitchen table, and opened a can of soup for us to share. Or I made cheese sandwiches and coffee, whatever I could do to get her eating again.

It was almost as if she'd stopped living because her husband was gone. I couldn't help but wonder if I'd be like that. If I were to lose Fredo, would I sink into a shell, like Mama did? Would I behave like my life was over too?

After Fredo died, I got a taste of Mama's grief. I felt like a part of me had died with him. Maybe that's why I try to hang onto memorabilia that has lost its usefulness. Some of those things help to keep my husband alive, if only in my heart.

I doubt Dorothy will ever understand that.

CHAPTER TWENTY-ONE

THE BRONX

1940-1942

Fredo continued to pick up day labor jobs with his two buddies. Pietro didn't care what he did, as long as he had a few bucks in his pocket. But John? He could tap into his family's wealth anytime he wanted to. Yet, out of some strange loyalty, he stuck by his two friends. John didn't care whether he found a job. To him, it was more about friendship and staying together.

He didn't even seem to mind Pietro's ridiculous stunts. Like the day that idiot stood on his hands on a girder fifty feet above the ground. Fredo froze in shock and called to him to come down. But, John cheered him on from the street below.

I lost count of how many times Pietro cheated death. I could only pray that he wouldn't take my husband with him. The incident at the forest camp had left a permanent scar on my mind. They both could have been lost in the river. Pietro had no regard for human life. Not his own or anyone else's.

Sadly, the day jobs didn't come easy for Fredo and Pietro. My husband came home in the evening, a cloud of dejection on his face, his pockets empty.

"The work bosses—they pass us all-a time. We immigrants. We strong. But no matter. They choose Americans."

"What about John?" I said. "He's an American."

"They pick him, but he no leave us. He say we stay together, like buddies."

I stroked his back. "It's okay, Fredo. You'll get work, I know you will. You're not a quitter." Even while I said the words, I knew the odds were against him.

The discrimination continued until the day John threatened to go to the newspapers. All three of them got on the truck that day. Even so, the bosses tried to cheat Fredo and Pietro out of some of their wages.

"They no pay us twenty-five cents an hour, like the others," he told me. He held out his day's pay, a mere handful of change. "We get fifteen cents. When I speak up, they poosh me to back of crowd." He shook his head. "I no get much work after that."

Despite such treatment, the immigrants fared better than the African-American laborers. Fredo told me the blacks were often left standing on the curb when the truck pulled away. In those days, there was no NAACP to protect their rights.

"They good workers," Fredo said. "Bosses do what they want, so nobody win."

With Fredo getting almost no work at all, our savings dwindled until we had only the change in the Mason jar. Back then, we had no credit cards to bail us out. We either had the cash, or we did without. For the time being, we discontinued our trips to the movie house. I stopped buying chickens and coffee and relied on Giuseppe's leftover fruit and vegetables. Occasionally, Fredo swallowed his pride and joined the people standing in lines for bread and soup.

Mama was struggling too. She showed me her empty cookie jar. By this time, Tomas and his wife had three children and another baby on the way. He still managed to give Mama a few dollars. She spent it the same day.

Mama's one joy was the occasional letter she received from Benito. She shared them with me whenever I came to visit. That boy scribbled pages about Hawaii's tropical setting, the lush vegetation, the abundance of fruit and vegetables, his acquired taste for pineapples and coconuts. He even gave details about his weekend leaves, the guys he hung out with, and the girls at the dance club. He'd met someone, an American girl who'd moved there with her father, a captain in the Navy.

I made the right decision quitting school, Benito wrote at the bottom. *This has been an educational experience. Even better than college. I love it here. Well, gotta run. The guys are waiting.*

While Benny was describing his time in the service like he was on some kind of a vacation, and Fredo and I were still struggling to make a living, Ariella was filling us in on the situation in Europe. Because of my friendship with her, I developed more of an interest in what was happening overseas. In the evenings, Fredo turned on our radio, then he and I cuddled on the sofa-bed and listened to the latest reports.

It troubled both of us that Hitler's army had invaded several European countries and had moved on to the Netherlands. Then France surrendered to the Nazi forces. A few days later, Germany and Italy became allies. The news kept getting worse and worse.

Fredo was quick to express his concern. "I no trust Hitler. He talk too loud. He look mean. No? And Mussolini? Watch-a what happen with those two. Not a good thing with them together. Joost-a watch."

Some nights, John, Katie, and Pietro came over and sat

around our apartment listening to static-filled accounts about the war in Europe. But, that wasn't all. On the other side of the globe, Japanese fleets had invaded several small islands in the Pacific. Until then, we hadn't considered Japan a threat to America. After all, an entire ocean separated us. Now they were creeping closer to Hawaii.

"My brother Benito is there," I said. "I hope he's safe."

The others just sat there and stared at me with sympathy in their eyes. No one could say a word. We had no idea what might happen from one day to the next.

John was the first to say aloud what the rest of us couldn't admit. We were sitting around the apartment, snacking on hot tea and hard biscuits. He turned from the radio and stared at each of us, his sharp green eyes darkening.

"There's going to be a world war," he said. "I can feel it. Eventually, America's gonna have to choose a side."

Pietro lit up a cigarette and shrugged. "Roosevelt says we stay out."

John shook his head. "False promises, my friend. It's only a matter of time before the United States gets sucked into the conflict. It's inevitable."

"So we go to war." Pietro blew a circle of smoke into the air. "I fight. You fight. We all fight. Then, we come home."

I set down my teacup and caught my husband's eye. "What about you, Fredo? You registered for the draft. What will happen if they call you?"

The three guys turned to look at me. Pietro's eyes flashed his excitement. "What you think, Angela?" he said. "We fight. Together. Like always. Where Pietro goes, John and Fredo go." He burst out laughing and popped the top off of a bottle of beer.

John looked at me with compassion in his eyes. "It'll be all right, Angela," he said, his voice soft. "The three of us will stick together. Like always. If one comes home, all of us will come home."

His promise sounded weak. He might as well have said, if one dies, all three will die. My eyes tearing up, I sent a silent plea to my husband. He smiled and let out a nervous chuckle. Then, he took my hand and leaned close to me. "No worry, Angelina," he murmured. "I'm still here. I no leave yet."

For a while, there were two separate wars—one in Europe and one in the Pacific. John's prediction came true, though America's intervention came in stages. At first, FDR gave financial aid to Britain. Then, he and Winston Churchill agreed to set up military bases throughout Europe, to protect the trade routes, they said. John insisted it was a military strategy.

The five of us made a pact of our own. In order to maintain our sanity, we stopped listening to the news reports and started looking for ways to enjoy ourselves. One weekend, John treated us to a night at the movies. Pietro had other plans that evening, so only the four of us went to see *The Wizard of Oz*. We came out of the theater skipping, with our arms linked, and singing, "Over the Rainbow."

We were almost to the apartment when John stopped walking and drew up in front of us. "We're the characters in the film," he said, and his face lit up. "Fredo's the scarecrow. Look how skinny and floppy he is."

He pointed his thumbs at his chest. "I, of course, am the cowardly lion. It took me a long time to get up the courage to kiss my girlfriend." He planted a kiss on Katie's cheek. "You're Dorothy," he told her. "You're the star of the show." Katie giggled and batted her eyelashes at him.

I placed my hands on my hips. "Okay, John, who am *I*, then?"

He poked my arm in fun. "Angela, you're the tin man. You have a tough outer shell, but really, inside you're a bundle of nerves. You need a good oiling now and then to loosen you up."

I laughed, but secretly I was groaning. John had spoken the truth. I had been trying to appear tough, but I hadn't been able to hide my anxiety. I was afraid my husband might make another decision that would tear us apart. Though John had mocked me in fun, his remark struck a chord. Had I turned into a worrywart who didn't trust her husband to make the right decision? I didn't want to be that way. Yet, every so often, that part of me surfaced unexpectedly.

Like the first weekend in October, 1941. All five of us had gathered in our apartment to listen to the final game of the World Series between the Brooklyn Dodgers and the New York Yankees. The guys had taken opposing sides. When the game ended, Fredo jumped up and screamed in Italian at our radio. Scowling, he handed a five-dollar bill to Pietro.

I sprang to my feet. "What are you doing, Fredo? That's a terrible waste of money."

Then, I stepped back, horrified that I had reacted on impulse. Only days before, I had vowed to be more like Mae, and here I was failing again. The guys laughed and popped open a couple more beers. Embarrassed, I slunk off to the window, stared out at the heavens and berated myself for acting so rashly.

Katie came up beside me. "It's okay, Angela," she murmured. "They didn't even notice."

"*I* noticed," I told her. "So did you. For a split second I didn't like who I was." I turned and stared into her innocent green eyes. "If you marry John, don't ever do what I just did. Be a good wife."

Katie nodded and gave my shoulder a tender squeeze. "You're absolutely right, Angela. I want to be a good wife—exactly like you."

Then she tossed her head. Her auburn curls bounced and settled around her face.

"I have something for you," she said.

She hurried to the sofa-bed and grabbed her purse.

The guys were sitting around talking like we weren't even there. Fredo stuffed his pipe with tobacco. Pietro lit up another cigarette and offered one to John. He held up his hand and shook his head.

Katie returned to my side with her purse in her hand. She pulled out a strange looking lump of fabric. It fell apart revealing a pair of sheer stockings.

"Look, I bought you these nylons." She said, smiling. She held them toward me. "Feel how soft they are. Now you can get rid of those scratchy things you've been wearing."

Awestruck, I handled the silky fabric. "Katie, I love them." I shook my head. "You shouldn't have spent your hard-earned money on me."

She shrugged. "I wanted to. Mae told my mother how faithfully you work at the soup kitchen. You deserve to have something special."

"You've already given me so many things. The scarf you knitted for me, and those pretty handkerchiefs you embroidered. I'll cherish them forever."

Katie wrapped an arm around my shoulder. We stood at the window and looked out at a starlit sky. We didn't speak, but a definite conversation was taking place. In that moment, I experienced a friendship that went beyond anything I could have hoped for. While someone else might have criticized me for the way I jumped on my husband, Katie withheld judgment. Isn't that what a real friend does? They accept you even when you've done wrong?

I'd like to say I changed that night. But, ever since John made that comment about America going to war, I felt a constant quivering inside my stomach. I couldn't restrain my curiosity. Once again, I started tuning our radio to the news. Japan invaded China. The Japanese emperor offered to withdraw if the United States would resume trade with them. Roosevelt refused. Japan made a pact with Germany and Italy. The globe instantly grew smaller, and both sides were closing in on America.

Nevertheless, Roosevelt kept promising, "*This country is not going to war.*"

Then came December 7, 1941. Fredo and I listened in horror to a radio announcer describe a surprise attack on our American fleet at Pearl Harbor.

Japan has made war upon the United States. His voice cracked with emotion. *About fifty planes participated in the attack on the Hawaiian Islands ... anti-aircraft guns went immediately into action and were responsible for bringing down many of the Japanese planes.*"

I backed away from the radio and choked out my brother's name. "Benito."

Fredo reached for me. A chill passed through me and I felt as though I would faint. I collapsed in a chair at our kitchen table and gazed out the window. The sky had turned a dismal gray, much like the wave of darkness that swept over my heart.

I put my face in my hands. "My brother," I sobbed. "He's there, in the middle of that horror. Please, God, let him be safe."

Fredo tried unsuccessfully to soothe me. I cried and paced and sat and wept. A newsboy came to our corner and untied a bundle that had been dropped off by a panel truck. The boy waved a newspaper over his head and shouted, "Extra! Extra!"

Fredo scrambled down the stairs and bought several newspapers, then rushed back up upstairs and spread them on the table. I stared at the headlines. *Japanese Bomb Pearl Harbor* and *War Begins!*

Horrified, I read the stories aloud, word for word, omitting nothing. Fredo leaned over my shoulder and wept with me. For the rest of the week, whenever we were at home, we kept our radio on and listened to the updates. More than 2,400 Americans were killed.

Fredo turned up the volume.

"Names," I pleaded. "Give us names." I turned to Fredo and raised my eyebrows, hoping for an answer he couldn't give me. "There's a chance Benny could still be alive, isn't there?"

He didn't have to say a word. The lines on his face, the sadness in his eyes, confirmed my greatest fear. My husband wasn't the type to give me false hope. He could only hold my hand and pray.

Until the attack, most of us had assumed our nation was invincible. We lived in the land of the free and the brave, the land of opportunity. So, what had become of opportunity? And how long would we remain free and brave?

The attack set off a landslide of retaliation. The United States and Britain declared war on Japan. Germany and Italy declared war on us. Just like John predicted, America had been drawn into the conflicts on both sides of the globe.

My mind drifted back to the New York World's Fair. Visitors from every nation had streamed in and out of Japan's pagoda-style pavilion, with its enchanting rock garden, fresh-water pond, and flowering cherry trees. The Japanese had led us to believe we were at peace. Now, a mere two years later, their planes had brought death and destruction.

One other thought brought the war right into my living room. Fredo wasn't about to sit back while his buddies went off to fight. They had registered with the draft together. If the government called them to service, they'd have to go.

Inside, I was fuming. My husband had been home for only a few years and I was about to lose him again. Maybe for good this time.

My first thought was, we should ignore the summons when it came. We could run off together—to Canada, or to the countryside where Fredo might find work on a farm. Maybe Ariella's parents would take us in. I laughed at my innocence. My husband would never run away from his duty to the country he had come to know and love.

At one point, he waved a fistful of newspapers in front of me and shook his head. "So many killed. So many."

I turned away from him, unwilling to hear him say what was in his heart. But, he didn't need words. His thoughts penetrated my mind as if we were one person, breathing the same air, feeling the same pain. He paced the floor behind me and let out a stream of curses in Italian, then he left the apartment. I stood frozen at the window as my husband marched down the street, his footsteps firm, his shoulders back.

He returned at dusk, a determined smile on his lips.

A chill ran through me. "You're going, aren't you?"

He nodded. "Pietro and John and me—we Marines."

With those words, my husband plunged a dagger into my heart. I blinked back a surge of tears. "Fredo, you promised you wouldn't leave me again." My voice was weak.

He shrugged. "Yes, *mio amore,* I remember promise. But, please, forgive me. I must break my word." His sky-blue eyes shone with determination. "How can I stay home when so many go? I serve for a little while. You will see. I be home before you say—*come si dice?*—"

"Jack Robinson?" I mumbled.

Then my knees buckled. I stumbled to our sofa-bed, dropped on it, and buried my face in my pillow. A retching erupted in the pit of my stomach and rose to my throat. I succumbed to an uncontrollable sobbing. No amount of Fredo's stroking and murmuring could ease my torment. This time, he wouldn't be cutting down trees or digging ditches. He'd be going into combat, face-to-face with the enemy. I'd read about the atrocities of war in Ernest Hemingway's first few novels. Perhaps, if I had never read those books I might have been spared the horrors my imagination was stirring up at that moment.

Three days later, my despair sank even deeper. My brother Tomas came to our apartment, his face drawn, his eyes lined with red. He didn't have to say a word.

"Benito?" I said.

Tomas nodded. "His ship was hit bad." Tearfully, he choked out the rest of his message. "No survivors, Angela. No survivors. Not Benny, or anyone else on that ship."

I fell into my brother's arms and we wept together. My

whole body went limp. Tomas held me. We stood there for a long time, retching and wailing into each other's necks, until I heard Fredo's step on the stair.

He opened the door to our apartment and froze in the doorway, his mouth open, but nothing coming out. Strange how some of our worst fears, when they're confirmed, don't need to be expressed with words. People who are close to you can read the answer in your eyes. I went to my husband. He slid his arm around me and held me close.

"You Mama, she's alone?" Fredo asked my brother.

"No, Donatella's with her. We left the kids with my mother-in-law." He sighed heavily, like a man does when death would feel better than a broken heart. "We should go to Mama. My car is outside."

The three of us hurried to my mother's apartment. A spirit of doom hovered there. We found Mama sitting on the sofa, sobbing. Donatella was by her side, a wrinkle of helplessness on her forehead. Mama looked up and spotted us in the doorway. She slid to the floor and doubled over. Her entire body lurched with every anguished cry. I rushed to her, knelt close, and kissed the tears from her face. Fredo reached down and lifted her onto the sofa.

"*Mio ragazzo.* My boy," Mama wailed. *O, Dio mio, perche? Perche?* Why you take my Benito? He was a good boy. Why you take him from me?"

She turned her watery eyes in my direction, as if she expected me to answer for God. But, how could I, when the only knowledge I had of him came from the hymns Mae sang and the prayers she and Colleen said? Though I'd sat in church as a little girl, I often escaped from the boring liturgy through fantasies I'd read in books. I didn't know how to pray, or to sing hymns, or to figure out what God might say to Mama.

My own pain was so great I didn't think I could help anyone else. Yet, Mama needed me, her daughter, the only one who could understand her broken heart.

Fredo sat nearby, his eyes closed. He was either weeping or praying. Either way, I appreciated his silence, and I think Mama did too. We stayed with her throughout the night. The tiny apartment sank into a morgue-like quiet, as though the angel of death had come to stay. Mama refused to turn on the lights. In the end, she sobbed quietly for a while. Then, she fell asleep, whimpering, in my arms.

Other than a telegram confirming Benny's death, we received no mention about whether they were shipping his body home or burying him at sea. The following weekend, we held a memorial service at Mama's church, and the weeping and wailing started all over again.

Needless to say, my anti-government sentiments grew. I'd lost my brother to a war I didn't support. And, for the second time in my young marriage, I was about to lose my husband. In a few weeks, Fredo would head off to basic training. He'd put on a uniform and would fight for a cause I didn't understand. I hated the idea of war. How could I trust a government that sent young men into danger, to be wounded, or worse, to die?

And where was God in all of this? Even as the question surfaced, Mae's voice kept coming back, telling me to trust the Lord. Trust him with what? My life? Fredo's life? What about all the people who already had died? Benito. And thousands of others?

A sick feeling settled in the pit of my stomach. Some

mornings I barely made it to the bathroom before I started vomiting. I wept easier than I ever had. And, I woke up in a cold sweat in the middle of the night, my nightgown clinging to me, my hair hanging in damp spirals around my face. I felt as though I had stepped onto a runaway train and I didn't know how to get off.

That imaginary train switched tracks the day Fredo left for training at Parris Island, South Carolina. While my husband packed his bags and kept going at high speed, my own life suddenly had come to a halt.

CHAPTER TWENTY-TWO

THE BRONX

1942

The day of Fredo's departure, Katie and I trailed behind our men on their way to the bus terminal. The three buffoons strutted ahead of us, swinging their suitcases, their excited voices sailing back to us. They laughed and chided each other and poked one another in the arm. I shook my head and scowled. My husband was acting like a little kid running off to a playground. Except this playground was littered with land mines. Snipers hid in the brush. Tanks came out of nowhere. Didn't he know he could be maimed? Or worse?

What's more, Fredo had never fired a gun in his life. John and Pietro had gone rabbit hunting, but their flimsy air rifles didn't compare with the guns and grenades they'd have to carry. They had killed small animals. Not people. Except for maybe Pietro. One night, when the three of them sat around our apartment drinking beer, the idiot bragged about having killed a guy in the old country. Not with a gun, with his bare hands.

"We fight over a girl," he said, a little too casually. "I no remember her name now." He let out a loud laugh. "Joost a stupid, drunken brawl, that's all. The guy say he kill me if I no kill him first. So, what-am-I supposed to do?"

Pietro. He was a cross between Rocky Balboa and Sonny

from *The Godfather*—all brawn and no brains, and with a quick temper that often got him into trouble. He ran the gamut of emotions—one minute, angry enough to pound the stuffing out of our sofa-bed, the next minute, laughing hysterically during a *Marx Brothers* routine. He cried like a baby when we lost our dear Benito. Then he put his fist through the wall and cursed the Japanese planes that had rammed Benny's ship.

Just thinking about my dear, innocent husband running off with the likes of Pietro had me chewing my fingernails to the quick. Fredo was going to war with a wild man—the same fool who nearly got him drowned at the forest camp. I'd have to trust John to stay close to Fredo. My husband didn't need protection from only the enemy. He needed protection from Pietro.

When we arrived at the bus depot, John set down his suitcase and came up beside me, his eyes brimming with sympathy. "I want you to know, Angela, I'm determined to come back. I have good reason." He glanced at Katie. "Trust me. I'm coming home. And I won't leave Fredo behind." He wrapped his arms around me. "I'm gonna stick close to your man. We're fighting for a lot more than this country. We're fighting for the two women who'll be waiting for us." He gazed into my eyes and nodded. "We *will* come home."

Then, he went over to his true love and gathered her in his arms. Katie clung to him and pressed her forehead against his neck. Ever since the World's Fair, those two had been inseparable. John gave Katie an engagement ring the day he enlisted. I've never seen her so happy. Come home? Nothing would stop him.

Fredo approached me, a sheepish grin on his face. He

needed me to say it was all right if he ran off with the boys again.

"I'll wait for you, Fredo," was all I could say before he engulfed me with an embrace that would rival any love scene in the movies. I cherished those last few minutes, wished I could extend them into more days, or weeks. Fredo held me so close I could feel his heart pounding through his shirt, its steady rhythm matching my own. I melted against him, aware that the moment would have to hold me until he returned.

"C'mon! What's-a matter for you?" Pietro's gruff voice broke through our momentary escape. Fredo clung to me.

"One more kiss, an' that's all," the bully shouted at us. "Bus coming. We gotta go."

Men were lining up at the curb. Pietro joined them, looked back, and gave a frustrated wave at Fredo. The door hissed open. Pietro smirked at me, as if to say, "You lose." I glared back at him. That man never offered one word of comfort to me. He just laughed, like the whole thing was one big joke.

Fredo held onto my hands. "Take care, my Angelina. I love you."

The next thing, he grabbed his suitcase and headed for the bus. Tears soaked my cheeks. I choked back a sob. Fredo slipped in line and moved closer to the bus and farther away from me. Suddenly, he hesitated, dropped his bag and spun around. In seconds he was back at my side, wiping away my tears, stroking my hair, his cool blue eyes penetrating mine and sending a message of comfort and love.

"I'll be back, *mio amore*. I promise."

I swallowed hard and sputtered out something about being careful and how I'd be waiting for him. Then he was gone.

He blended in with the other guys. Some of them looked

no older than seventeen. Boys going to war. Untrained fighters. Immigrants. No restrictions. Not their age, their nationality, or their physical ability. The war didn't discriminate. Then, reality struck me. Many of them would not come home.

Fredo and John grabbed window seats and peered back at us through the glass. Katie and I waved, tears streaming down our faces. After the bus pulled away, we remained in front of the terminal, holding hands. We stayed long after the other women walked away. Instead of going home, we took a walk in town and talked about the things we would do to keep busy while our men were gone.

The lump in my throat stayed there for several hours after.

A few days later, a thought hit me like a bolt of lightning. With most of our men going off to war, jobs might open up for us women to fill. I'd heard that the defense department had set up plants all over the country. Six million jobs had opened up. Within the week, I landed an assembly line position in a munitions plant in a building that once housed a shoe factory. I'd never done assembly-line work, but I could learn. The point was, I'd found something to keep me busy until Fredo returned. And I could earn a decent living. I wanted to put away enough money so when Fredo came home we'd have a good amount to make a fresh start. I wanted to make sure he never had a reason to leave me again.

Katie and her mother also fared well. Colleen got a contract sewing uniforms for the military. They moved to a larger shop, one that had an upstairs apartment. Colleen hired four women who could sew. She had so much work, she often extended their hours to include Saturdays.

I worked long hours too. Exhausted, I'd drag myself up the stairs at the end of the day and collapse, fully dressed, on my bed. I'd rise again before daybreak so I could get a prime spot on the assembly line.

Sometimes, at lunchtime, I headed over to God's Kitchen to help Mae and Andrew. Things had changed there too. Against his parents' wishes, young Ronnie had joined the Navy. In his absence they could use my help in the kitchen. Our "guests" had dwindled to about a dozen people. Mae told me several of the men had signed up for different branches of the military. Some of the women also had gone off to be WACs and WAVEs, or they had taken jobs like the one I had. We served the remaining few at one sitting. No more long lines. No one turned away.

One day, Mae stepped close to me, a knowing smile on her face. "When's the baby due?"

I rested my hand on the little bump over my abdomen. "I didn't think it showed yet." I smiled. "The doctor said by the end of August."

"Have you told Fredo?"

I nodded. "Yes, in my last letter." I blinked against the sting in my eyes. "I don't think he'll be home in time for the delivery."

"Angela, you need to keep strong for your baby. Not just physically, but emotionally too."

"I don't want my baby to grow up without his father." My chin began to tremble and tears shot like needles to my eyes.

Mae shook her head at me and grabbed my shoulders. "Angela," she said, frowning. "Haven't you put your husband in God's hands?"

"I'm sorry, Mae, I-I don't know how."

"It's like my son, Ronnie. I didn't want him to go, but I had to accept it. I had to leave him in God's hands."

I bowed my head. "I believe there's a God, but I'm afraid to trust Him. It's been my experience that he gives and takes away, gives and takes away. I'm afraid to trust him with Fredo. He might take him away for good."

Mae shook her head so hard, her bun came loose. "My girl, you still don't understand, do you?" She reached up and twirled her bun back in place. "You start by giving Jesus your heart. Then, you give Him everything else, including Fredo."

She poked a finger against my chest, gently but firmly. "It's a personal thing, Angela. Start here, in your heart. Faith isn't only about attending church and lighting candles and reciting prayers from a book. Those things are okay as acts of worship, but you need to move beyond them. You need to receive Jesus and accept his plan for your life. Until you do that, you'll have a void in your heart, one that only God can fill."

The overhead light cast a radiance on Mae's face that nearly turned her skin to porcelain. She had to be hurting over Ronnie leaving, yet her countenance literally glowed.

"Remember, dearie," Mae said, a tender smile on her lips. "Nothing can happen to Fredo unless the Lord allows it. The only thing you have to do is step back, let go, and wait for the miracle. Think about it, Angela. You have a miracle growing inside you right now."

She turned away and went to the cupboard where she kept her purse. When she came back she had a small, leather-bound book in her hand.

"Take this." She thrust it toward me.

I hesitated. "It's your Bible, Mae, I can't—"

"Take it," she insisted. I opened my hand and she gave me

her most prized possession. A day didn't go by when she didn't read a passage in that book.

She didn't flinch. "Listen closely," she said. "This isn't one book, Angela, it's a whole library of books. I want you to begin with the *Gospel of John*—back here." She indicated the place. "Then, read the letters of Paul, starting with *Romans*. And don't forget the *Psalms*." She pointed to the middle of the book. "Make time every day. You'll find strength in these writings. What's more, you'll learn how to be a supportive wife to your husband, when he comes home."

When he comes home. She didn't say *if*. She said *when*. Mae had demonstrated a confidence I hadn't seen in any other woman, not even my Mama. That confidence had helped Mae keep the soup kitchen going even when supplies ran short. She also had demonstrated her faith in God in the way she comforted people who came through the door. She treated them like friends and relatives, never looked down on anyone, but always had a kind word for each one of them.

And Mae had shown me how a wife should behave toward her husband. She'd built up Andrew with praises, she'd laughed with him, shared his dreams, joined his plans. Because of Mae's unwavering support, that little man strutted around like he was ten feet tall. I wanted to be that kind of wife to Fredo. So far, I'd given him only grief.

For the last couple of years, while helping out at God's Kitchen, I'd actually been in a classroom of sorts. Because of Mae, I learned about life, about poverty, about survival, and about a husband-and-wife relationship that went beyond earthly pleasures.

One day, Fredo would leave the battlefield. He'd need to

come home to a place of contentment and peace. Because of Mae, I had the tools to provide such a home.

That afternoon, I walked out the door with Mae's Bible inside my purse. After supper, I read the first chapter of the Gospel of John. Every night after that, I read more passages before going to bed. I awoke the next day surprised to find I'd slept better than I had in weeks.

The day came when God's kitchen closed its doors. I said a tearful good-bye to Mae and Andrew, gave Ariella a hug, and left with a promise to stay in touch.

Andrew took a job as a cook in a high-class restaurant, and Mae went to work cleaning rich people's homes. They hadn't heard from Ronnie in months. Ariella stayed at her parents' farm in the country. They had taken in some of their Jewish relatives who'd fled from Germany, including Rachel and her parents.

Ariella's boyfriend, Max, went off with the Army Air Corps. And old Jake? I came upon him one day, sitting on a park bench, tossing breadcrumbs to pigeons, and mumbling to himself.

On Sundays, Katie and I met for lunch at a bus stop located halfway between our two places of work. We showed up with brown bag lunches and shared letters from our guys. We wept together, laughed together, and prayed together. Sometimes, we took in a movie, or we settled for an ice cream or a quick cup of coffee.

I continued to visit Mama whenever I could. She'd smile and ask when the baby was coming. The next time I visited, she'd ask me the same thing all over again. She kept busy knitting little baby sweaters and blankets, like she'd done for Tomas' four kids. Only this time, she rarely smiled. I made sure she had enough yarn in green or yellow or pure white. Back then, we didn't have ultrasounds, so I didn't know if I was having a boy or a girl.

It didn't matter to Mama. Donatella and Tommy had two of each. As for me, the sex of my child wasn't as important as having Fredo there when I delivered. But with war raging on both sides of the globe, I doubted he'd be home by August.

CHAPTER TWENTY-THREE

THE BRONX

1942-1944

Within the first few months I had accumulated a nice stack of letters from Fredo. His first few filled me in on the rigors of boot camp. There was the sergeant who mocked the new guys and called them sissies. The vaccinations, with Pietro falling to the floor in a dead faint. The embarrassing physical exams. The uncomfortable cots that had to be made up just so every morning. The early wake-up calls, the long marches, the weapons training.

Then there were the psychological examinations. *They try find out if I loco,* Fredo wrote. *Already send two guys home. Say they no fit to serve. I fraid they maybe fire Pietro, but he know how to fool them.*

My greatest thrill came from the photo Fredo sent after he'd been issued a uniform. His prideful smile nearly jumped off the picture.

John say I handsum, he wrote. *What you think, Angelina? Handsum or no?*

I put the photo in my wallet, so I could have my husband with me wherever I went. At a whim, I could pull it out and gaze at my Fredo. I could show his picture to anyone else who cared to see it. Yes, to me, he was very handsome.

One of Fredo's last letters sent ripples of terror through me.

The three of them had signed up for the Fleet Marine Force. I'd read about that amphibious team. They were trained to hit the beachheads ahead of the heavy artillery. One night, I woke up sobbing. I had dreamed about Fredo, marching along a dirt road, the enemy hidden behind trees and rocks. The flash of gunfire and my husband going down. I leaped out of bed and turned on the light. I reread his letter. His words were filled with pride, yet they had filled me with fear.

We infantry, he wrote. *We get ryfils, bayonetas. Marines best in world. But no worry, mio amore, I take good care. Pietro and John and me, we make vow, watch each other backs.*

I suppose his words were meant to comfort me. Instead they drove shrapnel into my heart. All I could think was, Fredo is going into battle with a lunatic and a love-sick puppy. And they were going to be armed. Already, I imagined myself a grieving war widow.

If I didn't get my mind on other things, I'd go crazy with worry. So, I put aside Hemingway and I read books about baby care, took walks, cut salt out of my diet, and concentrated on my work at the munitions plant.

Day after day, I sat on a stool beside a moving belt. Bullets and gun parts streamed in front of me, stark reminders of where my husband might be heading. I prayed over those bullets and hoped one of them might end up in Fredo's gun and maybe save his life. I had to keep reminding myself what Mae had said, that I needed to put my husband in God's hands. At night, I went back to the Scriptures for my own ammunition. I needed to fight off the anxiety that was threatening to destroy me.

Katie and I continued to get together on Sundays. We shared the letters we'd received from our men, and we talked about our plans for when they came home. Katie's eyes danced with delight, a positive balance to my fretful comments and the wringing of my hands.

"It's going to be all right," she assured me. "Before you know it, Fredo will be home. Don't forget, John already knows how to handle a gun. And, trust me, he's not going to leave Fredo's side."

"I wish I had your confidence, Katie."

"You *can* have it. Simply trust God. Put Fredo in *his* hands." Mae's message was echoing off my friend's lips. I couldn't escape what they were trying to tell me.

About the time I began to assimilate those words for myself, Fredo's next couple of letters unsettled me even more. He talked about long marches that left him falling into bed at the end of the day. They staged fake conflicts, giving him a taste of battle. I sensed a change in his thinking, like he had drifted into Pietro's world of kill or be killed. Not long after that, the three of them graduated from boot camp and were getting ready to ship out to England.

Their trip took two weeks by ship, so I didn't hear from Fredo for more than a month. His next letter had me smiling. Poor Pietro had experienced a terrible bout of sea sickness. The big oaf had scrambled to the deck, leaned over the rail, and retched his guts out. I caught myself smirking. If nothing else, the image gave me a slight sense of satisfaction.

Ironically, ten years before, Fredo and Pietro had traveled across the Atlantic in the opposite direction. They'd gone from a port in Italy to New York's harbor, eager to start a new life in America. Now they were on their way back to Europe, this time to fight a war on behalf of their adopted country.

Adopted country? Fredo had struggled to make a living the

entire time he lived here, and now this so-called "land of opportunity" had sent him back across the sea, possibly to die for opportunities he never got to enjoy.

A month went by before I received another letter. The guys had transferred to a secret location in preparation for deployment to some unknown battlefield. I don't know what was worse, me waiting at home worrying, or Fredo getting ready to move into enemy territory? I pulled out the photo he'd sent from the forest camp. Fredo with a stupid grin on his face, and his two friends striking a silly pose on either side of him. While they were traipsing through back country in a foreign land across the sea, my world was transforming before my eyes.

Abandoned storefronts were now being used as factories for the production of boots, gun belts, and helmet straps. Restaurants reopened. Banks offered accounts with no fees and promised backing by Roosevelt's FDIC, whatever that was. Stubbornly, I continued to stash my money in shoeboxes until I had three, four, then five boxes, bulging with cash and standing in a row like ready soldiers under our sofa-bed.

The government issued War Bonds as a way of supporting military operations. I didn't bother to buy any. Why should I pay to have my Fredo killed? I wanted the war over. I wanted my husband to come home.

War and *death*. Those two words meant little to me in the past; but now they were nagging at me from beyond the grave. I'd lost my brother to the war. Mae was praying for her son, Ronnie. Ariella had been separated from her true love. And I had no idea if or when I'd see my husband again.

More stark realities struck the day I picked up a Life magazine. I stared in shock at the cover's black-and-white photo of naked people being ushered into a prison camp. I flipped to the inside. There were more graphic pictures and a full article about persecution of the Jews and anyone who tried to help them. I thought about Ariella's anxiety for her cousins and finally understood why she felt so strongly about the Nazis.

The article mentioned concentration camps—a new word for me. "Death camps," the writer called them, and I shuddered. He also wrote about gas ovens where men, women, and children went in and never came out. There were photos of firing squads and skeletal humans standing beside empty graves they had dug for themselves. I crumbled into a ball on my sofa-bed and wept tears of compassion for those people.

I asked God, "Why?" over and over again, not only for them, but for Fredo, and for me.

No audible answer came. And I didn't feel any peace as Mae had predicted would happen if I prayed. Perhaps my heart wasn't ready for that kind of peace.

I took the Life Magazine to work with me. Some of my coworkers insisted the stories were nothing but propaganda meant to rile up Americans. Others shouted them down and said they were true. All I knew was, Fredo was heading right into the midst of all that horror. He wasn't the type to stand aside while another human being suffered. He'd already risked his life to save Pietro. Wouldn't he do that again?

I pleaded with God to end the war and to bring our men home, safe and in one piece—with all of their body parts intact. Without Mae to run to every day, I had nowhere else to turn but to the Bible she had given me. The Psalms encouraged me to trust in the Lord with all my heart, and to praise him, despite my circumstances.

Then, a desperately needed letter came from Fredo. Though it didn't offer much comfort, I hung on his every word.

We do gard duty at Navy base. England our ally. John happy we close to Ireland, but no chance he go there.

Sargent bring books to camp. Men all jump on them, so I no get one. That ok. I read poor.

Bombs drop in city at nite. Some close, but miss our camp. Peeple use blackout shades. You must do too. Keep you safe.

I try make riting better. John help sometime. Spell a werd for me, then I write.

My husband's atrocious spelling didn't bother me. His words were clear enough for me to know what he was trying to say. I cherished his letters, bound them with yarn, and put them in a drawer with my nightgowns.

Ariella telephoned me about once a week. More Jewish refugees had come over from Europe, including a large number of children who had escaped on what they called "kinder trains." They were searching for relatives or someone—anyone—to take them in. Ariella's parents had converted their barn into sleeping quarters so they could house more people. To me, they were saints, taking in strangers along with their own relatives.

Ariella was certain Max was involved in the Army Air Corps bombings in the Pacific. She hadn't heard from him in weeks and only knew he'd been sent west after his initial training.

I counted the money in our shoeboxes. That had always been Fredo's job. Now it was mine. I sorted out the paper bills the way he used to by putting a different denomination in each shoebox. All the while I thought about the day my husband would come home and take over the counting. He was in for a big surprise. I'd already saved enough to buy him a new truck.

We were still receiving ration books for sugar, gasoline, milk, and coffee. I visited Mama as often as I could and made sure she had food in the house and was doing okay.

Fredo's next letter nearly sent me over the edge. His company was still encamped outside London. He spoke about cold nights, guard duty, the drone of enemy aircraft, the darkness shattering, as bombs lit up pockets of the city.

What he said next turned my blood cold.

They say we go on destroyer soon. Secret mission. I proud be American. I fight for my new country. I fight for you, Angelina, my love. No cry.

Of course, his telling me not to cry had the opposite effect. I read his letter again and shed a bucket of tears. When I didn't hear from him for several months, I paced the floor, unable to eat or sleep. The Bible passages about trust and peace failed to encourage me. I turned to my best friend, Katie, for comfort.

From the day our men left, she hadn't wavered. I knew I could depend on her. I hurried to her mother's shop and pulled her away from the khaki-colored jacket she was sewing. She looked into my eyes and let out a heavy sigh.

"Listen to me, Angie. Our men can't always communicate with us. John warned me this would happen."

I shook my head. "What keeps you going, Katie?"

She simply smiled. "When John told me he was going to war, I put him in God's hands," she said. "Once I did that, I couldn't take him back."

I bowed my head. "I said the same prayer for Fredo," I said, weakly. "Mae told me I should do that, and I did."

Katie sighed and wrapped an arm around me. "But, you took him back, right? You put him in God's hands, but you never let go."

Heat rushed to my face. I shrugged. "I guess so. I can't help it, Katie. Maybe I listen to too many people at work. They say the Italians have joined forces with the Germans. They're fighting against the allies." I looked her in the eye. "Fredo is *with* the allies. There's a possibility he'll have to fight his own countrymen. Do you actually think Fredo will defend himself against men who used to be his neighbors? Or his own relatives?"

Katie shook her head and grabbed my hand. "You've got to stop listening to those stories. Listen to me. Even before Fredo fell in love with you, he fell in love with America. What's more, his love for you will remind him what he's really fighting for. Now, what *you* have to do—what you *must* do—" she gently squeezed my hand with every emphasized word, "—is *stop* this ridiculous *worrying*."

Katie was right. I was on an emotional roller-coaster. I prayed every day and felt uplifted. Then the newspapers and radio broadcasts brought the war right inside my living room, and I plunged. I had no idea where my husband was, marching ahead, perhaps lying in a ditch, maybe even dying on some battlefield, perhaps calling my name with his last breath. The war effort was hurting those of us who remained at home as much as those who went into conflict.

I couldn't stop the stories that flew back and forth past my station at the munitions plant. At times, I'd burst into tears and have to break away for a few minutes. A co-worker tacked a poster of Rosie the Riveter on a nearby wall. The funny girl with the red bandana and muscular arm gave me a slight boost of confidence. The poster's words, "We can do it!" became a mantra for us women. We'd look at Rosie, then someone would thrust a fist in the air and we'd all shout, "We can do it too!"

By July, I was eight months pregnant and suffering from the heat. My ankles had started to swell and no amount of fanning could wipe the sweat off my brow or keep my blouse from sticking to my chest. The doctor ordered me to quit my job. He wanted me home with my feet raised. I bought a little fan and set it on the kitchen table in front of the only window. Sometimes, on stifling days, it merely blew the hot air around.

Two weeks before my baby's due date, I felt like a bowling ball had settled in my abdomen. I couldn't get comfortable sitting, standing, lying down, or walking. I couldn't take a deep breath.

The pains started coming on Thursday, August 13. I watched the clock. The skin around my abdomen tightened and released, first at ten-minute intervals, then closer together. I struggled into the stairwell. Bracing the bottom of my sagging stomach with one hand, I hung onto the railing with the other, and I hollered for Giuseppe. After my third and loudest cry for help, he stumbled from his shop, his forehead a twisted bunch of wrinkles.

"O, Dio mio," he shrieked. "We go. We go to hospital."

Trembling, he assisted me down the steps. He fumbled with his keys, dropped them on the floor, picked them up, and somehow, though his fingers were shaking, he locked the door of his shop.

"Careful, careful," Giuseppe mumbled. He slid his hands under my arms and eased me out the door. I stopped to catch my breath. "You okay?" he said. "Not now, Angela, please, not now."

After the contraction passed, he picked up our pace, shoved me into his truck, and, before I could get settled, he slammed the door, ran around to the other side, and got in the driver's seat. He cast a frantic glance in my direction, then he peeled out into the street, the walls of the truck rattling, the tires squealing on the pavement. I fell against the door, grabbed the dash, and slid back in the seat, just as another contraction started.

What luck. My dear husband was somewhere in Europe, and I was bouncing around in a truck driven by a wild-eyed grocer. Not only that, but it was five o'clock in the afternoon—rush hour. Traffic blocked our every turn. We inched along to the hospital. I gasped, then let out a cry in the midst of another contraction. What a horrible turn of events if I should deliver my first child on the floor of a beat-up, old vegetable truck.

Once we got to the hospital, everything moved quickly. With a sigh, I lay back on the gurney and left everything up to the hospital staff. We sped off to the labor room, leaving Giuseppe standing in the hall wringing his hands.

Five hours later, I was in a regular room holding my daughter in my arms. I gazed down at her, my little pink angel, swaddled in a blanket, her watery dark eyes gazing back at me, trusting me. I thought my heart would burst.

It was nearly midnight, so I waited until the next morning to call my brother, Tomas. He picked up Mama, and the two of them came in together.

"What about your job?" I asked him.

"Don't worry. I told the boss my kid sister was having a baby.

He let me off for a few hours, said I could claim sick time."

"You have a nice boss."

He grunted. "Don't worry. He'll call me in on a Saturday to make up for it."

The nurse brought my baby in, and Mama nearly fainted. "She look-a just like you, Angela. You were pink like that, and you had lots-a black hair, like your baby's."

On the other side of my bed, Tommy smiled and cooed. "What did you name her?"

"Dorothy," I said, smiling. "After the girl in *The Wizard of Oz.*"

"What?" Tommy straightened. "You pick a movie character instead of a relative? Donatella and I named our twins after my two grandmas. We named our boys after my grandpas. You could have at least named her after Mama. Catherine is a nice name."

I ventured a look in Mama's direction. She didn't appear to be offended. She may not have heard our conversation at all.

I glared at my brother. "So what, Tommy? It's my business what I name my children."

I looked down at the sweet infant in my arms and my heart melted. Mae was right. I'd witnessed a miracle. How sad Fredo hadn't been there to share my joy. He'd been my rock for the last seven years. Now it was *my* turn to be a protector, *my* turn to care for someone and make sure she was safe and healthy and happy.

Here I am, sixty-six years later, and that tiny baby has grown into a one-hundred-and-sixty pound bully who's taken over my house. I've become the dependent one, and she has assumed complete control over me. Back then, I adored my little baby girl. Now I'd like to choke her.

Sometimes, the only way I'm able to keep loving my daughter is to think back to those early days when I took Dorothy home from the hospital. My apartment came alive overnight. For the first time since Fredo left, I had someone to love and care for. Dorothy kept me so busy with night-time bottles and diaper changes, I didn't have time to dwell on her daddy's absence. I wrote to Fredo twice a week and kept him informed of his daughter's milestones—the first time she slept through the night, her first doctor visit, the morning she woke up and smiled at me, the first word out of her mouth. "Da-Da." How could that be? Her father was nowhere around, yet she'd said "Da-Da." I rationalized that maybe it was the easiest word a baby could say. "Ma-Ma" would surely come soon.

Though I checked the mail every day, it took weeks for Fredo's responses to reach me.

I father now, he wrote. *My wife. My baby girl. I tell men in barracks. They pat my back, smile, make jokes. Pietro give me cigar but I no like. Took maybe one puff, then throw away. But I happy. Waiting to see you both, my two ladies.*

Weeks passed before another letter came. Even while I read it, Fredo had moved on somewhere else. Such was his new life. Transient. Secretive. Always on the move.

With a growing baby to care for, I rarely had time to cook. I bought a variety of Campbell's soups. They cost nine cents a can and took mere minutes to heat on the stove. I also kept my pantry stocked with rice, Kellogg's Raisin Bran, and a supply of jarred baby foods, the hottest new thing on the market. Giuseppe gave me left-over vegetables at the end of each week. I cooked and pureed them for my daughter.

I took Dorothy to Mama's house at least twice a week.

Having a grandbaby around lifted Mama's spirits. She actually started reminiscing about the birth of her own babies. She shared stories about Tomas and Benito and me as little kids, running around the apartment and giving her headaches that later made her laugh.

We were visiting Mama one day when two sailors knocked on the door. They presented Mama with Benito's Purple Heart. She wept profusely. Then she pinned it to her dress over her own heart and wore it there every day until she died.

Dorothy was eight months old when Mama passed the following spring. The week before Easter Sunday, I stopped by to see how she was doing. We were sitting on the couch and were in the midst of conversation, but I couldn't hold her attention. Her eyes strayed to the window and settled on the brick wall of the building next door. She placed her hand over Benito's Purple Heart and whispered something in Italian.

I spoke a few words of comfort. She stood up and walked right past me, as if she hadn't heard a word I'd said. She shuffled off to her bedroom but never made it to her bed. The doctor said it was heart failure, but Tommy and I knew the truth. Mama had died of a broken heart.

CHAPTER TWENTY-FOUR

JACK'S VISIT

2008

My son's coming home today. I asked Dorothy to take me to the beauty shop this morning so I could get my hair done. After we returned home, I took a shower, then I put on my aqua blue dress and slipped my little silver hoops through the holes in my earlobes. I hardly ever wear earrings anymore, unless it's a special occasion, and, by golly, *this* is a special occasion. I even gave my fingernails a fresh coat of polish, pink this time, and I tried to apply a little matching lipstick, but my hand shook so bad, I had to wipe off the smudge and leave my lips bare. I checked my appearance in a full-length mirror, fussed with my hair, brushed the wrinkles out of my dress. I'm as giddy as a schoolgirl getting ready for her prom.

Butterflies have been jumping around in my stomach ever since I woke up this morning. I hope they settle down before Jack gets here. He doesn't need to walk in on a nervous old woman.

As they had planned, Jack and Amy spent the night in a hotel in Orlando. They visited Epcot this morning. It'll take them about an hour to drive here. I can't sit still, but neither can I walk around. I'm a prisoner in my own body, stuck here in this chair in front of the TV.

You would think I might have learned something about waiting during the months Fredo was away. Hopefully, I'll settle down before Jack and Amy get here.

It's been two years since they last visited. My son spent a few hours with me, then he left for a conference in Orlando. Amy stayed and kept me company. That girl is like another daughter to me. In fact, sometimes, I feel closer to Amy than to my own two girls. She pays attention when I talk to her. Not like Patricia, who always has something better to do. Nor does she argue with me like Dorothy does. If I could have had a third daughter, I would have wanted her to be exactly like Amy.

I check the clock on the wall. It's almost noon. They're probably stopping for lunch. Maybe there's something good on TV. I fiddle with the remote control and settle on a game show. I reach for my sewing bag. This handkerchief needs finishing. Dorothy threaded a bunch of needles for me this morning. All I have to do is pull one off the pin cushion and start sewing.

For a while, I shift my attention between the snarl of daisies on my lap and the game show. The winner is screaming and jumping up and down. I shake my head. Even on my best day, I never jumped up and down over money. I reserved that sort of foolishness for something special—like getting a letter from my husband, or finding out I was pregnant, or watching my baby take her first step. Even today, with Jack coming, I'd jump up and down if I could.

I love Jack more than life itself. Though my kids came out of the same womb, they have different personalities and different abilities. Dorothy's doing what she does best, tearing through someone else's house and getting rid of everything.

She loves to make decisions that have little to do with her own life but drastically affect the life of someone else.

I hardly got to know Patricia. She wanted to leave us almost as soon as she could walk. She married way too young. Her marriage failed. She moved in with us for a while, but she paced the house like a caged tiger. I wasn't surprised when she left and moved back north. She returned only once, five years ago, for her father's funeral. Except for a brief phone call once or twice a month, and cards on Mother's Day and my birthday, I never hear from her anymore.

Then, there's Jack. Dear, sweet Jack. He was the baby of the family, the child I bonded with from the beginning. I guess, like they say, boys *are* drawn to their mothers. He used to follow me around the kitchen like a little puppy dog. When the time came for him to start school, he didn't want to go.

"I don't like school," he said in a squeaky, little voice.

"How do you know you don't like it? You haven't even gone yet. Give it a chance."

"I want to stay home—with you, Mama." He wrapped his arms around my leg and wouldn't let go.

Of course, in time, he adjusted, not only to school, but to sports, and ultimately, to girls. But, Jack never left me, not completely. Even after he went off to college, he came home on weekends. We'd go on mother-and-son dates, order pizza, stay up after Fredo went to bed, and talk until midnight.

Then, Jack met Amy, and he didn't come home on weekends anymore unless he brought her with him. Then they'd cut out and head for the beach or a theme park or a party with friends. I didn't mind. She made Jack happy, and that was good enough for me.

Another game show is starting. Somebody just asked for an

"A." I turn off the TV and concentrate on the handkerchief. It's a simple pattern with stitches I can easily work using my good hand. The tiny loops take me back seventy years to Colleen's sewing shop. Katie leaned over my shoulder and laughed at my first awkward attempt at rose buds. I must have ruined a dozen handkerchiefs before I caught on. Then, one day, my creations actually started to look like flowers.

I'm so intent on sewing this little bud, I didn't hear Dorothy come in, but there she is, standing before me, with a smile on her lips. I stop sewing, raise my chin, and squint at her. What does *she* have to smile about? She opens her hand, palm up, and reveals a little band of gold with a pea-size diamond.

"Does this look familiar?"

I blink. "It's my engagement ring."

"What about this?" She brings up her other hand and shows me Benito's Purple Heart, one of the few treasures Mama left to me after she died. She left Tomas her cookie jar, but she gave me her most prized possession.

I squeeze my eyes shut against the sudden sting. Tears gush out.

"I found these in your jewelry box," Dorothy says, her voice thick with emotion. "They're precious, really precious."

I glance from the ring to the Purple heart, and my heart surges with love, not for the material items—they'll fade away one day—but for the people connected to them.

Dorothy's still smiling at me. In a rare moment of compassion, she pulls a tissue from the box on the end table and presses it in my palm. "I'll leave them in your jewelry box, Mother. Would you like that?"

All I can do is mop my face and nod.

She heads back down the hall toward my bedroom. I heave a sigh. I'm suddenly in my mother's darkened living room. She's clutching Benny's medal and we're grieving together. I drift farther back to a happier time in that same room. Fredo is going down on one knee and he's extending that little ring toward me. Those two items may be trinkets from the past but to me they're symbols of life and death, sacrifice and honor, hope and a future.

I return my attention to the handkerchief and take another stitch. My fingers don't move as fast as they used to. I'd like to finish this project today and give it to Dorothy, to show my appreciation for those rare moments when we've connected.

The doorbell's ringing and my heart leaps. Dorothy emerges from the bedroom and breezes past me on her way to the front door. I turn my upper body to get a better look.

"Hi, it's good to be home." A flutter erupts in my chest. *Fredo?* For a micro-second I'm in our tiny apartment in the Bronx, and my husband has walked through the door.

But, it's not Fredo. It's Jack, of course. He has his father's voice. He strides into the room and approaches my chair. In his hand is a bouquet of cut flowers, and on his lips is one of his father's silly grins, straight across his face, with long creases down the sides of his mouth. I gape at my son and I see Fredo, home from the war. I blink away the image. It's Jack, with his father's blue eyes and a patch of gray at his temples. He lays the bouquet on top of the handkerchief, wraps his arms around me, and nearly lifts me out of my chair with a bear hug. I lean back and gaze at him through a blur of tears.

"It's good to see you, Mom," Jack's tone is tender, loving. "Did you think I wasn't coming?"

I gasp for a breath, then I find my voice. “Of course not, Jack. You never let me down.” I give him my biggest smile.

I have to crane my neck to look past him, but there’s Amy standing in his shadow. “I’m so happy to see you both,” I say, and I mean it. Amy’s been like a daughter to me.

Amy moves closer and rests a gentle hand on my shoulder. “We’re happy to see you too, Mom.” She plants a kiss on my forehead, then pats my hand. Her own hand is cool and smooth. “Are you doing okay?”

“Oh, yes. I’m fine.”

I glance at Dorothy. I lied, of course. I’m not fine. I’m being evicted from my home. But, for now, I’ll say I’m fine, until I get a few minutes alone with these two.

“The doctor said my left hand is improving. He wants me to keep doing physical therapy. Pretty soon, I’ll be able to do everything I used to do, before I had the stroke.”

Jack and Amy are smiling at me. Neither one of them says a word.

“There’s no reason I can’t stay right here in my own house.” I’m rambling now.

Jack’s eyebrows have slanted to a point in the middle of his forehead. Dorothy’s stepped up beside him, her arms crossed in front of her. She’s stopped smiling. Amy’s staring at me with sympathy in her eyes. I’m the center of attention. The three of them have crowded around my chair, their eyes focused on me, like they’re viewing a corpse in a casket. *Will somebody please break the silence?*

I open my mouth to say something. Anything, when Jack moves away and grabs a place on the sofa. Amy settles beside him, the same way I used to sit beside Fredo when he was here. Dorothy hasn’t budged.

Jack clears his throat. I know the sign. His father used to clear his throat before saying something important. I clutch Jack's flowers to my chest. A few petals spiral to the floor.

"Mom," Jack begins, and a lump comes to my throat. "We came to see you because we've missed you, but also to help Dorothy with your move. We'd like to find something more suitable, a place where you'll be comfortable and not have to work so hard."

My heart plummets.

"Dorothy's done a great job of organizing your move." He glances at his sister. She's still standing beside my chair, a little too close for comfort. I stuff her unfinished handkerchief in my sewing bag.

Jack's leaning toward me with his elbows on his knees. "You have a lot of things, Mom. I hope you don't mind my helping Dorothy sort through them. She needs my help, especially with the heavier items—you know, the furniture and whatever's inside Dad's tool shed." He pauses and stares into my eyes, like he's trying to read my reaction. He clears his throat again. "We may have to give away some of your belongings, but only those items you don't need anymore. Are you okay with that?" He tilts his head.

My mouth is dry. I don't know what to say. I had hoped to find an ally in Jack.

My son's brow creases the same way Fredo's did the day he told me he'd joined the Marines. I couldn't hide my disappointment then and I can't hide it now. I look from Jack to Amy and back again.

No one moves. No one says a word. It's like they're waiting for me to say it's all right if they tear my life apart. Somewhere deep inside me another woman is resurrected. She's the one who waited alone while her husband went off to war. She's the one who worked in a munitions factory and saved half of every dollar she earned. She's the one who nursed a broken war hero back to health, who raised three children, who made important decisions inside and outside the home, who survived the most traumatic period that ever hit the nation.

I straighten my back. "Son, I don't know what Dorothy has told you, but I don't *want* to move." Dorothy lets out a huff, but I continue. "Your dad and I spent many years in this house. We made a lot of memories here. Everything works fine. The worst that can happen is I'll need to hire a housekeeper and get someone to mow the lawn."

Dorothy opens her mouth like she's about to protest. Jack raises his hand and silences her. But, instead of speaking in my defense, he shakes his head and gives me a patronizing grin.

"Mom, I know you want to stay here, but you have to understand Dorothy's view. It's become difficult for her to run back and forth to check on you. We're all worried about you. One of these days, you might need help. Or there might be a fire. Or—"

"I can dial 9-1-1."

"Not if you can't reach the phone."

"I can get one of those alarm thingies to hang around my neck."

Jack shakes his head. "Mom," he says chuckling. "Those are fine ideas, but you need to be somewhere safe, where people can look after you, cook for you, drive you to the doctor's office, make sure you take your meds. I don't see that happening if you stay here by yourself."

I shrink back and let the flowers slide off my lap to the

floor. Jack gathers them up and sets them on a side table.

"Please understand, Mom. We're concerned for your safety. You think you can take care of yourself, but you can't. Not anymore."

"I tell you I'm fine, Jack. My left hand is doing better. I have some feeling in my fingers. I just need a little more time. Please, give me more time."

Jack lets out a sigh and settles back in his seat. Amy slips her hand through his arm. She's smiling, but there's a sadness in her eyes. The truth hits me. I don't have a single ally in this room.

Jack cocks his head to one side. "You have a couple of options, Mom. Though Amy and I would love to take you to California with us, we don't have room for you right now."

I nod my head. "I know." I bite my lower lip to keep my chin from quivering.

Jack shifts in his seat and goes on. "Patricia's in her own little world. Think about the last trip you took up there. You turned right around and came back to Florida the next day."

Again I nod.

"Now." Jack's voice has taken on a business-like tone. "You can go into assisted living. Or, you can move in with Dorothy and Barry. They have plenty of room. You'll have your own bedroom and bath. It'll almost be like living on your own."

"I *am* living on my own. I have a whole house to myself and I like it this way."

"It's not the same. You can't drive. You can't get to the doctor or go shopping. And, how about maintaining this old house? From what Dorothy tells me, it's starting to fall apart."

"Your father showed me how to keep things running. If something breaks, I can call a repairman."

Dorothy unfolds her arms and places her fists on her hips. The movement is sharp and aggressive. "She's being stubborn." She says, and glares at me, then she turns toward Jack. "Look. I didn't call you here to humor Mother. We don't need her approval. I'm not going to fool around with needless arguments. We have to get this job done and get her out—"

Jack rises to his feet. "Settle down, Dorothy. Mom's not a child. She's an adult with definite feelings about her life. We need to make sure she's okay with whatever we decide."

Dorothy steps closer to Jack, her face inches away from his. "Either you're going to support me in this or you can go back to California."

Amy stands up and heads for the kitchen. "I'm starving," she says. "If it's okay, I'll fix us some supper." I watch her go and think, *Smart girl.*

With a wave of her hand Dorothy beckons Jack to the hallway. "Follow me. You've *got* to see *this.*"

Like a little puppy dog, Jack follows her to the spare bedroom.

Alone now, I settle back in my chair with a sigh. My initial joy at seeing Jack has deflated like a popped balloon. Things haven't gone like I had hoped. It's obvious Dorothy has sucked her brother into her plan.

I reach for my walker, intending to follow after them, but Amy rushes to my side.

"Come to the kitchen." Her voice sounds sweet and inviting. "You can help me fix something for us to eat."

I cast a longing look after Jack, turn away and edge my walker to the kitchen. Amy has set a stack of bread on the table along with a platter of lunch meat and cheese.

"You can layer the meat and cheese on the bread and I'll

add the mayo, the sliced tomatoes, and the lettuce," she says, her voice cheerful, like she's directing a child to help with a birthday party.

She gets me settled in a chair in front of the sandwich fixings. I smile. Amy has brought a spark of life to my lonely kitchen. From the day Jack started dating her, I never considered her a threat. Not when my son told me he'd fallen in love. Not when he spent every free minute of his time with her. Not even when they moved across the country to settle down near her folks. They were behaving the way Fredo and I did in those first few months of our marriage. We wanted to be together. Just the two of us.

"After dinner, we can go outside for a while," Amy calls over her shoulder from the sink. "We'll use your wheelchair, and I'll take you for a walk in the park across the street. Would you like that, Mom?"

"Sounds good to me."

"When was the last time you went down to the park?" Her voice rises above the spray of water.

"Let's see, I went down there a few days before I had my stroke."

Amy turns toward me and frowns. "Are you kidding? No one has taken you there in six months?"

With my one good hand, I reach for a piece of ham and lay it on a slice of bread. I keep going with the cheese and the roast beef.

"You must miss it," Amy says and starts slicing tomatoes on the cutting board.

"Yes, I do. When Fredo was alive, we went down there almost every night after supper. We used to stroll along the path that circles the pond. Then, we'd come home and sit on the porch for a while and watch our neighbors take *their* evening strolls. Even after Fredo passed, five years ago, I'd go down there sometimes and walk, or I'd sit on a park bench, like we used to do. In a way, by maintaining that routine I kept my husband close. Then, I had that stroke—

Amy gives me a wink. "Well, you're going to get out there again, but this time *I'll* go with you. Maybe Fredo will be there too. We can talk about him and the life you had together."

"It sounds wonderful." It's amazing how much that girl understand those of us who can't let go of the past.

There's a shuffle at the door and Jack comes into the kitchen. He's carrying two shoeboxes. Amusement is written all over his face.

"Mom, can you explain this?"

Dorothy is close behind him. She stops in the doorway, her lips scrunched up like a sourpuss.

My hand freezes in midair. A slice of cheese slips from my fingers and drops to the table.

"Mom." It's Jack again. Quizzical lines trail across his forehead. "Where did all this money come from?" He flips open one of the lids. Several bills spill to the floor. He shakes his head. I suck in my lower lip, feeling much like a child that's about to be scolded.

"I don't understand, Mom. There's a perfectly good bank a couple of blocks away. Why didn't you put this money in there?"

I shrug. "Your father and I decided long ago never to use a bank. They can't be trusted."

He glances at Dorothy. She folds her arms and says nothing. Jack shakes his head and smiles at me. He sets the boxes on the floor and kneels in front of me, his face close to mine.

"Mom, you're a gem." He gives me a kiss on the cheek. "Don't you know? These days, the banks are insured. You don't have to be afraid to put your money there."

I shake my head. "Your dad and I did the best we could, Jackie. Our banking system may not make sense to anyone else, but it worked fine for us."

"So, all those years while we were growing up, every time you needed cash for food or clothes or something for the house—every time I asked for a couple of bucks to go out with friends—you dug it out of a shoebox?"

I nod and pinch my lips together. Amy steps up beside me and places a comforting hand on my shoulder.

Jack's laughing now. I'm not sure if he's happy or if I'm the butt of a joke. He rises to his feet.

"Dorothy found several more of these boxes in the spare room closet," Jack says. "She's already counted the money, Mom. You have more than $34,000."

"So?"

"So, you could have been robbed. Or what if there was a fire? You would have lost everything."

"Well, we didn't get robbed, and we didn't have a fire."

Jack wipes tears of laughter from his eyes. "I love you, Mom, but—"

"I love you too, Jack."

"Now, what do you want us to do with all this money?"

I suddenly have a solution that may satisfy everyone. "I don't really need all that cash. Why don't you kids divide it up between the three of you? I can keep going on your dad's Social Security."

Jack's face crinkles up the way his father's used to whenever I said something that shocked him. "Are you kidding, Mom?"

"You heard me. Divide it up. All of it. Give some to Dorothy, and some to Patricia—if she wants it—and you can keep the rest. Help young Freddie and his family. I don't care. Let me live out the rest of my life in peace."

Dorothy bends over, picks up the wayward bills, and stuffs them in the shoebox. With Barry out of work, they could use a little extra cash. Maybe this is just the thing that'll get her off my back.

I relax for the first time since Jack walked in. He said I have more than $34,000 in those shoeboxes. It's a lot of money, for sure. But it's a drop in a bucket compared to what the guys are gonna find when they tackle Fredo's shed. I don't know how, but I definitely want to be there when they open the drawers on his big red tool chest.

CHAPTER TWENTY-FIVE

ANGELA AND AMY

2008

With dinner over, Amy brings my wheelchair around from the front closet. She helps me slip into a sweater, a soft blue cable-knit my friend Katie made for me about ten years ago. Everyone else runs around in shirtsleeves, but I don't have much meat on my bones anymore. I need a little extra something to keep out the chill.

Amy leans close to me and I catch the scent of lavender soap. She helps me slip into my wheelchair and off we go, out onto the porch, down the ramp, and across the street to the park.

I take a deep breath of outside air, glad to get out of the house for a change. After we finished off those sandwiches, Dorothy and Jack disappeared in the back of the house. They were still going through my closets when Amy and I slipped out the front door.

We leave my porch down a side ramp and travel cross the street. After viewing this scene through plate glass, it's good to get into the heart of nature once again. The world seems brighter, more colorful, more full of life when you can touch it and breathe it and savor it. I take a deep breath. Someone's tending a barbecue behind one of the houses.

A family of ducks waddles along the edge of the pond.

Their backsides jiggle from side to side. Locusts chirp in the treetops. Two squirrels chase each other in circles, then dart up and down the trunk of a pine tree. I feel the warmth of the sun on my back.

Amy positions my wheelchair next to a park bench and locks the wheels. Then she settles on the side of the bench closest to me. A nearby oak casts a sprinkle of shade over us, just enough to protect my eyes from the glare of the sun off the water. I wish I could remove my shoes and run through the grass the way Jack and I used to do in our backyard up north.

Amy takes my hand in hers. "So, what shall we talk about, Mom?"

I give her a sideways glance. "I don't know. Any ideas?"

"Why don't you tell me about Fredo and what your life was like after you moved here."

I smile. Maybe her husband isn't the only therapist in the family. I love to reminisce. Now I have someone who actually wants to listen.

With a surge of enthusiasm, I unravel my recent past. "Moving to Florida was one of the best decisions Fredo and I ever made. We didn't like the cold weather. Not anymore. We wanted to spend our senior years in a warmer climate. Lots of folks do that." I gesture toward the pond. "We used to love to walk along the path over there. We'd take a bag of bread ends with us, break them up in tiny pieces, and feed the ducks." I chuckle. "One day, a whole family of them came flocking around me. I dropped the bag and almost fell over backwards. Fredo rushed to my side and shooed them off."

Amy laughs. She may be in her sixties, but she's still got the heart of a child, a great quality for someone who's already a grandmother.

"I'm glad you had your hero with you to rescue you," she says.

"Yes, I could always count on my Fredo. He was my protector. My prince." I punch my good hand in the air. "My *Superman*."

Amy sighs. "You know, I feel that way about Jack too. He was always ready to rescue his damsel in distress. He must have learned that from his father."

I turn to look at her. "When did Jack rescue you?"

She smiles shyly, like she's about to spill a secret. "One time, a couple of guys tried to pick me up in a coffee shop. Jack was just coming in the door to meet me there. He was at my side in two seconds. He gave those guys a threatening look, didn't have to say a word. They practically ran out of there."

I nod. "My son, a superhero."

Amy sparkles with fresh enthusiasm. "Another time, we were walking across a parking lot and a car came barreling around a corner. Jack pulled me to safety and shouted something I can't repeat."

"Yep, sounds just like his dad."

I'm suddenly back in the Bronx and it's 1938. I tell Amy about the young man who mugged me on the street and then came to our apartment.

"Fredo came in like one of those last-minute heroes in the movies. He tackled the guy and saved my life."

"That's amazing. Your husband wasn't a big guy."

"No, he wasn't, but he was tough, and when he saw me being attacked, his adrenaline must have gone into overdrive."

We fall into more laughter. Then Amy pats my hand. "I'm glad he saved your life. Otherwise, we wouldn't be sitting here right now, talking and enjoying this wonderful evening." She breathes a sigh and turns her attention to the park.

Two little boys run past us and head straight for the playground. Their mother trots along behind them. The distraction paints a smile on Amy's face.

"I can't believe how fast my little Freddie grew up," she says. "It seems like only yesterday, he was running around in a playground. Now he's a grown man with kids of his own."

"I know what you mean."

Amy leans back and takes a deep breath of fresh air. We sit in silence for a few minutes.

Then Amy shifts toward me. "It must have been difficult, living through the Great Depression and World War II."

"Well, you know, Fredo was somewhere in Europe when I gave birth to Dorothy in 1942."

"That must have been tough, having your first child while Fredo was far away."

"My baby was a part of Fredo the war couldn't take away from me. No matter what happened, I had his child. My daughter filled my days and sometimes my nights with so much activity I didn't have time to fret about her father."

I smile at the memory. "She was a precocious, curly-haired baby, crawling around our little apartment and getting into things she shouldn't be touching. She had so much energy, I had to set up barricades."

"Our Freddie was the same way. I was always chasing after him, trying to keep him safe and out of trouble. I lost all the weight I had gained during my pregnancy. You might say he kept me in shape."

"You raised him well. Freddie grew into a fine young man."

"I have to admit, sometimes I miss the bond we had. There's nothing like a mother-and-son relationship. I sense that you had the same connection with Jack."

"I'd never say this to my girls, of course, but he was my favorite." I check Amy's reaction and find surprise on her face. "I'm only being honest, Amy. Jack and I had a unique relationship." I shrug. "My daughters and I have clashing personalities. Patricia took off on her own almost from the get-go. And Dorothy? Maybe she and I are too much alike." I pause and try to figure out my own responsibility for the barrier between us. "I wonder, if I'd done things differently..."

Amy pats my hand. "You didn't do anything wrong, Mom. Our kids make their own choices. They drift away from us. They make plans, sometimes they make mistakes. We can't take the blame for everything. And if we wait, they come back. My Freddie did."

Amy stretches her arms and yawns. "Isn't the pond lovely, with all the lily pads floating around, and the pink flowering shrubs along one side?"

Amy's face glows. She's the picture of gentleness and peace.

"I understand your husband was a Marine," she says.

I nod and allow more memories to rise up from the past. "Yes, and he was proud of it. The sad part was, he went away for a long time. The letters were few and far between. Most of the time, I didn't know where he was or what kind of danger he might have been in. If I wanted to find out what was going on during the war, I had to rely on the newspapers and the radio."

I'm suddenly overtaken by a coughing spell. I reach for a handkerchief in my sweater pocket.

Amy straightens. "Would you like a bottle of water?"

"Please." I cough into the handkerchief, then dab at my lips. Amy's already on her feet.

"I should have brought some water with us," she says. "I'll run up to the house and get us a couple of bottles."

I settle back and wait for Amy to return. I'm glad Jack married that girl. She treats me like an equal, not like some burdensome old woman who doesn't have anything useful to say. I can tell when someone's faking it. She seems to really care about me and the things that concern me. I can't say the same thing about everybody in my life.

I close my eyes and wait for the sound of her footsteps. I smile to myself. Amy wants to hear more stories. If nothing else, she'll get to know me better. And Fredo. And maybe even Jack.

Someday, Amy will pass my stories on to my grandchildren, and they'll pass them on to my great-grandchildren, and so on. Isn't that how people stay alive long after they've passed away? Somebody keeps telling their story.

CHAPTER TWENTY-SIX

REFLECTIONS ON 1944

I open my eyes to find Amy standing in front of me. She slips an open water bottle in my hand. I take a long drink of the cool liquid. It feels good going down and temporarily relieves my coughing spell.

Amy resumes her place on the bench next to me. "Okay." She takes a sip of water and tilts her head toward me, like she's ready to pick up where we left off. "Go ahead. Take me back in time. I want to hear more about your life with Fredo. I want to get to know the man you married, the little Italian I met years ago when I first got with Jack."

I give her one of my quizzical looks. I want to make sure she's serious. "It's a long story," I tell her.

"I know. We've got lots of time. If I remember correctly, when I met your husband, his health had begun to fail. I want to meet the other Fredo, the guy who won your heart back in the 1930s. Will you tell me about *him*?"

I nod. "That's easy." I place my water bottle in the cup holder on my wheelchair and take a deep breath. In seconds, I'm at the refrigeration plant and Fredo is walking through the door.

I glance at Amy and smile. "My Fredo wasn't the typical Italian. He wasn't loud, didn't pound the table with his fist like my Papa did when he wanted to make a point, didn't sit around with other Italians chewing the breeze. He was the main bread-winner in our home, and a gentle father who bounced his kids on his knee and sang lullabies in Italian. Of course, as our children grew older, they saw him as the banker they could run to whenever they needed cash. He rarely denied whatever they wanted. The two of us did without nice things for so long, he didn't want his kids to struggle like we did."

"I hope they appreciated all your husband did for them."

I raise my eyebrows and grunt. "Looking back, I think it might have done them some good to struggle. In a way, we spoiled them. Once they became teenagers, they decided we didn't know very much. Jack was the only one who went to college. The girls trained for careers that paid well. Neither Fredo nor I had finished high school. That made us ignorant, I guess."

"That's true of many families. People of your generation worked hard to give their kids things *they* never had. Some of those children grew up spoiled. You went through the Great Depression. Your kids didn't. Then there was World War II. Your kids were babies then. They didn't have a clue."

"Sometimes I wish they had experienced a small taste of what we went through. Maybe, if Dorothy had a more difficult life while growing up, she wouldn't be so cocky today. And Patricia might actually say thank you for all we did for her, instead of running off like she did."

"And Jack?"

"Sad to say, he's the only one who ever mentioned the Great Depression to me. The only one who ever asked about it."

"I'm not surprised. Jack has a very inquisitive mind." She

sips her water then leans back and shuts her eyes. "So tell me about it, Mom. Take me back to the worst of times."

I take another swallow of the cool water and gather my thoughts.

"Well . . ." I stare out at the pond. Memories come tumbling across the water. I spill them out of my mouth like a fountain.

"Fredo was far from home when Dorothy started to walk. The two of us did okay on my income, plus I was putting money away for when my husband returned. People kept saying the war brought us out of the Great Depression. I'm not sure it did. Up until the mid-1940s things were still pretty rough. Nearly everything was rationed—even shoes."

Amy opens her eyes, a shocked expression on her face. "Did you say, shoes?"

I chuckle. "Jack told me about your collection. He told me he had to install a couple more shelves in your closet. He said you could have opened your own shoe store."

Amy blushes and lets out an embarrassed giggle. "You're right. I love my shoes. I'm a shoe-aholic. I admit it."

I burst out laughing. "Try going without shoes for a while, Amy. You end up cutting out newspapers or strips of burlap to put inside your old ones. They smell to high heaven, but at least they stay warm and dry."

She's shaking her head and smiling. "I can't imagine."

I release a sigh. "Shoes were the least of our worries, back then. We rarely had meat on the table. Or butter, or salt, or cheese. Imagine cooking a meal without them."

"Wow. I'm okay with giving up meat. I'm almost a vegetarian anyway. But butter and cheese? And salt? I don't know." She pauses and takes a drink. "Okay, so times were tough. How did you keep going?"

"I didn't see my husband for two long years while he was involved in the war. I waited for his letters. Lived for them. He moved around so much, a lot of time went by until the next one came. My favorite song back then was "By the Light of the Silvery Moon." Fredo and I used to cuddle on our sofa-bed and gaze out the only window of our apartment at a starlit sky. Then, when he was away, every time that song came on the radio, I pulled out Fredo's letters and reread them, and I cried and cried and cried."

Amy rests her hand on mine and begins to sing softly, "By the light of the silvery moon, I want to spoon, to my honey I'll croon love's tune—"

I jump in, my own voice breaking as I sing out the words. "Your silvery beams will bring love dreams, we'll be cuddling soon."

We finish together, "By the silvery moon," and we collapse in giggles.

Tears are running down my face. Amy brushes a tear from her own cheek. We sit in silence for a few minutes. I gaze out at the pond. I can picture Fredo standing there. He's tossing pieces of bread to the ducks. He turns to smile at me.

Amy shifts toward me and draws me back. "You had no idea where Fredo was? Or if he might be alive?"

I shake my head. "Nope, none at all. The military kept everything secret. In his last letter to me, Fredo said he and his two buddies were getting ready to head out to sea. He didn't tell me anything about their mission. Said he couldn't." I give Amy a smug look. "Top secret." Then I settle back in my chair, wet my lips with another sip of water, and continue. "I followed the news reports and tried to figure out where they might be heading. A couple of weeks later, the allied troops took part in a huge invasion. They later called it D-Day, June 6, 1944. I figured Fredo was involved."

"So, Jack's dad went on the beach at Normandy?" Amy raised her eyebrows and twisted her upper body toward me.

I nod. "He opened up about it later, but not until a long time after he came home. Until then, I didn't know where he had been or what he had done."

"That must have been a trying time for you."

"While I was worrying about Fredo, I didn't know how long we'd be safe here at home. Our President's health had been failing for sometime. He had polio for years, but nobody knew how bad off he was. They even elected him to a fourth term."

"So, America had an ill President while a world war was going on?"

"That's right. We had to take precautions. Sirens went off at all hours of the day. Mostly they were tests, but I trembled inside as if they were the real thing. I was all alone. I put up one of those ugly dark shades in our one window. The whole town went pitch black after nine o'clock. The shops in my neighborhood shut their doors and turned off their lights. All the street lamps went out. Even the nighttime baseball games were canceled. If you didn't have the darkening shades you couldn't have any lights on at all, not even a candle. I began to wonder how close the enemy had gotten. They'd already bombed England, so why not us too?"

"Did you ever see any enemy planes?"

"No, but one night, I heard a droning in the distance. I turned off the lights and peeked out the side of my black shade. The streets were dark. The droning grew louder. A large, cigar-shaped object with flickering red and blue lights cruised overhead and set off a rumble that shook our building.

A couple of my dishes fell off the shelf and shattered on the floor. I let go of the shade, ducked under the table, and didn't come out until the droning faded."

"What a frightening experience. Did you ever find out what it was?"

I bob my head. "The next day Giuseppe, the man who owned our building, told me an American airship, a dirigible, had flown by on some sort of surveillance mission."

"That must have been a relief."

"It should have been, but I decided you don't have a watchdog unless there's something to watch out for. The enemy might show up at any moment. You can bet I pulled that shade down every night after that."

"And Fredo?"

"I didn't hear anything from him until he phoned me from the hospital in Paris. He'd had an operation to remove shrapnel from his leg. Sad to say, they couldn't remove all the shards."

"I remember he walked with a limp."

"He did. And he could predict when the weather was going to change."

Amy shakes her head and smiles.

I sit back and continue. "He came home at the beginning of August, just in time to celebrate Dorothy's second birthday. A few months later, he received a Silver Star and a thousand dollars for his two years of service. He healed okay—physically—but it was a long time before he recovered emotionally."

"I understand. It's like the soldiers who came back from Vietnam and the Middle East conflicts. They didn't have a name for the condition until 1980. They call it post-traumatic stress disorder."

"That's what my Fredo had."

"One of Jack's colleagues at the clinic works with veterans. According to him, they tend to revisit those traumatic situations, over and over again. They have nightmares. They withdraw. They cry for no reason. And, they avoid talking about the war, the very thing that might bring healing."

I nodded. "My husband clammed up for months. He went to work, came home, played with his little girl, and, more often than I like to admit, he escaped into his own world. Nighttime was the worst. Sometimes, he'd wake up sobbing and tearing at his bedclothes. I tried to comfort him, but I finally had to let go. He needed to release the trauma on his own."

"How awful for you."

"What made things worse, about that time, Dorothy entered the terrible twos. I had a husband who wouldn't talk to me and a daughter who wouldn't shut up."

The image sets us both laughing. We drink our water, let out a couple of long sighs, and giggle together again. Then we look at each other and fall into hysterics.

Amy wipes tears from her face and starts laughing all over again.

I double over to ease my aching ribs. Finally, we settle down and I continue to draw on the past.

"The next couple of years had us trying to be a family. Fredo used his military earnings to buy another truck. He hooked up with a produce company and started delivering fruits and vegetables to markets and restaurants. Giuseppe, our former landlord, became one of his buyers. Fredo's business started to take off."

"So, things were getting better."

"They were. Then Franklin Roosevelt died in April, 1945. He'd been our President for more than a dozen years. I'd heard his voice on the radio. I'd read about him every day in the papers. It was like losing an old friend. Fredo sat with Dorothy on his knee, and we drew our chairs close to the radio and listened to a live account of the funeral procession. The announcer's voice cracked as he described the scene—grown men weeping, people lining the street, holding hands, heads bowed, voices praying in unison. Sadly, Roosevelt didn't live long enough to see the end of the war. A couple of months later, Germany and Italy surrendered, then Truman made the decision to drop atom bombs on two Japanese cities. Lots of innocent people died."

"That's a shame."

"Yes, but America came out of the war as both a military and an economic power. That's when things finally started to pick up."

Amy gestures toward the front of my house. "Jack's dad used to fly the American flag off your front porch," she says. "What became of it, Mom?"

I look her in the eye. "I'm afraid my Italian husband was more of a patriot than I was. It's funny, isn't it? Fredo came here from another country, but he loved America, and he kept on loving it, even after he got battered up in the war. And I? I'm ashamed to say, I didn't like how the government tore apart our happy home. We were newlyweds. We barely had a chance to enjoy each other when we separated, first to survive and then to help our country survive."

"You were apart twice?"

"That's right. The first time, Fredo went off to a forest camp to earn money in one of the President's restoration programs.

Two years later, he went to fight a war—the same war that killed my little brother and almost killed Fredo too. Fly the American flag? I don't think so. It's been standing in a corner in Fredo's shed ever since the day he died."

A few minutes of strained silence pass between us. I don't like coming off as a bitter rebel, but Amy wanted honesty. The government didn't give me anything for my part in the war effort. Why should I pretend to be grateful?

"So," Amy says, blinking. "Fredo returned home. You already had Dorothy. Then Patricia came along. And finally, Jack."

"Um-hmm. Patricia was born in September 1945. Jack followed two years later, in December. He was the son Fredo so desperately wanted—a male heir to carry on the Busconi name."

Amy laughs. "And, thankfully, we have young Fred and his sons to do the same."

I smile into Amy's twinkling eyes. "I'm glad Fredo had the chance to see his grandson before he died. After all, you named your boy after him. To an Italian, that's the greatest compliment of all. Your Freddie had three sons of his own. Three, Amy. Triple the blessing to carry on my husband's legacy."

"Yes, and honored to do it." She pats my hand and smiles. "And, what about *your* three children? Did you raise them all in a tiny, second-floor apartment?"

"Oh no." I laugh and shake my head. "Fredo's business was doing so well he bought two more trucks. He hired a small crew and a secretary. He made me treasurer. By the time Jack came along, we had moved into a nice little house in the suburbs. We paid $5,000 for it. At last, my girls didn't have to sleep in dresser drawers. Plus, they had a backyard to play in. And a public school was a block away."

"Sounds like the all-American dream."

"For *us* it was. We had lived like paupers for so long, we didn't know how to handle our newfound prosperity. I continued to make my girls their dresses until they got into high school. Then, they fussed that they wanted new clothes from a department store. Patricia was the worst. She even took a part-time job dipping ice cream at the local drugstore, just so she could help pay for her expensive new dresses."

"Mm-hmm." Amy stares off at the pond. "What were your kids like while growing up? They each seem so different from one another."

"Let's just say they each had their own individual strengths and weaknesses. Dorothy was tough, almost a tyrant when it came to wanting her own way. After the other two came along, she fell right into the roll of big sister. Actually, she was more like a *Gestapo*. She bossed the other two around and doled out chores for them to do."

"And, they accepted it?"

"No, they let her think so. They made faces behind her back and walked away without doing whatever she had ordered them to do." I chuckle. "I wish I could do that right now, just ignore her, stick out my tongue, and walk away."

Amy lets out a ripple of laughter that brightens her face. I can understand why Jack fell in love with her.

"Patricia was the exact opposite of Dorothy. She loved to dance and perform on the stage. We used to call her 'Miss Prissie.' Of our two girls, we figured Patricia would be the one most likely to succeed. She proved us right. Before we moved to Florida, Patti did a little fashion modeling. She even made the cover of a couple of magazines."

"Then she married Ed Carpenter and her career went to

pot. Their marriage failed several years later. By that time, Fredo and I had moved south. She came down for a while, but, she didn't stay. She and Dorothy didn't get along. So, Patricia moved to Burlington, New Jersey, and got a job as a buyer at Riche's Department Store. After that, she ran with an elite crowd and forgot about the rest of us."

Amy's eyeing me with interest. "And Jack? Tell me something I don't already know about him."

"Jack was my little prince. He never gave me a moment's grief. He did well in school, played Little League baseball, and worked a paper route to earn his own spending money." I chuckle. "You should have seen him with his dog. Jack called him Buddy. He was a scruffy little mutt, but he gave our boy hours of fun."

"Jack did well in school?"

I lift my chin. "He graduated with honors and earned a scholarship to UF. It's where you two met. Then you got married, the two of you took off for California, and the rest is history."

A sadness clouds Amy's eyes. "I'm sorry, Mom. I didn't mean to hurt you. We *had* to move. My parents—"

I smile and gently pat her hand. "Don't you worry about it, dear. I never resented you for taking Jack so far away. I knew he had to make a life for himself. And you and I clicked, didn't we? Do you think maybe it's because we both love Jack so much?"

"I think so."

"Anyway, you have your own problems."

"Yes, we do. We're worried about young Fred and his family. Jack warned him not to take a newspaper job, but that's what he always wanted to do. These days, people are turning to the Internet for their news."

"What'll Freddie do now?"

She leans back and gazes up at the sky, like she's searching for an answer between the drifting clouds. "We don't know," she says. "Jack doesn't push him. Fred has a minor in English, so he could teach, I guess. Or he could go into TV news. We're letting him make up his own mind."

"I hope he finds something soon." I heave a sigh. "Amy, I want to thank you for doing this—for coming here. For taking me to the park. For listening."

"It's no trouble. I love you, Mom, and I want you to be happy."

"Happy? How can I be happy when my daughter wants to kick me out of my own house? I wish I had my old life back, Great Depression and all. At least all my body parts worked, and I was able to make my own decisions."

I gaze at Amy. Years from now, she might go through something similar. Her son will take over her life, and she'll remember how I was controlled by someone too.

Amy points toward the pond. "Look, Mom; ducks."

At the edge of the water, a mother duck leads her brood into the shimmering pool. They cruise toward the center leaving a wake behind them. Then they move in a straight line toward the opposite shore.

"Why don't humans do that?" I muse aloud. "Why can't we moms and dads lead our children along a safe path and why don't they trust us to take them to the other side?"

"I think maybe things start out that way."

"Yes, but babies grow into teenagers, and they begin to make their own way. Then, we grow old, and *they* lead the way and expect us to follow. What a twist of fate."

The warmth on my back begins to diminish and leaves me shivering. I tug my sweater a little tighter around my shoulders. The setting sun paints orange streaks over the pond and leaves lengthening shadows on the ground in front of us. Two distinct silhouettes appear, Amy's and mine, leaning toward each other. It's a comforting image.

Amy rises. "We should go in. It'll be dark soon."

A sadness sweeps over me. I'm not ready to let this moment go. Amy points my wheelchair toward the house. I turn my head and take one last look at the pond. The ducks have reached the other side. The little ones are clustering around their mother. A tear comes to my eye.

With great effort, Amy maneuvers my wheelchair up the ramp to the house. At the top, she pauses to catch her breath. Muted laughter erupts from inside. Jack and Dorothy must be having a grand old time going through my things.

"Let's see what they're up to." Amy wheels me inside and down the hallway to the master bedroom.

Jack is holding up my lacy red nightgown—the one I bought from Frederick's of Hollywood thirty-five years ago. Dorothy's gripping her right side and laughing hysterically. They catch sight of Amy and me. Dorothy's laughter sputters to a chuckle. Jack winks at me and sashays in front of the mirror. He presses my nightgown against his shirt and tilts his head from left to right, admiring his own image.

"I think you should find something in your own size," I tell him.

"Do ya' think so?" he says, feigning a high-pitched voice. "I don't know. I kind of like this one."

We erupt in hysterics. I relish the moment. We're getting along, my kids and I. There's no talk about moving, no mention of my treasures, no arguments, no nasty looks. We're having fun, and I'm loving every minute of it.

CHAPTER TWENTY-SEVEN

NEW YORK
1945-1957

A different man came home from the war than the one who'd left. Fredo walked in the door, a mere hint of a smile on his face, his eyes void of the former sparkle. Our embrace lasted for several minutes. He didn't say a word. Tears streamed down his cheeks. I nestled my forehead against his neck and cried with him.

Dorothy also started to bawl and drew our attention across the room where she squatted on the floor, a pile of blocks in front of her. Fredo released me from his grasp and went to our baby girl. His smile broadened, but a distressing sadness lay beneath the cooing that rose from his throat.

The next day, nothing had changed. Or the next. Except for Dorothy's outbursts, our apartment settled into a disturbing silence. Where there should have been joy and celebration, there was an uncomfortable sensation that a stranger had come into our home. Not even Giuseppe's humorous stories could rouse my husband back into the fun-loving, vocal Italian he once was.

At night, Fredo shattered the stillness with tormented cries. During the day, he went through the motions of being a husband and father. But something had stolen his life. Questions remained on the tip of my tongue. They went no farther.

At mealtimes he sat across from me at the table and picked at his food. I stared into lifeless eyes. Our conversations settled around the mundane—Fredo's job hunt, what to have for supper, our next get-together with Katie and John. We both avoided the real issue. The war and what had happened out there. Me out of respect for Fredo, and him from some trauma that roiled inside him. He behaved like he hadn't returned from the war at all, like a part of him was still on the battlefield.

After several weeks, Fredo began to seem more like himself again. Not the fun-loving, jokester who'd left on a military bus two years before, but a more serious version of the man I married. The day he went out to buy another truck, a spark returned to his eyes. He shared stories from his day at work, interesting interactions he'd had with his clients, his amazement at how the city had changed during his time away. The increased traffic, the shops that had opened, the new products on the shelves.

He came home each night, ate supper, and afterwards, he got down on the floor with Dorothy and they built things out of her blocks, or he read a story out of her growing stack of children's books. There were times when she actually had him laughing again.

A twinge of jealousy struck me. Dorothy was able to draw him out, when I couldn't. After he tucked her in bed at night, he retreated to that far-off place I couldn't enter. I felt like he needed to punish me for his own suffering. For the first time in our marriage, a resentment built up inside me. Try as I might, I couldn't stifle my bitterness.

Despite the trauma of war, Fredo's patriotism didn't wane. He continued to stand up whenever the "Star Spangled

Banner" played on our radio. I gritted my teeth and turned away. One day he came home with an American flag tucked under his arm. The swath of fabric measured three feet by five feet, and it came with a long staff and a bracket. Fredo showed it to me with a stupid grin on his face.

"You silly man. We live in a one-room apartment over a grocery store. Where do you expect to hang that thing?"

"I keep," he said. "Someday, we buy a house. Our flag tell people, 'veteran live in this-a house.'"

I shrugged off the idea, but gave him no further arguments. Fredo put the flag in the back of our clothes closet. As far as I was concerned it could stay there forever.

Then, new life came to our little apartment. Patricia was born on September 9, 1945. Our upstairs flat was hardly safe enough for a toddler and a crawler. Fredo put double locks on our apartment door. We moved our kitchen chairs away from the window, and we placed a wooden barrier in front of the stove.

Late at night, after the girls fell asleep in their individual bureau drawers, Fredo and I sat at the dining table and talked about our future plans. My dream always included a house with a big backyard, new furniture, and a packed pantry.

Fredo dreamed the way most men do. "Someday, I drive big Cadillac—with fins an' fancy hood animal," he said. "I smoke a pipe—like-a you daddy—eat steak, drink brandy—like-a rich people do."

One day, Fredo *would* drive a Cadillac, with fins and a hood ornament, and I'd have a station wagon for grocery shopping and for hauling our kids to their ballgames and dance recitals. Hoover's promise of "a car in every garage" would finally come true for us more than thirty years after he'd said it. Not just one car, but two. And his promise of "a chicken in every pot?" Eventually, Fredo surprised me with a side-by-side refrigerator. We packed the freezer with chickens and lots of other kinds of meat. And fish. Plenty of fish.

Though Fredo had come out of his shell, and though he went through the motions of being a husband and a father, he avoided talking about the war, though I felt he needed at some point to address the worst trauma in his life. My husband might have been sitting inches away from me, but he was missing in action.

Our situation improved when Jack came along in December, 1947. There were times when Fredo held his baby boy and I thought the buttons would pop off his shirt. He'd laugh out loud, make funny faces, and roll on the floor with the kids. Then, during the night, he'd get out of bed, tiptoe to the bureau, and he'd watch our children sleep.

As for Fredo's buddies, all I knew was, Pietro had died on the beach at Normandy. John carried my husband back to the ship, then he returned to the beachhead to find more of the injured until he also was hit. He came home a month after Fredo did and had several operations to remove shrapnel from his back.

John and Katie were married two days after he was released from the hospital. John teetered on crutches and grinned at Katie as she walked down the aisle in a dress her mother made. Of course, John asked Fredo to be his best man, and I was Katie's matron of honor. In her wedding vows Katie promised to take care of her husband during his recuperation and beyond.

"In sickness and in health," she said with a smile.

While still under a doctor's care, John tapped into his

inheritance, and he and Katie started a garment business. They hired Colleen to design many of the clothes they produced. Their business quickly grew, and so did their bank account.

The four of us were inseparable. John and Katie bought a house on Long Island. Fredo and I settled in the suburbs north of the city. We got together on weekends, took in a movie, sat around and played cards, or went dancing, just like before the war, only this time with plenty of food on the table and John's brand new Oldsmobile for transportation. Fredo and John never talked about Normandy.

Our lives might have gone on like that indefinitely, if not for one sweltering evening in August, 1957. John and Katie came to our apartment and ordered us to dress in our Sunday best. They'd left their two daughters with Colleen, as usual. Dorothy, who was now fifteen, agreed to watch over our two, though I suspected she'd immediately turn into a master sergeant the minute we went out the door, and the other two would probably hide out in their own bedrooms until we returned.

We often went out on the town with John and Katie, but this time they wouldn't tell us where we were going.

Fredo froze with a puzzled expression on his face. I looked at Katie for an answer. She pressed her lips together and shook her head.

John waved his hands at us. "Hurry up. Get dressed. I don't want to be late."

I narrowed my eyes. "Late for what?"

Katie merely smiled. "Don't ask."

John checked his watch. "C'mon, you two. The program starts at 7:30. I want to get a good seat."

I looked at Fredo and shrugged. We trusted John. He'd never given us reason not to. Giggling, I hurried into our bedroom. Fredo came in behind me. I slipped into a green dress and high heels. Fredo put on his favorite suit, a gray one with wide lapels. He stood in front of a mirror adjusting his tie. A wisp of a smile appeared on his face.

We barely had time to say goodbye to the children when John whisked us out the front door and into his car. Despite my prodding, he refused to tell me where we were going. I watched his face in the rearview mirror. He had a mysterious grin on his lips. Katie turned around from the front seat and cast a tight-lipped smile our way, then she slid close to John.

An hour later, we parked on a side street a couple of blocks away from Madison Square Garden. Then we walked to the arena. I looked up at the marquee. *Nightly at 7:30, Billy Graham New York Crusade, Air Conditioned, All Seats FREE.*

"Billy Graham?" I said. "Isn't he that evangelist?"

Katie nodded and kept walking.

I shrugged. "Well, at least it's air conditioned."

Fredo hesitated at the entrance. Other people streamed past us.

John beckoned us to follow him. "C'mon." He said. "You need to hear this guy."

Fredo glanced at John, then at me. I gave him an encouraging nod. He stepped forward, slowly at first, then he took my hand, and we blended in with the crowd.

The arena quickly filled up. John located four empty seats half-way from the stage. A huge choir, all of them clothed in white shirts, began to sing. I surveyed the auditorium. American flags were draped on the walls and on the front rails. Fredo settled in a seat, then sat with his hands clasped in his lap, his eyes on the woman's hat in front of him.

Moments later, the audience stood and joined in the singing of "To God be the Glory." I didn't need a hymn book. The lyrics rose from the depths of my memory. Mae used to sing them while setting up lunch at God's Kitchen. I moved my lips and softly mouthed the words, my thoughts on Mae instead of on the One who was being praised.

Fredo stood beside me, like a pillar. He didn't flinch, didn't sing, didn't show any sign of emotion. When we settled into our seats, he remained rigid but directed his attention to the speaker.

So that was Billy Graham. I knew about the young evangelist but I had never heard him speak. Now his voice echoed throughout the arena. "The Bible tells us the Christian is a soldier."

Fredo straightened his back as Billy went on to compare a soldier's responsibilities to a Christian's duties at home and in the world. My husband leaned forward in his seat. He didn't budge, but listened intently to the entire message.

Then Graham invited people to come to the floor of the arena. "If I had a doubt in my heart that I was a Christian, you couldn't drag me out of Madison Square Garden until I settled it," he said.

The choir began to sing another hymn, "Just as I am." I stared wide-eyed as people stood up throughout the auditorium. They stepped into the aisles, streamed down the stairs, and crowded together before the stage. I spun around and looked behind me. More people flowed into the aisles on either side of us. I turned toward Fredo, but his seat was empty. In a panic I scanned the room, checked the exit doors, searched the lines of people still moving in a steady cascade to the front.

I turned to my other side and nudged Katie. "Where's Fredo? Did he leave?"

She smiled and pointed. I caught sight of my husband moving with the crowd toward the podium. I leaped from my seat and stumbled into the aisle. Keeping my eyes on Fredo, I hurried down the stairs. At the bottom, I drew up beside my husband and grabbed his hand. Billy Graham was praying aloud. People in the crowd were repeating his words. My husband's lips were moving. Something had changed. His back was straighter. His eyes shone. Then he turned toward me and he smiled. For an instant I was looking at the humble Italian who stood by my desk more than twenty years before.

We rode home in silence, but it was a different type of silence than what had settled on our home for more than a decade. This was an electrified silence. It had a life of its own. Even John and Katie refrained from talking. They didn't come in for a nightcap as they usually did. Somehow they knew Fredo needed to be alone.

After the kids went to bed, my husband asked me to dig out the Bible Mae had given me years before. I searched through all the cupboards, emptied storage boxes, and checked the attic. Finally, I found Mae's Bible collecting dust on the top shelf of our bedroom closet. Fredo grabbed it from my hand as though he were starving and the book was a sandwich. He sat on his recliner, opened the Bible, and read silently.

Thus began Fredo's nightly ritual of Bible reading. Every day, like clockwork, he'd come home from work, he'd take a quick shower, and he'd sit in the living room with Mae's Bible on his lap. I didn't mind losing my husband to the

Good Book. Whatever he found in there had put a new spark in his eyes. He smiled more often. Even laughed more often. And he talked with passion about his plans to improve his business.

Then, one Saturday, while the kids were at the park, he opened the Bible to a marker where he had left off the day before. I was busy in the kitchen preparing a chicken salad sandwich for his lunch. I kept glancing in his direction, but I kept my mouth shut. He seemed engrossed in what he was reading. Then he looked up, put a finger to his lips, and stared at me.

"Angelina ..."

I figured he was ready for his sandwich. I added a handful of potato chips to the plate and poured him a glass of lemonade. Then I set everything on a TV tray in front of him. I started to turn away, when he grabbed my arm.

"No leave." He looked at me the way he used to, before the war, with a twinkle in those cool blue eyes. My heart leaped and I caught my breath.

Fredo ignored the sandwich. He patted the sofa beside him. "Sit, *mio amore*."

Tears filled his eyes and his cheeks flushed a deep pink. Trembling, I settled beside him, my own eyes swimming in a pool of tears. For the first time since he came home, he opened up to me about the war.

Instantly, I was on the ship with him, approaching the shores of Normandy.

"Many men with me," he said, his voice soft. "No one speak. No one breathe. We see the beach. My heart pound. We train for this but no expect it really happen. Now we get close. I look at my buddies—Pietro an' John. They stand each side of me. We still a team. Pietro's eyes fill with fire. John look scared—like-a me, but energy build up. We no can stop. No chance to turn back.

"Then ramp go down, an' we take off like bullets. We hit the water, splashing all around—cold, so cold. Men fall. On my left. On my right. In front. Behind. I keep going. Hard to move. Water strong. Mud thick. John beside me. Pietro move ahead. I try reach him, but he too fast. Like a big, angry ox, he hit the beach, firing his rifle.

"Pretty soon, mud drag my feet. My boots, they sink in, but I keep going. Slower, but still forward, splashing. Lifting my feet. No more see Pietro. John by my side, joost-a like he promise. Then, men run between us—push us apart. Gunfire all around. Noise. Blasting noise. Over and over."

He paused and placed his hands over his ears. "Loud. Too loud." Then he lowered his hands and took a couple of deep breaths before continuing.

"My leg burn. Hot pain, like fire. I go down. Drop my rifle. I drag my leg. Try to crawl to rocks. All of a sudden, Pietro beside me. He come back, Angelina. *Mio compagno,* my friend, he come back. He no leave me."

Fredo looked in my eyes. Tears spilled from red-lined sockets onto his cheeks "Pietro." Fredo choked out his friend's name. "He pull-a me, and pull-a me, and pull-a me. He drag me to the rocks. Blasting all around. And noise. Loud noise like I never hear before. Bright gunfire like lightning over my head.

Pietro—the big, dumb monkey—he lie on top me. More gunfire. His body jump, two-three times. He say, '*Caro Gesu, perdonami.*' Then he—*come si dice?*—he collapse—an' he go still."

I sat back, my mouth open. "Are you telling me Pietro saved your life?"

"*Si.*" Fredo nodded and more tears fell. "Like Billy Graham say, come joost-a like you are. Pietro say, 'Dear Jesus, forgive me.' Only he no say in arena. He say on the beach. And then he die."

My husband began to sob. "Oh, Pietro, Pietro, *mio compagno*. He save my life, Angelina. He save me. He gone, an' I live."

Still in shock, I felt helpless to comfort him. He lifted the napkin from his tray and wept into it. His body racked and lurched as years of pain spilled out. I leaned close, wrapped my arm around his shoulder, and kissed his cheek. I had no words to soothe the trauma, so I simply made my presence known with a touch, a kiss, a stroking of his back.

After a while, he lowered the napkin and took a deep breath. "My head go black. I wake up on ship. Still no John. No Pietro. Many others lie on deck. Some scream. Some lie quiet. And me? Hot pain in my leg. Medic come, put bandage on, give me shot. Morphine I think. Next thing, hospital. Doctor say operate on leg. Then, I sleep long, long time. I ask for phone, call you one time. Then, home. Like a big *tempesta*. Everything go fast."

Fredo ended his traumatic story with a long, shaky sigh. He drew the napkin to his face again and wiped away more tears. I stroked his arm and rubbed his back. My Fredo, my dear love, had released so much pain, but the telling of the most traumatic experience of his life had freed him from the prison he'd been in for more than a decade.

He leaned back and smiled at me. "*Grazie, mio amore.* You listen. No words. Just listen."

I pointed at the Bible, still open on his lap. "You must have read something in there, something that helped."

He nodded. "It say man who give life for friend. No greater love. Pietro give his life an' I live. Pietro that kind of friend."

He took a breath and grabbed my hand. "Angelina, I need you forgive me."

"Forgive you? For what?"

"I no be good husband since I come home." He shook his head, a sadness clouding his eyes. "No good father. I what they call, absent."

"You did all you could, Fredo."

"No, what I do, not enough. My wife, my babies, they need me. I fail. But now, I change. This book help me do better."

My heart swelled with admiration for my husband. Silently, I thanked God for Billy Graham's message, and for our friends, John and Katie, who refused to give up on us. If they hadn't taken a chance, hadn't risked Fredo's rejection, my husband might never have escaped the trauma that had held him captive for so long.

I got up and left Fredo alone to eat his sandwich. I cleaned the kitchen, ventured an occasional glance in his direction, and mulled over what he'd said about Pietro and his pathetic cry for forgiveness. Was that all it took? A plea for forgiveness? Billy Graham had said it was.

I considered Pietro's simple prayer and I asked Jesus to forgive me too. But, forgive what? I hadn't lived the kind of life Pietro had. That man had a lot of reasons to ask for forgiveness. But, what had I done? I was a good wife and mother. I cared for my own mother until she died. I even went to church on occasion. I certainly never killed anybody.

But something nagged at the back of my mind. Something

Mae had said long ago. Her words came back to me with full force. *You need to receive Jesus and his plan for your life. Until you do that, you'll have a void in your heart, one that only God can fill.*

I looked at Fredo. He had devoured his lunch and had turned his attention back to Mae's Bible. A veil had lifted from his face. The troubled lines had dissolved and an aura of peace remained. I wanted that peace too. Again, I reiterated Pietro's prayer, *Dear Jesus, forgive me.* This time, I had no expectations.

Of course, my opinion of Pietro had changed in an instant. I regretted every evil thought I ever had about that man. The big oaf had sacrificed his life to save my husband. The Bible said there was no greater love.

CHAPTER TWENTY-EIGHT

THE AFTERMATH

After Fredo's breakthrough, he talked freely about the war. Not like he did that first day when he unleashed all the trauma. Now he spoke of some of the lighter moments. For weeks after, he told stories about his two best buddies, how they helped each other through the grueling rituals of boot camp, Pietro's tendency to get into trouble, and John bailing him out, time after time. Fredo had me laughing and crying, sometimes over the same incident.

With the release of pent-up emotions came renewed confidence. Fredo built up his trucking business with more trucks and more drivers. We started putting money aside for the kids' future needs. For two weeks in the summer, Fredo left his manager in charge of things and we went on a holiday, usually to a campsite on Lake George, or to a rented cottage on Cape Cod.

Our friendship with John and Katie remained strong. We got together on weekends. Dinners out. Movies. Sunday picnics with the kids.

Then, one rainy afternoon, Katie phoned me with bad news. Her voice broke and I could hardly understand what she was saying.

"My mum has ..."

"What? Your mum has what?" I knew before she said the words.

"She's gone home to be with the Lord." Katie broke down then. Several minutes passed before she was able to speak again. I waited, listening to her sobs, and wishing I could wrap my arms around her.

"I found her this morning, Angela," she said at last. "She went peacefully in her sleep."

I grabbed my coat. "I'm going to Katie's house," I called out to my daughter, Dorothy. "Take care of your sister and brother. I'll explain when I get back."

Three days later, our family attended Colleen's funeral in a Catholic cathedral a few blocks away from their house. I sat with Katie in the front pew, held her hand, speechless, for no words could fully express the pain we both felt.

Katie smiled at me through tears that made her green eyes shimmer. "I know where my mum is. But, oh, the loss is so great, I can hardly bear it."

Such losses mingled with milestones and celebrations. In June 1960, Dorothy graduated from high school and immediately landed a job as a secretary for an insurance agency. Patricia was modeling teen dresses for a local department store. And Jack played baseball for his middle school team. He got high marks in all his classes. Like my brother Benito, Jack would be the only one of our three kids who would attend college.

When John F. Kennedy gave his inaugural address, he touched a nerve when he said, "...man holds in his mortal hands the power to abolish all forms of human poverty and all forms of human life." I shook my head. Didn't he know poverty still existed on our city streets? The jobless were still with us. So were the homeless. I saw them on street corners, holding signs that said *Will work for food*, or something of that nature.

Even now, seventy years after the Great Depression, people are selling their homes or letting them go into foreclosure. Dorothy hasn't been able to find a job. And Barry's about to dip into his IRA.

Like Sam, my former boss, said, there's a pattern. A cycle. "You only have to watch for the signs," he told me.

And so, I pay attention. The cycle has already begun. And, it's happening right under my nose. After all my years of collecting and saving, I'm about to lose everything. Dorothy's turned my house into an empty shell. Barry took my furniture and used the big pieces to stage one of the houses he's selling. Dorothy has packed away my china and silver. Yesterday, she took several boxes of clothes to the shelter across town. And now Jack and Amy are here. Dorothy has them cleaning out the attic.

Many of my treasures have disappeared into boxes or into the trash. Sadly, Mae's Bible has vanished too. Dorothy made some off-hand comment about it's battered cover. Sometime later I remembered that worn book when I read a comment attributed to a nineteenth century preacher named Charles Spurgeon. *A Bible that's falling apart usually belongs to someone who isn't.* I know this to be true. I saw with my own eyes how the word of God transformed my husband and helped him find wholeness again. As long as he had that book in his hand Fredo wasn't falling apart anymore.

CHAPTER TWENTY-NINE

ANGELA

SEPTEMBER 2008

We slept at Dorothy's house last night. Jack and Amy took an upstairs spare bedroom. I was relegated to the old lady lockdown off the kitchen. I might as well get used to it. I'll be spending the rest of my life in there.

Now I'm looking across the breakfast table at Jack, and I see so much of my Fredo in him. I'd like to rush over and give him a big hug. But rushing isn't part of my life anymore. It's a blessing if I can feed and dress myself.

"Let's go. We have a lot of work to do." It's Dorothy, barking orders again.

Like obedient children, we finish breakfast, gather our belongings, and head out of the house. Barry and Jack help me down the ramp and into the backseat of Barry's van. I no sooner get my seatbelt fastened when Dorothy starts her stuff.

"Okay, here's the plan." She says with an air of authority. "Amy and I will wrap up the rest of the breakable items. I picked up some packing paper at the U-Haul office the other day. Jack, you help Barry clean out Dad's shed. There's such a mess in there, it's gonna take you guys all day. Save whatever you think we can use and run the rest to the dump."

Nobody argues with Dorothy. Not even Barry. It's no

wonder I've lost respect for that man. He abdicated his throne two years after they married.

Jack winks at me. "What about Mom? Do you have a job for her?"

I know what my daughter's going to say long before she says it. "Mom? What can she do with one hand?" She turns around in the front seat, makes eye contact with me, and sighs. "Oh, all right. I guess we can find *something* for her to do."

"Why don't we let her sort through those old photo albums?" Barry tilts his head in Dorothy's direction. "She can look at them while she's sitting at the kitchen table. It'll keep her busy and out of the way. We don't want her getting hurt."

I sneer behind his back.

Dorothy's nodding with enthusiasm. "There's a ton of albums in the back closet. She can toss out pictures of people she doesn't know anymore and hang onto our family photos."

I've had enough. "Will you people please stop talking over me like I'm not even here? I can still speak for myself."

"Sorry, Mom." Jack sounds genuinely remorseful. "What would *you* like to do? Name it."

I hit him with an idea I've had rolling around in my head ever since my son arrived yesterday.

"I want to go with you to Dad's tool shed."

"What?" Barry flashes a glance in the rearview mirror. "Are you kidding? It's a mess in there."

"You might need to ask me about some of Fredo's things." My eyes dart from one to the other. "I won't get in your way. I promise."

"Are you crazy, Mother?" Dorothy's voice has gone up an octave. "It's dusty and dirty in there. You'll end up with one of your coughing fits. What are we supposed to do? Drop everything and rush you to the hospital?"

"Oh, it's not so bad," I tell her. "Dad kept it clean. I went in there lots of times with him."

Jack's lips part in a silly grin, like he may be considering my request. "I don't know—"

If I can reach anyone, it's my boy. "C'mon Jack. I'll be a fly on the wall. There's plenty of room for my wheelchair in the corner. Anyway, it'll do me good to look through some of Dad's old stuff."

Fredo's shed was more than a place to store broken things. Sure he accumulated a lot of junk—a broken lawn mower, a rusted electric can opener, a lamp with a stuck light bulb, and just about anything my husband could find in the dumpster down the street. I loved watching him transform a worthless item into something useful. With Jack and Barry pulling everything off the shelves, it'll be like my husband came back from the grave and is tinkering around in there.

But there's something else. Something I'm going to keep to myself. It'll do my heart good to watch them open the drawers on Fredo's big, red tool chest.

I blink my eyes and give Jack my most imploring smile. "I won't bother you, son."

Dorothy spins around, scowling. "Mother, please. We're trying to get this place cleaned up. *Today*."

I ignore the sharp tone in her voice. "Jackie?"

He lets out a sigh. "All right," he says, more to Dorothy than to me. He lifts his hands, palms up. "Don't worry, Sis. I'll look after Mom."

Dorothy's objection freezes on her tongue. She still has her mouth open as we pull into my driveway. Jack springs into action, grabs my wheelchair from the back of the van, and gets me into it. He wheels me around the side of the house to the front of the shed and locks the wheels.

I turn to look at him. "Thank you, son," I whisper.

He pats my shoulder, then he goes into the house and, a few minutes later, he comes back with Fredo's keys. Dorothy's blocking his path with her arms crossed. Jack sidesteps around her, releases the padlock, and swings the shed door wide open. With a huff, Dorothy turns away and stomps toward the house. I don't care. Jack's taken control, if only for the moment.

My son pushes my wheelchair into the shed and I move from blinding sunlight into cool blackness. Barry hits the wall switch and the shadows dissipate. Jack wheels me into a corner, and parks my chair in front of Fredo's American flag. I sit with my hands folded and wait for the two of them to start going through my husband's things.

Barry heads for a row of jars on Fredo's workbench. "Look at this." He opens one of the jars and dumps a pile of tiny metal spikes into his palm. "Nothing but rusty screws and bent nails. What did your dad think he was gonna fix with these?"

"And look here," Jack calls from the other end of the shed. He's gripping a carving knife. "Who would use something like this? The handle is about to fall off. The two pieces are bound together with nothing but a bunch of rubber bands. I don't know how my dad expected to use it. He would have ended up cutting *himself*."

I leap to my husband's defense. "My Fredo didn't waste anything. Why, he could pound those nails straight as a pin, Barry. And the rusty ones? Whenever he needed some, he'd soak 'em in a jar of gasoline. They came out good as new. And, don't worry about that knife, Jack. Your dad used it lots of times. He never cut himself, and the handle never fell off."

Their eyes meet for a quick exchange, then they turn away and head for different parts of the shed. They're probably sorry they allowed me to come in, but after a while, they pretty much forget I'm here. I keep one eye on the big, red tool box. I straighten the collar of my blouse, fiddle with the fringe on my shawl, twirl my wedding band around the finger of my left hand, and bide my time.

"There's nothing but worthless junk in here," Barry says. He dumps handfuls of rubber bands and twist ties into a trashcan.

"Right." Jack points toward a shelf lined with oil cans. "What about these?" He shakes a couple. "They're all empty."

"Dump 'em."

He tosses them in the trash setting off one clank after another. "It looks like my father saved everything. Like my mother." He grins in my direction. "Look at this pile over here." He bends over and sorts through the mix. "Broken tools, rubber hoses, hunks of wood—and what's this? Work gloves with holes in the fingers." He's shaking his head and chuckling.

My son-in-law has moved to another corner where Fredo kept larger items and left-over parts. Barry puts his hands on his hips. "Hey Jack, what do you want to do with these lawn mowers? There must be three or four of 'em over here. All of them with missing parts."

Jack sidles up to Barry and peers over his shoulder. "I don't know. What do you think?"

"I suppose we can take the useable pieces, put them together, and maybe come up with one good lawnmower."

"Do you want that job?"

Barry frowns and shakes his head. "I vote we take 'em to a metal recycling center." He gestures toward the far corner. "Look around, Jack. Nothing in this shed is worth keeping, except maybe that tool chest over there. We can save time by trashing everything else."

Jack nods and scrunches up his lips in thoughtful agreement. He walks to the workbench and lifts a ring of keys off a hook on the wall. He fingers through them. "One of these should open the lock on the tool chest. What do you think, Barry?"

My son-in-law answers with a silent nod.

"Will you look at this?" Jack pulls a small, flat key from the ring and laughs. "I swear, this little key looks like the one Dorothy used to adjust her roller skates when she was a kid. Do you think she'll want it—you know, as a keepsake?"

"Nah. Dorothy's not one to keep anything. Your mother turned her off to collecting, a long time ago. I'm tellin' ya', Jack, you won't find a single knick-knack in our house. I guarantee it."

It's true, Dorothy did give me a hard time on Saturday mornings when I made her dust my curios before she could go out and play. I was trying to teach her to take care of precious things. I suppose it had an opposite effect.

All three of my kids had Saturday morning jobs. Patricia had to gather up everybody's laundry and start the wash. Funny thing. She was the one I expected would balk, but she never did. She liked taking care of the family's clothes. No wonder she ended up working in the garment industry.

As for Jack—every Saturday morning, he helped Fredo with the lawn and garden. Their chatter sailed over the rumble of the lawn mower. Bursts of laughter rose above the scratch, scratch of their rakes. And their voices went back and forth across the yard as they gathered up piles of leaves or pulled weeds from my garden. I didn't see the two of them until lunchtime. They came in chuckling and stomping their feet, like they'd had a grand old time out there.

The sunlight spills through the open door and my attention wanders to my backyard garden. The flowers withered and died months ago. The lawn hasn't been mowed in two weeks. But then, fall has arrived. Even in Florida death overshadows an untended garden.

When spring comes around again, a new owner will tackle the landscaping and will hopefully bring it back to life. Somehow I'll have to resign myself to the fact that my house and my entire world are slipping away from me. They'll soon belong to someone else.

I turn back to the inside of the shed and I perk up. Jack has spread Fredo's keys on the workbench. He tries one key after another, but, so far, none of them have turned the lock on the tool chest. He lets out a long sigh, tries another key, and there's a click. He shoots a smile at Barry and pulls open the top drawer, which emits a loud screech, evidence that Fredo's tool chest hasn't been opened in more than five years.

Jack looks inside, then lurches backward. "Of all the—Mom! What's this?"

Barry moves closer. "What's the matter, Jack? Are there bugs? Spiders? I hate spiders."

Jack shakes his head. "Not bugs or spiders. Something else."

Barry cranes his neck to get a better look. They gape at each other, then they both turn to look at me, their eyes wide.

Jack reaches inside the drawer and pulls out several rolls

of bills, tightly bound with rubber bands. A chuckle escapes from my throat as he opens drawer after drawer, revealing more of those precious green bundles, each of them in different denominations. My chuckles explode into uncontrollable laughter. I wipe tears from my cheeks.

Jack's scowling at me now. "Mom, what in the world?"

"Yeah, what's going on here?" Barry's face is contorted in shock and surprise. "This isn't funny, Angela. What did you and your husband think you were doing?"

Still laughing, I grip the arms of my wheelchair to keep from falling out of it.

Jack grabs a paper grocery sack off the bottom shelf of Fredo's workbench. The two of them stuff the rolls of money in the bag. Then Jack stands in front of me, the bulging sack in his hands.

"Can you explain this?" I don't like the sharp tone in Jack's voice. He sounds like a male version of Dorothy. "Mom? What's going on?"

I stop laughing and frown at him. I straighten my back and look him square in the eye.

"Now you settle down, Jackie, and I'll tell you."

My tough sounding answer backs him up a step. His mouth is hanging open. I let him sweat it out for a few more seconds. Barry's in no better shape. He's frozen like a statue.

I take a deep breath and I look from one to the other. Then, satisfied that I have their attention, I clear my throat and lift my chin. "If you must know," I tell them. "The money you found in Dad's tool chest belonged to him." I let that register for a couple of seconds. "And you know the bills Dorothy found in those shoeboxes?" I jerk my head toward the house. "Those belong to me. I saved that money. I could use it for whatever I wanted." I nod toward the bag in Jack's hands. "So could your Dad. We had our own special banking system—with separate accounts."

"Banking system?" Jack's face has turned crimson. "This is lunacy. Are you telling me your banking system consisted of a tool chest and shoeboxes?" He shakes his head and the lines on his face suddenly soften.

"Tell me, Mom," he says. "When did you start collecting all this money?"

I look at the ceiling like I might find a calendar up there. "Let's see now. We started back in the 1930s. We didn't trust the banks, so we used a cigar box. When we needed something bigger, we chose shoeboxes. Of course, I didn't have that many shoes. Most of those boxes we found in people's trash. Now, you can't tell me our system didn't work. You're holding the evidence right in your hands."

Jack looks in the bag, then back at me. "Are you saying, when we moved south, you lugged all this money with you from New York to Florida? And, even after moving here, you refused to use a bank? You kept putting your money in shoeboxes?"

My son turns toward Barry. "Did you and Dorothy know about this? Did this money hoarding take place right under your noses?" Jack's tone has sharpened again.

Barry backs away and puts up his hands. "Hey, Jack, I left your Mom's care up to Dorothy. All I know is, her Social Security check comes in every month and covers her expenses. I had no idea she's been stashing away all this dough."

Jack looks inside the bag again and shakes his head. "What do you think we should do with all this money, Mom?"

"I don't know. Do you have any ideas?"

"Well, there's enough here to pay assisted living expenses for the rest of your life. Dorothy said she's checked out a few places. They're like miniature country clubs. They have restaurants where you can eat all your meals. You won't have to cook a thing. They bring in entertainment. You can play cards or watch TV with people your own age. You can make friends. And somebody will do your laundry and monitor your meds."

"Or, you can come and live with Barry and me." Dorothy steps inside the shed and peers into the open bag in Jack's hand. "What's this? More money? I don't believe it." She scowls in my direction. "It seems *Mother* knows how to keep *secrets*." She hasn't taken her eyes off of me. They're hard as stone. "So where will you go, Mother? My house—or Palisades Care Facility?"

"How about *my* house?" I tell her.

The shed goes silent. I glare at Dorothy, then at Jack, then at Barry, and back to Dorothy again. "You can shut your mouth, Dorothy. I love you, but I want to stay—in—my—own—house. I have enough money to pay my bills and take care of anything that needs fixin'."

She crosses her arms and lets out a noisy huff. "It's not about whether or not you can maintain your house. It's about your health. The stroke left you nearly an invalid. Who knows what will happen if you have another?"

"Yes, dear, and you might drive your car off a bridge. I don't live on *what if's*. Never have, and neither should my daughter." I settle back in my chair and cross my own arms. "Listen, you people—" Again, I glance from one to the other. "You don't have to worry about me. I had enough sense to put this money away and I have enough sense to spend it the way I want to. I can keep it for a rainy day, or—"

"Stop, Mother. Just stop." Like a knife, Dorothy's rebuff cuts into my heart.

I stare at her and wonder where my curly-haired angel has disappeared to.

"Tell you what," she says, her tone sweeter but still firm. "Give us a day to think about all this. We'll decide tomorrow where you should go—after I have a chance to think things through."

There's no question what that means. Like always, Dorothy's in control again. My sudden burst of strength is slipping away. Jack has failed me. He hasn't come to my rescue like I'd hoped. I can tell he loves me and wants to do what's best for me, but Dorothy's in charge, and she's convinced him to side with her. He never stood up to her in the past, so why should he start now?

CHAPTER THIRTY

DECISIONS

SEPTEMBER 2008

We spend the next hour with Dorothy directing, and Jack and Barry gathering up the trash to haul to the dump. When they finish, Dorothy grabs the paper sack of money and carries it to the house. Except for the workbench, a couple of shelves, and the big, red tool chest, Fredo's shed has been swept clean. My husband's American flag is still standing close to me in the corner, right where I put it after he died.

I reach out and finger the stiff cloth. Fredo had gone through a couple dozen flags before he bought this one. He insisted on hanging it outside our house every day as long as it wasn't raining. I draw the cloth across my lap, and stroke the red-and-white stripes. The silvery stars draw me back to a time when there were fewer of them. When Alaska and Hawaii joined the union, Fredo poured himself a glass of wine and sat on the front porch, toasting the new entries.

An intense shame washes over me now. All those years of resistance, all those times when I justified my stand against the government and the decisions our leaders made, yet my husband remained loyal. He wasn't even born here, yet he was a more faithful patriot than I was.

Fredo never complained about having to leave home, never

once shirked his duty. The truth hits me like a tidal wave. How could I have loved the man and not loved the country he served? How could I cherish those years we spent together and not honor the time we were apart? How can I enjoy all the freedoms our soldiers won and not pay homage to the flag they fought for? I'm brought to a bitter place of repentance. Not only did I fail my country. I failed my husband and every male and female veteran who ever lived.

I'm still wiping away tears when Dorothy comes back to the shed. She doesn't stop to ask if I'm all right, just wheels me to the house and gets me settled at my kitchen table. Then she disappears in the back room. When she comes back to the kitchen, she's cradling a pile of photo albums in her arms. She drops them in a noisy cascade on the table in front of me.

"There," she says, her voice curt. "These will keep you busy for a while."

Amy's standing nearby. The sadness in her eyes speaks of her concern. But she doesn't say anything. Like Jack, she's bowed to Dorothy's rule.

My daughter grabs Amy by the hand and they head down the hall together. Their chattering fades, and I'm left alone with my albums. I heave a sigh. More memories. *More junk,* according to Dorothy.

I scan the pile. One of the albums has a faded pink cover with tiny tears in the fabric. I pull it toward me and flip to the first page. A sepia-toned photo shows Papa seated in his high-backed chair, his ever-present pipe in his hand and Mama hovering behind his left shoulder. Mama's smiling. I had forgotten how beautiful she was when she smiled. She's wearing a print dress with a lace collar, and she looks so young, the image takes my breath away.

The next few pages contain black-and-white baby pictures of Tomas, Benito, and me, followed by more family photos. I reach a break in the pages, then there's a whole slew of pictures John shot with his little Kodak Brownie camera. Most of them are from the 1939 World's Fair. The pavilions, the rides, plus multiple shots of Katie in different poses. Those pitiful black-and-white images don't do justice to her flaming red hair and green eyes.

I reach for another album, slowly turn the pages and stop at a spread of photos someone shot of Fredo and his two buddies at the forest work camp. Here's the one of their little skit when Pietro dressed like a big, ugly woman, and the other two vied for "her" attention. There are a few from military training, and some scenic shots of England and France. John arranged them like a museum art show. I always said he should have become a professional photographer.

Five years after the war, Fredo paid $90 for a Polaroid Land camera. We filled an entire album with instant photos of our kids—playing baseball on the front lawn, riding a pony, building sand castles at the beach, and sitting around the kitchen table with their favorite board games. Tears come unexpectedly. I can almost hear the giggles and the shouts, can almost envision the friendly battles over rent fees on a Monopoly board.

I linger over the images. Here's Fredo's military photo. My heart swells with love all over again. Three pictures, lined up in a row, show my kids in their caps and gowns, diplomas in their hands. Wedding photos—Fredo and me, John and Katie, Dorothy and Barry, and, sadly, a blank spot where Patricia's wedding picture used to be. The next few pages hold photos of our many family reunions, with all of us grouped together like a human quilt.

Dorothy's not going to like this, but I haven't come across anything I'd want to throw away yet.

A blue-and-yellow album beckons to me from the bottom of the pile. I slide it out and flip open the cover. Some of the photos take me back fifty years or more. Fredo's posing beside the truck he purchased with his military stipend. The cargo bed was much nicer than the first one. This truck was completely enclosed, with a back door for loading supplies. Fredo's resting one hand against the side that bears his company name in black letters—*Busconi's Produce Delivery*. A few years later, he had a whole fleet of trucks—professionally painted—and a dozen employees.

Here's a photo of our favorite grocer standing on the sidewalk in front of his store, his arms crossed above his bulging stomach and a proud grin on his face. The man was literally married to his store. My heart sinks. A few years after he closed his store, Giuseppe died of a heart attack.

I have a couple of photos of Mae and Andrew vacationing in the Bahamas. Mae lost about sixty pounds, but she had the same smile. I'd know her anywhere. The two of them retired in 1965 and moved to Boca Raton. Fredo and I drove down there a couple of times and visited them. I noticed with sadness how they had aged. They both had gray hair, and Andrew had developed a slight case of osteoporosis.

They told us Ronnie had followed his dream and was an architect in New York City. They showed us pictures of his wife and children. The girl looked an awful lot like Ariella, but I didn't say anything. The next time we visited, Mae and Andrew repeated the whole scenario all over again, like they'd forgotten they already said all that before. The two of them passed away ten years ago, within six months of each other. I've heard such a thing often happens to people who've been together so long they're closer than skin. One dies, and the other soon follows.

The next two pages hold several pictures of Katie and her mother. I miss Colleen's melodic Irish lilt and all the bits of wisdom she ladled out along with her Irish stew.

My friendship with Katie lasted nearly seventy years. Even after Fredo and I moved to Florida, she and I kept in touch. We sent Christmas cards and birthday gifts. We called each other on the phone at least once a week. Katie and John took a couple vacations to Florida and stayed in our home for several days.

About the time I lost Fredo, five years ago, Katie's telephone voice got a little muddled. She often drifted back to the past and talked about things that happened in the 1940s and '50s. She mentioned people and places I knew nothing about. Once, she even called me by the wrong name. From then on, John took my calls. He kept me informed on how my friend was doing, and he promised to relay my messages to her. The last time we talked, he tried to answer all my questions, but his voice broke and he had to cut our conversation short.

John took care of Katie until she died, last year. He phoned me one more time to tell me. I wanted to attend the funeral, but I didn't have the strength to make the trip. Anyway, I preferred to remember my friend the way she used to be—a fiery-haired sprite who kept me from falling into a pit of grief during the most difficult years of my life.

My eyes sting. Some might think those were the worst of

times, but, because of Katie and Colleen and Andrew and Mae, and Giuseppe, and so many others, I often think of them as the good ol' days. *My* good ol' days.

I have a couple of photos of Ariella. My, she was beautiful. No wonder Ronnie couldn't take his eyes off her. The thing was, she also had a beautiful spirit, which showed in the way she cared for the homeless people who used to come to God's Kitchen. Not only that, but she and her parents dedicated their lives to helping other Jewish refugees find a place to live and work in America.

Ariella wrote me after Max came back from his military service, a decorated war hero. Impressed by his loyalty to America, her parents finally relented and gave the two of them their blessing. Ariella and Max were married in a mixed religious ceremony with a rabbi and a priest sharing in the rituals. Of course, Fredo and I attended, happy to witness Ariella's dream come true. I have a picture of the two of them striding down the aisle after the ceremony, a glowing smile on her face, and a proud look on his.

The last photo taken of my brother, Tomas, shows him seated at the head of a dinner table with his brood of kids and grandkids and Donatella standing to his right. Tommy died in a car accident the next day, struck head-on by a drunk driver. The guy's father was a millionaire. He made sure Donatella and the kids had whatever they needed. Every one of them got to go to college.

Another album contains photos of Fredo's relatives in Italy, plus some of the vacation sites we visited when we made a long-overdue trip there in 1970. Fredo had a ton of nieces and nephews that produced more offspring.

I pause for a moment and think of people who aren't

in my albums. Like Cappy and his family, and little Tanya, who died before her time. Fredo and I ran into Cappy about thirty years ago, while we were in Miami on a mini-vacation. We stayed at a little motel near the beach. A custodian in a denim jumpsuit was gathering up palm fronds and placing them in a barrel. We passed close to him and I got a funny sensation. I glanced at his face, then did a double-take. There was something familiar about the man. His hair had gone salt-and-pepper gray, but he had the same proud stance, and a long scar stretched from the corner of his left eye to the side of his mouth.

"Cappy?" I drew closer. "Is that you?"

He turned toward me, and his tired lines sloughed away, replaced by a smile of recognition. "I'd know that voice anywhere," he said and stepped back to get a better look at me. "Well, look at you. Little Angela all growed up and in her prime."

I laughed. "Well, if you want to call sixty years old in my prime."

I moved toward him and raised my arms to give him a big hug. He dropped the frond he'd been holding and put up his hands. "I'm dirty, Ma'am."

I shook my head and continued toward him. "You've never been dirty to me, Cappy." I wrapped my arms around his shoulders and clung to him for several seconds. Then I stepped away and searched his face. He had tears in his eyes. I swallowed hard. We stood staring at each other for a while, then I remembered to introduce him to Fredo. After they shook hands, I tilted my head and eyed Cappy with concern. "How's your family?"

"Mah wife still good. All mah kids, too—'cept of course, little baby Tanya. She done g—"

I put up my hand. "I know," I said. "We found out."

He nodded. "The others, they all workin' an' married and puttin' out babies and granbabies. They doin' jus' fine."

I smiled. Cappy's family had survived the worst years in American history. Another miracle, as far as I was concerned.

I brought him up to date on my own life, then we fell back into the past and mulled over stories about the soup kitchen people. After a while, a shadow clouded his eyes.

"I need to finish mah work," he said. "Boss might be comin' out soon."

We said our good-byes, and I left with a big lump in my throat. Now the lump has come back.

I flip through the rest of my albums and pause over each photograph. The faces come to life again. Decades have passed, but they're all here, preserved in print. I've all but forgotten what's happening to my house.

I bring my hands to my face. Tears ooze through my fingers. A wave of conviction sweeps over me.

I cast my eyes around the room. Most of my belongings have been hauled away. Those items I called my treasures have disappeared. For days, I've been sitting here, fretting over mementos that were thrown into the trash and wishing I could retrieve it all.

I haven't seen the truth until this very moment. The realization came from the pages of those albums. More tears flow as I reach out and caress the tattered covers. Now I know without a doubt what my real treasures are. They're the people in those photos, people who came into my life, if only for a season, friends who made an impact on me during the most difficult days of my time on earth. Friends who stood by me when Fredo left to fulfill his responsibility as a husband and then as a patriot. And my family. Mama and Papa. My brothers. And my children. All those faces came into my life for a little while and then they went away, only to return this very day as I look through my albums.

These are treasures no one can take away, not even Dorothy.

I think about how focused she's been, how she insists she's doing all this for me. I didn't know it until now, but *she's* one of my treasures too. In spite of everything, I love my daughter, and I wish the best for her. It's like that Bible verse when Jesus warns his followers not to trust in earthly things that moths eat up or in things that can rust and rot away. *For where your treasure is, there will your heart be also.*

The truth is, my heart is and always has been with the folks in my picture albums.

I expect more tears to come, but, instead, an overwhelming peace consumes me, and I'm content. It no longer matters where I live or don't live, which possessions I take with me or which I leave behind. God has blessed me with a life full of treasures. They're in these photo albums, and I can take them with me wherever I go.

With a heavy sigh, I reach for another album but stop. There's a tapping at the side door.

"Someone's knocking." I direct my voice to the hall.

Nobody answers. The girls continue to gab and giggle in the back room. The guys have driven away in Barry's van, most likely taking a load of trash to the dump.

I set down the album in my hand and throw my voice toward the door. "Come in."

The knob turns, the door swings open, and I let out a gasp. "Patricia!"

My youngest daughter in coming in with two large suitcases in her hands. She sets them down, smiles, and rushes to my side. There's a rustle of silk. Patricia wraps her arms around me. I smell lilacs. She plants a lipstick-coated kiss on my cheek. I don't mind. My Patricia has come home. We're having a family reunion. They came one-by-one. First Jack and Amy. And now Patricia.

I hear footsteps in the hall. Dorothy emerges with Amy close behind her. My oldest daughter stops short and stares at her sister. Dorothy's eyes grow wide with a mix of surprise and suspicion.

"Hello, Patricia." Icicles drip from Dorothy's voice. Her eyes fall on the two suitcases. "Moving in?"

Patricia purses her lips and gives Dorothy a nod. She backs away from me and straightens to a height three inches taller than her older sister. I can't believe Patricia's really here—my prodigal daughter—that untamed spirit—coming home to see her mother.

"How long can you stay?" I ask her.

"How long can I stay? Well, Mother..." She glances at Dorothy then at me. "I'm moving in with you. If you'll have me."

Shocked, I open my mouth but nothing comes out. I simply nod and smile.

Patricia rests her hand on my shoulder. "We'll fix up this place and turn it into a bachelorette pad for the two of us. What do you think, Mother?"

I glance at Dorothy's angry puss. She can fret and fume all she wants. It won't make any difference now. Jack will have to support Patricia's decision. It'll be the three of us against one. Or two, if Barry backs up his wife. The odds are still in my favor.

"Of course," I say, at last. "That would be the most wonderful thing in the world."

My Patricia has come home. I don't need to know why. I won't ask her any personal questions. Nothing about her boyfriend or her job or anything. I'm just happy to see my daughter again. Like Mae taught me years ago, I put Fredo in God's hands, and God brought him back to me. Then I put Patricia in God's hands, and now he's brought her home too.

I ignore Dorothy's smirk and focus on my younger daughter. "We're gonna do this, Patti—you and I. Don't worry about a thing. I have enough money to take care of us for the rest of our lives. We'll fix up this old place. We'll put life back into it."

"Yes, Mother." She looks around and I'm guessing she's noticed the bare walls and lack of furnishings. "We'll add lots of color," she says. "New furniture. New curtains. A whole new look. I can paint, and clean, and hammer a nail or two. And you can direct me."

We're holding hands now. Amy rushes past Dorothy and wraps an arm around Patricia. The sparkle in her eyes tells me she's happy about our plan. Dorothy doesn't have a chance. I lean close to Patricia and lower my voice, as if I have a secret to tell her.

"Patricia, dear. Before we do anything else, will you do me a favor?"

She nods and smiles sweetly at me.

"Go outside to Dad's tool shed and get the American flag that's standing in the corner. Take it to the front porch and slip it in the bracket your daddy installed out there. Make sure you unfurl the cloth so the colors hang real nice, the way your father used to do." I gaze into her eyes. She doesn't flinch. "Will you do that for me, Patti? Right now? I think your daddy would like to see it flying again."

DOROTHY

2012

Four years have passed since Mother and Patricia settled down together in the old house. Barry's real estate business continues to suffer. He sold only four houses in the last year, and they were short-sales, which didn't bring him much of a commission. Thank God for the $10,000 their mother provided out of her shoebox savings. Dorothy was able to pay off her credit cards. But it was only a Band-Aid, a temporary fix, until Barry cashed in his IRA.

Patricia used her $10,000 to redecorate Mother's house. Jack gave his share to young Fred, so he and his family could settle into a three-bedroom rental. Two months later, Fred landed an editorial job at a national magazine.

Though Dorothy put in applications all over town, she hasn't been able to land a job. She tried going back to school to learn about computers, but she couldn't keep up with the twenty-year-olds, so she dropped out during the second semester. What difference does it make? More than twelve million people are out of work, and she's one of them.

A few months ago, Barry let their house go into foreclosure. Then, he put a small down-payment on a two-bedroom condo in a less affluent part of town.

Today is moving day. Dorothy's boxing up her dishes and

cleaning out her kitchen cupboards. Barry's been up in the attic all morning, sorting through piles and deciding what to give to their daughter and what to throw away.

She hears his step on the stair and turns as he enters the kitchen.

"What should I do with this stuff?" he says, puffing. He's holding an open box.

She peeks over the flap. Inside is a collection of toys—cars, trains, a football—things Barry bought for the son they never had. Dorothy's third miscarriage was a boy. She'd carried him for seven months. Other than their daughter Carrie, she never got pregnant again.

She hesitates, chokes back a sob, then gathers her composure.

"Give them to the shelter," she says. "They must have lots of little boys over there. Let somebody else enjoy them."

Barry sets down the box and wraps his arms around her. Nestled close to his chest, Dorothy releases her pain. For the first time in months, she's letting the tears flow. Until recently, she's been able to hide her frustration, never allowed her mother or Barry or anyone else to see the anxiety she's been holding inside. The tough exterior she'd developed over the years had proved to be a worthy shield.

Most of all, she wouldn't want Patricia to see how she was hurting. Much to Dorothy's surprise—and envy—her younger sister had fulfilled her promise to take care of their mother. Dorothy hadn't expected Patti's moment of insanity to last very long, but the two of them were doing just fine. Meanwhile, Mother regained full use of her left hand, and she's been walking with a cane. She and Patti have been having a ball, going out to flea markets, movies, and lunches at the Tea Garden, Mother's favorite restaurant.

Barry waited a full year before turning the little bedroom back into a dining room. "What a waste of time and money," he grumbled.

How ironic that now they're having to do the same thing to their house that they tried to do to Mother's four years before.

Dorothy pulls away from Barry, avoids looking at the box of toys, and returns to the stack of dishes on the table.

"Make sure you hang onto my favorite pans," Barry says. "And that metal thing I use to flip pancakes and turn steaks."

"Why don't you stay and help me?"

He nearly turns away, then stares into her eyes and relents. "Okay, what do you want me to do?"

Dorothy gestures toward a row of boxes, clearly marked *Charity, Family, Yard Sale,* and *Condo.* "You can help me decide what goes where," she says. "And the junk can go in that metal trashcan in the corner."

A Golden Oldies station is playing Frank Sinatra's *New York, New York.* Dorothy hums along with it. "Do you ever miss New York, Barry?"

"Nah." He shrugs. "Okay, so the money's better up there. I pulled in a good income selling cars. But, I like living in Florida. At this stage of my life, I wouldn't go back."

He lifts a large electric griddle to the table. "I want to keep this. Do you think that tiny kitchen will have room for it?"

"Sure, Barry. We'll make room."

A news break interrupts Sinatra's crooning.

"*The stock market took another dip this morning.*" The reporter's voice carries a somber tone. "*Eighty-five thousand homes have gone into foreclosure.*"

Barry lets out a grunt.

"The national debt has reached sixteen trillion dollars and

is still climbing," the reporter says. "Experts agree we're in the worst financial crisis since the Great Depression, and they can't promise things will get any better."

Dorothy flips off the radio. "Things won't get any better? Isn't there any good news anymore?"

She pulls a stack of Tupperware out of the cupboard and adds them to the pile on the kitchen table. "What do you think, Barry? Are we getting a taste of what Mother and Daddy went through?"

"Looks like it." Barry's busy stacking iron skillets beside his griddle. "Maybe we should try to save as much as we can—like your Mom and Pop did."

Dorothy pauses and stares out the window. Like an avalanche, her mother's stories about the Great Depression come barreling down on her. The bank closings, businesses shutting their doors, people begging on street corners, the robberies, the rations, the soup kitchen, the lines of people waiting for a loaf of bread. They weren't mere delusions concocted in the mind of an old woman. They really happened. And now they're happening again.

Dorothy pulls her stack of Tupperware out of a cupboard and sets it on the table. She takes a close look at the tomato stains, the scratches, the containers that have no lids. She eyes the trash can, hesitates, then she shrugs. Instead of dumping them, she gathers the bowls in her hands and places them in the box marked *Condo.*

"There," she says with a satisfied nod. "Who knows? We might need them someday."

ACKNOWLEDGEMENTS

Angela's Treasures would never have come to life except for my own mother and father, who served as models for Angela and Fredo and also survived the Great Depression. From my own mother, I learned to stretch one chicken into four meals, and I watched with chagrin as she stuffed plastic bags in a cupboard and washed plastic forks to save for the next picnic.

Like Fredo, my father was a humble Italian immigrant who worked hard and displayed great integrity and pride in everything he did.

I am grateful for my many readers who gave me feedback and criticisms, particularly my friends in the Word Weavers Ocala Chapter, and especially my daughter Joanna, whose keen eye caught the details that needed to be changed and improved.

Also, I want to thank my former agent, Les Stobbe, who advised me above and beyond his regular job requirements and also helped me come up with the title, *Angela's Treasures.*

Thanks also to WordCrafts publisher, Mike Parker, whose amazing editing skills made this novel so much better.

Last, but certainly not least, I thank and praise my Lord and Savior Jesus Christ, without whose presence I could not have endured the many hours of research and rewriting it took to complete this labor of love.

RESOURCES

Research for Angela's Treasures took me into some unexpected places, including into the living rooms of people who either had lived through the Great Depression or had parents and grandparents who had. Their stories confirmed and enhanced what I had already gathered from my own parents.

Beyond those visits, I delved into many resources that transported me to another time and place that was alien to me.

Books, Periodicals, and Electronic Resources:

The End of Affluence, The Causes and Consequences of America's Economic Dilemma.

The American Heritage History of the 1920s and 1930s.

The Great Depression, An Eyewitness to History.

The Coming Economic Earthquake.

Hard Times, by Studs Terkel.

The Forgotten Man, by Amity Shlaes.

The Great Depression, Turning Points in World History.

FDR's Folly, How Roosevelt and His New Deal Prolonged the Great Depression.

The Wild Bunch; The Great American West.

The Crash of 1929.

Rainbow's End, The Crash of 1929.

The Grapes of Wrath, by John Steinbeck.

Timetables of History.

America's Decades.

Field Guide to the U.S. Economy.

Politicians Still Don't Get It, New York Times column by Bob Herbert.

Time Magazine, The Roosevelts, special issue on 12/5/14.

Classic Films from 1931 to 1960, Gatehouse Media premium edition.

PBS: The American Experience.

The Great Depression, Vol. I, video, The Great Shake-Up.

www.access.gpo.gov/eop, Economic Report of the President.

www.Fedstats.gov.

www.Hyperhistory.com

www.content.time.com

www.eyewitnesstohistory.com.

www.infoplease.com.

www.amatecom.com/gd/gdtimeline.huml.

www.census.gov/statab/

ABOUT THE AUTHOR

Pulitzer Prize nominee Marian Rizzo has written four contemporary novels and two biblical era novels. She's been a journalist for twenty-five years with the Ocala Star-Banner Newspaper, part of the Gatehouse Media Group. Now retired, Marian has continued to work with the Star-Banner as a correspondent. She's won numerous awards in journalism, including the New York Times Chairman's Award and first place in the annual Amy Foundation Writing Awards.

Marian lives in Ocala, Florida, with her daughter Vicki who has Down Syndrome. Her other daughter, Joanna, is the mother of three children. Grandparenting has added another element of joy to Marian's busy schedule, which includes workouts five times a week, lots of reading, and lunches with the girls.

Visit her online at Marianscorner.com

Also Available From

WORDCRAFTS PRESS

A Purpose True
by Gail Kittleson

End of Summer
by Michael Potts

Odd Man Outlaw
by K.M. Zahrt

Maggie's Song
by Marcia Ware

The Awakening of Leeowyn Blake
by Mary Garner

Home
By Eleni McKnight